IN THE GROOVE

Life can be a bitch, as they say, but it does have its moments. One of them must surely be lazing on a bed, drinking beer, watching a strapping wench take off her clothes and display her body for your pleasure. When Jovial was naked, her skin as black as ebony with a polished sheen that seemed to glow from within, she stood still to let me look her over. I admired the merchandise: magnificent full breasts with nipples like thumbs, a narrow waist that flared out to rounded thighs and long shapely legs.

'Do I please you?' she asked.

No reply was necessary . . .

Also available by Lesley Asquith

Sex and Mrs Saxon
Sin and Mrs Saxon
In the Mood
Reluctant Lust
The Wife-Watcher Letters
The Delta Sex-Life Letters

In the Groove

Lesley Asquith

Copyright © 1995 Lesley Asquith

The right of Lesley Asquith to be identified as the Author of the Work has been asserted by her in accordance with the Copyright, Designs and Patents Act 1988.

First published in 1995
by HEADLINE BOOK PUBLISHING

A HEADLINE DELTA paperback

10 9 8 7 6 5 4 3 2 1

All rights reserved. No part of this publication may be reproduced, stored in a retrieval system or transmitted, in any form or by any means without the prior written permission of the publisher, nor be otherwise circulated in any form of binding or cover other than that in which it is published and without a similar condition being imposed on the subsequent purchaser.

All characters in this publication are fictitious and any resemblance to real persons, living or dead is purely coincidental.

ISBN 0 7472 4527 4

Phototypeset by Intype, London
Printed and bound in Great Britain by
Cox & Wyman Ltd, Reading, Berks

HEADLINE BOOK PUBLISHING
A division of Hodder Headline PLC
338 Euston Road,
London NW1 3BH

In the Groove

Chapter One

My immediate attention was drawn to the statuesque beauty standing amidst the chaos of Kampala bus station. All around, as I sat in the ancient bus taking me to yet another fresh start in my life, the sights and sounds of East Africa abounded. The girl stood black as polished ebony, a splendidly healthy specimen of young Ugandan womanhood, erect as a guardsman. All her worldly goods she balanced unconcernedly on her head in a tied cloth bundle.

The upright posture moulded her colourful cotton Busuti costume to the extravagantly ample curves of her high, thrusting breasts and flaring thighs. Despite the bustle and chatter around me from my fellow passengers and the view of a busy market place thronged with travellers, heavily armed soldiers, beggars and thieves, I could not tear my eyes away from such female magnificence. She had great tits, I had to admit, imagining them swinging free in all their naked glory. In my mind's eye, I pictured the firm fullness of them, perfectly matched twin mounds thrusting out so enticingly. My ever-responsive dick stirred and lifted at the delightful thought of seeing them naked,

In the Groove

of handling and kissing them. That was to come.

Beside her stood a woman similarly garbed, an older edition of the girl whom I took to be her mother. She held a small boy of perhaps two years of age. As passengers began to alight from the bus she handed over the child. Once in what was evidently his mother's arms, he drew aside the loose neck of her dress to reveal a large swollen teat. A few feet from where I sat, the boy fastened his mouth over a big purplish nipple, sucking contentedly. From the engorged round of the breast there was a more than ample supply. He was, I considered, somewhat old still to be breast-fed, but that was no doubt not unusual among African mothers as long as their milk was available. My observation of the scene was noticed by the girl. She grinned at me as I was about to look away, revealing perfect white teeth, then she poked out a long red tongue. In the same spirit, I smiled at her and she laughed. She drew aside the neck of her costume to free her other breast, cupping the luscious orb while hitching her boy over to that nipple. Having fed him and hugged him fondly, she handed him back, protesting, to the older woman. The girl gave me one last amused look, covered her lovely big breasts, and entered the bus.

It was already well filled, a good cross-section of my fellow passengers seemingly on the move along with every type of household article and a fair selection of livestock. There were cooking pots, basins, rolled mattresses and chairs as well as chickens, geese, even a goat. In the humid heat you could have cut the atmosphere with a knife and my clothes clung to me. The noise was quite deafening. As the only white face present, I was an object of some curiosity, a *mzungu* evidently too poor to own a car and therefore using public transport, an eccentricity never ever attempted by normal Europeans.

The truth of the matter was that my mode of transport had been made necessary. I was fleeing from a group of people after my blood in neighbouring Kenya, where my career as a bush pilot had ended with sudden drama through too many amorous misadventures. All I had in the world were the clothes on my back and the hold-all on my lap containing my essential documents: passport, pilot's licence, plus a small amount of money. But this was fine by me. I had always travelled light and savoured new situations, most of which, like my present predicament, had meant getting out in a hurry – and by the skin of my teeth.

Relieved to have escaped so lightly from various entanglements over the border, I looked forward to the next instalment of what could only be described as a rude, lewd life.* It had ended on a high note, even for me, when I was caught in bed with a mother and her daughter by a furious husband and father armed with his trusty elephant rifle. I felt lucky to be sitting where I was, my future precarious but interesting.

The girl I had admired came up the passageway of the bus, picking her way over bundles and baskets to sit beside me. '*Jambo*,' I greeted her in Swahili. '*Habari gani*?' This translates as 'Hello, how are you?' She gave her white-toothed smile and replied in good English. 'I am well, *Sibbu*. Why is a *mzungu* travelling on this bus?' She regarded me with a questioning eye. 'It is not usual—'

'I guess I'm not a very usual *mzungu*,' I replied, using

* See *In the Mood* (Headline 1992)

In the Groove

the word meaning 'peeled one' and referring to pale skin. 'This bus goes on to Entebbe, I've been told, where there's an airport. I hope to find work there and a place to live.'

'You will need a good housegirl to cook and clean for you,' she announced, no doubt offering herself. 'I go to Entebbe to find work also. I cook and clean very well, taught by the nuns at the Catholic mission at Kisubi. They taught me to count and read and speak English too. I could shop for you, do all duties very well—'

I liked the sound of the 'all duties' but was in no position to promise employment. 'What about your baby?' I asked. 'You've had to leave him—?'

'He is old enough now,' she said. 'My mother will take him back to our village and look after him. When I get work I will send money home to keep them. I must do it.'

I learned her name was Jovial Nkutu but when our bus got to Entebbe and we parted, I imagined I'd seen the last of her. First things first . . . I was directed to the Entebbe Club, the meeting place for Europeans. I went up stone steps to a long cool verandah. It was early evening and groups sat about being served drinks by African servants in white drill uniforms. The male club members looked well fed and prosperous, their women relaxed and good-looking – as well they might with their easy lives, their house-work done for them and their children away at boarding schools. Most were in golf or tennis clothes, enjoying a sundowner or two before changing to dine.

My appearance caused raised eyebrows and interested looks. I was immediately approached by an officious florid fat man in the regulation bush shirt, shorts and knee-length socks favoured by overseas types.

In the Groove

'Are you a member?' were his opening words, knowing bloody well I wasn't. 'It's members only in here, unless you know a member who can sign you in as a guest.'

It was politic to eat humble pie before such a pompous ass, for the sad fact was I'd have to kow-tow to men like him until I'd got myself 'in' with the local white community and obtained a pilot's job and a place to live. 'Tyler Wight,' I announced myself, offering a hand, which was accepted limply and with obvious reluctance. 'Forgive me for intruding but I've just arrived and I'm looking for somewhere to stay. I thought someone here might know of a place—'

All eyes were on me by then, taking in my travel-worn appearance. My type was well known, if thankfully rare, a renegade white shunned by the legitimate expatriate crowd who earned their place in the sun as British overseas civil servants or United Nations advisers to the now independent state of Uganda. I was unofficial, the kind who bummed around in a tropical paradise, an embarrassment, not beyond going native and drinking in township bars, and taking up with the local women. How wrong could they be? If offered the choice, I always enjoyed the best of both worlds.

'There's the Lake Victoria Hotel just ten minutes' walk from here – if you can afford their prices,' the fat one informed me curtly. 'We can't help you here. I suggest you leave—'

It was not an auspicious start, I decided. It was just my bad luck to meet such a pretentious prig on my first attempt to be accepted among what might be loosely termed 'my own kind'.

In the Groove

'Thank you,' I answered politely, in no way allowing him to think he'd put me in my place. At the same time I made a mental note to take the arrogant tub of lard down a peg if the chance came along. 'The hotel sounds all right until I find somewhere permanent,' I said. 'I'll trouble you no further, sir,' certain he'd appreciate that last bit of subservience.

'What is it?' enquired a shapely woman in her middle forties, wearing tennis whites. She regarded me with interest. 'What does this man want, Jumbo?'

I smiled at her, amused by her name for the fat man. Jumbo suited him perfectly with his trunk-like thighs and voluminous shorts. Her tits, I observed, filled her white tennis blouse in ample mounds, the nipples outlined clearly, bulging through the thin material. My look did not pass unnoticed. This was a woman worth getting to know, I decided, offering my hand which she shook in friendly fashion. 'Bev Marchbanks,' she introduced herself as I gave my name. 'Has my husband been giving you a hard time? He does take his position as president of our club rather seriously—'

'Quite right too,' I said levelly. 'Can't let any old riff-raff in, can one?' I saw by the glint in her eye that my reply amused her. 'Actually I was enquiring about finding a place to stay. A house or bungalow to rent—' Here at least I felt I'd found a human being, one who might be of help.

'I've directed him to the Lake Vic hotel, Beverley,' her husband cut in abruptly. 'No doubt he wants to be on his way, my dear.' He gave her a meaningful look as if defying her to say more. To my admiration and delight she ignored him completely and turned to face me.

'I'll be driving past the hotel on my way home,' Mrs

In the Groove

Marchbanks informed me. 'I'm leaving now, so I can give you a lift if you wish—'

I did wish, if only to see her husband go purple trying to stifle his displeasure. In the car beside her as she drove the half-mile to the hotel, I said, 'This is very kind of you. I hope it won't cause trouble with your husband. He did seem none too pleased—'

The woman laughed, obviously enjoying the situation. 'You have that effect upon husbands, don't you?' she said teasingly. 'I've heard about you, Tyler Wight, and your reputation with women. Usually the married kind too.' She glanced across, amused by my concern. 'I somehow expected you might turn up here—' She drew up before the entrance of an imposing hotel and leant back in her seat, savouring my discomfort.

'I've only just arrived in Uganda,' I told her. 'How could you possibly know anything about me, Mrs Marchbanks?'

'Call me Bev,' she said lightly, 'and it didn't take a genius. Don't worry, your lurid past in Kenya is quite safe with me – at least with your co-operation.' I remained silent as she continued gleefully. 'By chance I was in Nairobi when the great scandal erupted about you and those Gore-Blomley women. Mother, daughter *and* the aunt, wasn't it? The town revelled in talk of your sexual prowess. True?'

'There was some trouble,' I admitted ruefully.

'Indeed,' she smiled knowingly. 'You fled the scene, of course, but I reasoned you wouldn't go far. Africa is perfect for the likes of you. Since you are a pilot and Entebbe has a busy airport, I thought you might turn up. I was right, wasn't I?'

'You've got me,' I had to say.

'I intend to have you,' she informed me calmly, studying her painted fingernails. 'You saw my old man, Jumbo, and what a fat pompous ass he is. I haven't made love with him for over a year, and then it was not memorable. I'm told I'm not unattractive. Men like well-built women like me. And I'm in need of a good fuck—'

'There must be many local men, members of your club, willing to do the necessary—' I began.

'I wouldn't risk it, the place is a hot-bed of gossip,' she replied. 'Affairs never remain secret in such a tight community. You've had enough trouble, it got you kicked out of Kenya. Word of it here would finish you in Uganda. So you keep my secret and I'll keep yours. Bargain?'

'Here I go again,' I muttered and she laughed at me.

'Book a room and I'll join you,' Beverley ordered. 'My husband has a committee meeting all evening. Time's wasting.

Chapter Two

The room I booked into was part of an annexe to the main building of the hotel. It was suggested to me by Beverley Marchbanks as being more discreet because it could be entered by a rear door from the car park. It was cheaper too, which suited me, and the room itself was well fitted out with twin beds, adequate furniture and a bathroom with a shower. This I wanted to use right away as my clothes were sticking to me after my bus journey in oven-like heat. But Mrs Marchbanks joined me moments after I'd been shown into my room. She wanted something else.

'No,' she stated firmly when I suggested I sluice off the sweat of travel. 'I've had enough of clean sex to do me; we can shower later – together.' She raised an arm to sniff at her armpit. 'I've been playing tennis all afternoon and am rather high myself. I rather fancy a sweaty bump and grind for a change. Let's get on with it—'

The lady liked a bit of rough, I guessed, and I no doubt fitted the bill. As she stripped off her tennis outfit beside a bed, throwing the clothes aside and revealing herself, I had no complaints. She had an all-over tan which showed she sun-bathed nude, and her smooth skin had an exotic glow.

In the Groove

I admired the big ripe heavy-hung breasts, the ample thighs with the raised mound nestling between and the growth of thick pubic hair flattened by perspiration. There was nothing else for it but to enjoy and to hell with the consequences. She came to me, unbuttoning my shirt and pushing if off my shoulders. 'I want to see *you*,' she said, her hands unbuckling my belt and unzipping my jeans, pulling them down to my knees. 'Yes, oh yes,' I heard her murmur as my prick stood out horizontally in its semi-erect state. 'That is a *good* one. I shall love that up my cunt. It must be eight inches at least—' Her hand grasped it, fingers circling the girth, gently stroking. Under her manipulation the stalk tightened and thickened, grew in length. 'Nine or ten now,' she observed lewdly. 'My God, it is a prize specimen. Such a bulbous knob on it too. I've never taken the like—'

Looking down I was regaled by the lovely sight of her big damp tits nestling together in their fullness, the cleavage a thin line. I would have my dick between them as a future treat, I decided, wondering if her fat husband Jumbo had ever enjoyed that pleasant deviation.

She was still cooing over the size of my cock. 'I've never taken the like,' she repeated, impressed.

'It has always all gone in,' I assured her. 'Let me show you—'

'I want to ride on it,' she told me firmly. 'It's something I've always wanted to with an outsized cock. Lie on the bed, kick off your trousers and do as I say. Now, right away—'

I could think of lots of things to do with her – fondling her magnificent breasts, sucking the thickened nipples, touching up and tonguing her clitty. I enjoyed lengthy foreplay designed to have women begging to be fucked – always a powerful stimulant for both participants of a properly arranged fuck by a good cocksman.

But this woman was eager to ride on the staff she had in her hand, desirous of its pulsating hardness and heat inside her to grind down on, no doubt with her mind racing wantonly and rotating her fine arse ever wilder. It was a lazy way for a man to fuck but many women liked the change in position. It had its merits too. Lying back, one could enjoy the expression on the female features as her excitement mounted; the glazed eyes, the gaping mouth with its cries and moans as inhibitions were abandoned. There was also the spectacle of gyrating breasts before one's very eyes and the pleasure of watching them in flight.

'This is blackmail,' I taunted her, but she was beyond being amused by talk. I was almost thrown to the bed and she knelt over me, her strapping thighs parted, the plump split at their divide poised directly over my now rampant dick. She reached down to pull it upright, quite roughly rubbing the circumcised plum-shaped knob against her outer cunt lips. Then, with a low moan, she thrust down to impale herself on its rigid length, pubic hair to pubic hair. The hard fullness so suddenly embedded deeply within, made her gasp and remain still for a long moment.

'God, it's like an iron bar inside me, I feel filled to the stomach,' she gasped once she was accustomed to the feel of it. 'I couldn't resist trying it for size. No wonder the Gore-Blomley females liked it. Did you fuck them separately or all together? I want you to tell me—'

'Let's stick to the business in hand,' I said, now fully aroused by the delightful sensation of my dong enveloped deep in the moist soft folds of Mrs Marchbanks's tight recess. Her magnificent tits hung over me like two balloons, forcing me to reach up to heft their solid weightiness. I moved my hips, giving a little jiggle to shunt my probing dick into her. She in turn groaned as if in agony, at first gingerly grinding her cushiony arse to my tentative thrusts, timing her downward movements to meet my uplifting thighs. Once the lech proved too strong, she positively moaned with pleasure, working her pelvis ever faster, urging me on with the lewdest cries. She had been right. The lady needed a good fuck.

Her vocal accompaniments shouldn't have surprised me, but it always does when an outwardly sensible and respectable woman gives vent to the most obscene crudities when being fucked to a climax. I like it. It greatly adds to the occasion, heightening the lustful feelings, bringing out the real woman, the hidden side. 'Oh, God, fuck that thing up me harder, you bastard,' Beverley ground out ecstatically, leaning back from me, tits bouncing, neck craned and eyes wild, each utterance sounding more guttural and throatier. 'Fill my cunt, stuff it full! Shoot your load up me! Keep fucking, go on, go on – oh, I'm coming – COMING! Oh heaven!' Her bucking, grinding and furious gyrations gradually slowed. With much huffing and puffing she disengaged herself, falling sideways and face down across the narrow bed. 'You dirty sod,' she muttered into the coverlet. 'You raped me.' How like a woman to come out with that. If anybody had been raped, I had.

All the same it had been a memorable first ride with

a fine, full-bodied and undoubtedly frustrated female. I wondered if, now that she had tried me, it would end there. I'm not in any way reluctant to fuck any attractive woman, but screwing around was what had put paid to a very good life in Kenya, and here I was getting off on the wrong foot again so soon after my arrival in Uganda. Until I was accepted it was common sense to play it cool. Her husband, Jumbo Marchbanks, was obviously a pillar of the local white society, and would not appreciate my rogering his wife when I needed a job and a place to stay. I had money enough only for a few nights' stay in a high-class hotel, so I was dependent on being thought a dependable type by the stuffy expatriate community, worthy of paid employment and able to rent a bungalow or some reasonable residence. Thinking as much, I suggested to the lady lolling naked across the bed that she should dress and leave while the going was good.

Even while saying so I could not resist admiring the curve of her back, the sweep of splendid rounded buttocks so presented and my hand began to fondle each cheek, my middle finger idly stroking into the enticing parting. Deciding that such an action was hardly conducive to suggesting she leave, I stopped touching her up and instead gave her plump backside a good hearty slap.

'You big bastard,' she complained, 'I was just enjoying you feeling me up. Why do you want me to go?' She sat up, tits wobbling delightfully to face me, rubbing her smacked bottom.

'No sense being too blatant about you being with me, is there?' I suggested. 'You were a lovely fuck, let's call it quits.'

In the Groove

'Who's to know?' she said coolly. 'Besides, I can't leave until it's dark—'

'It's bloody dark already,' I said, for in equatorial East Africa night fell sharp at seven every evening like a curtain. I was laughed at for my concern, her big breasts jiggling.

'Getting cold feet are you, the infamous Tyler Wight?' she teased me. 'No one will miss me. I told you, my husband is chairing a meeting at the club. Jumbo is so long-winded it goes on for hours. Being president of a club out here automatically makes a man a prick, as if Jumbo isn't a big enough one naturally. Except where it counts, of course. If he can muster three inches with a hard-on, I've never known it. Do what you were doing to me just now,' she added, rolling over and presenting her lovely arse.

What could one do, offered such a tantalising sight? My hand went back to caress the firm moons and my finger slipped into the deep cleft between, finding it warm and damp and her cunt lips still pouting from the recent shafting. She gurgled her agreement as I probed and titillated a very engorged clitoris, stiff as a fingertip. 'That is *nice*,' she stated. 'Don't stop, I like it.' Her hands came back to pull apart the cheeks of her arse. 'When you are ready again, I want it this way this time. Doggy fashion I believe it's called, isn't it?'

'If you insist,' I grinned. 'Tell me, do you ever tell old Jumbo so matter-of-factly what your sexual preferences are? He might appreciate it. Most men would—'

'Never mind him. Tell me what you feel. Talk to me.'

'You have magnificent tits just made for a lovely titty-ride,' I told her, 'and a splendid arse built for a back-

In the Groove

scuttle. A cunt as tight as a mouse's ear too—' My hand was now in to the wrist in the hot dank cleavage of her raised bottom, clamped between the rounded cheeks, a curled finger in moist cunt-flesh idly circling the taut clitty. She moved her buttocks in a slow grinding movement against the captive hand, uttering little moans and sighs. 'Well juiced but tight as a mouse's ear,' I repeated.

'Only my husband has ever been there,' she admitted sadly. 'I married young, almost from finishing school, imagining a life of an overseas wife would be exciting. But Jumbo turned out to be a typical Foreign Office idiot, dressing for dinner in the wilds of Borneo, maintaining true Brit standards in all our postings in far-flung outposts. As a dutiful wife I was no more than a decoration, the perfect hostess. No more! I'm not getting any younger. I want to find out what I've missed—' She moaned again, tilting her cunt to my fingering. 'Are you ready to fuck me again? I need another of those lovely comes—'

She evidently didn't intend to rush off, and I've always revelled in unhurried sex-play – having the women with me getting impatient for the cock, having them completely uninhibited and eagerly revealing their innermost desires. No doubt long frustrated, Beverley wanted the works, with lewd vocal accompaniments. I withdrew my hand from her parted bum cheeks, eyeing up the downward bulge of her cunt before going in there with my face, tongue extended to snuffle like a hog after acorns.

'Oh, oooh!' she exclaimed in surprise. 'I've heard of *that*, but never experienced it. Oh, Lord, is that your *tongue*? Oh, oh, ooooh,' she groaned, bucking her arse, buffeting my face, her excitement mounting. 'You'll make me come, you devil! God oh god, I can't help it – I'm there – COMING! Dirty beast – Aaaargh!'

Her big arse swivelled and jerked in helpless convulsions, face buried in the pillows, on her knees and perfectly positioned for the rear entry I was now ready to accomplish. 'Stay still a moment, damn you, woman!' I ordered her sharply, endorsing that command with a couple of good smart smacks across her ample buttocks. On my knees behind her, my rejuvenated prick poised to penetrate her well-salivated pouting fig, she turned her head questioningly. All the same, when entered to my balls, cushioned in the warm folds of her bottom, she grunted as if in an agony of delight with the stiff intruder up her, muttering 'Yes, oh yes, give me that, every lovely inch of it, my darling—'

I fully intended to, altering the angle of entry as I shafted her, withdrawing to the knob and thrusting in again while she gurgled and gabbled helplessly in her pleasure. Like a veteran, she balled her arse back to me, rotated it, squirmed it into my curved belly as I crouched over her back like a dog on a bitch, hands grasping her down-hanging tits for anchorage. The heat in my balls boiled and released itself in a surge through my dick, arse thrusting ever faster as I jetted my load deep inside a receptive cunt. She too went out of control, crying out wildly as she climaxed. Finally she fell forward as if utterly spent. For long moments we could only gasp and regain normal breathing.

'Old Jumbo don't know what he's got or what he's missing,' I told her admiringly in time. 'That was a truly magnificent fuck, Mrs Marchbanks. Thank you.'

'The pleasure was all mine,' she said wickedly, sitting up beside me and fanning her face in mock gestures. 'I'm not sure how many times you made me come; more than enough for another man's wife, I'm bound to say. Now I think we should use your shower, Mr Tyler Wight. Then you'll be in time to dine here, the food is very good. You must keep up your strength for me. I shall want more of what we did, you know—'

I soaped her breasts and thighs, we dried each other, and she dressed and prepared to leave. 'There'll be a man here for dinner tonight,' she informed me, 'a Sam Bishop who you should introduce yourself to. He's flying home to England tomorrow and I've heard is seeking a caretaker for his house while he's away. It's the usual thing out here, unlived-in houses get robbed of one's things almost without fail while the occupier is off on home leave or safari. He'll be in the bar for sure after dinner if I know Sam Bishop. Cultivate him a little, let him know you are seeking a place to stay; he may well offer you his bungalow to caretake until he returns.'

She saw my hesitation and laughed. 'Don't worry, he's not a Jumbo-type, but a bit of a rough diamond himself – like you! Say you know me if that will help. I'll be interested to know how you get on. If you get his place as a temporary stopover while he's away, it would be ideal for me to visit you, situated by itself near the airport and not where the white community lives—'

'I'll seek him out,' I promised, 'but your offering to visit me, much as I'd like that, don't you think it risky? I don't need to look for trouble, it always seeks me out.'

'Don't worry,' she assured me. 'We'll be the soul of discretion. I won't look at you in the club when you get to join, as you no doubt will in time. I'll ignore you completely, but don't think after what you did to me this evening I won't want more. It was what I've fantasised and I'm not letting you off the hook.' Before she slipped out of the door to the corridor and the door to the car park, she clamped her arms around my neck and pushed her big cushiony breasts to my chest, kissing me lingeringly and sliding her tongue in my mouth. 'Our first kiss, and after all that we did,' she teased, 'there'll be more.'

Alone, I fished out a fresh shirt from my holdall, went through to the main building of the hotel and looked in the bar before going to the dining hall. It was modern and spacious with subdued lighting, tables and armchairs, decorated with the skins of the local wild game and mounted lion and leopard heads, large tusks. One or two couples sat at the tables but at the bar was a solitary man in a safari suit, drinking morosely. I went up to order a whisky and soda from the splendidly attired black barman in flunky's livery, and the lone drinker glanced at me, a heavy-set man with a large moustache. 'Join me,' he offered. 'I'll pay for that. You look like one of us, an Africa hand, not a bloody millionaire tourist. I'm going to get good and pissed tonight. Sam Bishop's the name. Keep me company.'

Chapter Three

That was an offer I couldn't refuse, seeing as I had hoped to meet up with the same Sam Bishop. Beverley's description of him being a rough diamond was about right. He was already half-sozzled, and I intended to state my case about needing a place to live before he got insensible. 'You got yourself a drinking partner,' I said, giving my name and offering my hand. 'Just arrived in Entebbe and looking for work and a place to stay. I enquired at the club but got short shrift—'

'Bunch of stuck-up bastards, full of their own importance,' Sam agreed. 'Me, I earn my living, got my own business here, built it up myself.' He brushed his moustache and steadied his eyes to focus on me. 'You ain't a government wallah, I take it. What'ya do?'

'I flew bush in Kenya, thought I'd try my luck in Uganda. Busy airport here, I'm a good pilot.'

'I intend to get an aircraft for my set-up,' he said. 'Photo Safaris, that's me, catering for the rubber-neckers who come to East Africa and don't want to shoot everything in sight except with a camera. Right now I run to a few LandRovers to take parties up-country, but I'm thinking ahead. Some of my paying customers don't like their rich arses jolted for hours over dirt roads to see the game. Flying 'em up will be the thing. Drop 'em right in prepared camps in the bundu—'

'I'm your man if you get an aircraft,' I offered grandly.

He considered that but said nothing, ordering doubles and swallowing his down. 'Who did you work for in Kenya?' he said when lowering his glass. 'Are your papers in order? Have you got a work permit for Uganda?'

'Nizar Ramji,' I answered. 'I flew a DH Dragonfly for him.'

'I know him, a shrewd hindi. Work permit's no problem here, a bribe will get one. You're not drinking—'

I downed my whisky, deciding to attempt to keep him sober enough to remember me, suggesting we go through to have dinner. At the table he regarded me afresh, screwing up his face as if to steady his brain. 'I'm off to England tomorrow,' he stated. 'Bloody wife trouble – she's with another bloke. I don't mind that, everyone's entitled to a bit on the side; I fuck every woman that lets me, black or white. But I need her here, she's a trained accountant, nobody better at keeping my books.'

'A good enough reason,' I agreed.

The food was excellent, a steak that was tender and well done, just as I like it. Sam Bishop toyed with his, agitated and drinking steadily. 'She's a fine piece, not just an accountant. I hope to Christ she agrees to come back. It's my fault she went off with this bloke. I encouraged it. Would you believe that?'

I had fucked men's wives in my time, while their husbands watched with mounting excitement at witnessing

In the Groove

their women being shafted by another man. If Sam was such, he seemed set to relive the experience. 'If you say so,' I agreed. My guess had been correct. He launched into all the lurid details.

'Tall, dark and handsome bastard,' he recalled, 'and a lot younger than my wife and me. Out here on a temporary assignment for some news agency and he hired my outfit to go upcountry. I drove him myself and got chummy. He could drink. All his talk was about the women he'd had, how good he was at it. Taking a piss with him in the bush one day, he flashed his dick at me, saying this was what made his army of females return for more.' Sam hiccupped. 'Christ, in its relaxed state you could have used it to whip cats from under the bed. Thick and bloody long, that dong. Never seen the like—'

'Lucky old him,' I put in. At least while he talked, warming to the subject, he wasn't drinking so much.

'Luckier than you think,' Sam continued. 'I told my wife about it and she got too interested. Bitch,' he added, but I detected a hint of pride for his game missis in his slurred voice. 'She made me describe its size and how many inches did I suppose it was? She had me hold up my hands like a fisherman describing the one that got away. I ain't exactly short in the dick department, mind you, but that woman was *intrigued*—'

I could guess what was coming next. 'I hope you didn't invite the big bastard home to meet her—' I said.

'Just what I did,' Sam nodded grimly, appreciating my showing interest. 'She received him all dolled up in her war-paint, looking a treat with her big tits and fine arse in a tight dress. We sat drinking and the talk got sexual. Big

Callum couldn't keep is eyes off her, fairly boasting of his success with women and hinting at the reason why—'

It was a familiar scenario to a wife-watching get-together, almost a ritual prelude necessary before getting down to the nitty-gritty. I had been there. 'You couldn't blame her too much if she was impressed with the guy,' I offered sympathetically, ingratiating myself as much as possible. The more he thought me a soul spirit, the better chance he might let me caretake his house when I suggested that later. Right then he was getting a kick recalling the night big Callum had patently screwed his wife. 'Somebody new and attractive,' I added. 'And the drink, the horny atmosphere at the time. His eyeing her up, probably flattering her too – what woman wouldn't feel sexually attracted?'

'Right!' he agreed. 'She was all for it, flirting back like a schoolgirl, starting to match his tales of having it off with stories of her past that I'd never heard myself Like when she was a teenager and her piano teacher screwed her regularly. Or at the bloody boarding house in Bournemouth where her parents went every summer. Seventeen she was and her ma caught her being laid by the bloke who owned the joint. That put paid to the holiday there. Christ, she came out with as good as she got, flaunting it—'

I could imagine how Sam and their guest had enjoyed her lewd confessions. What was more, I decided, I admired her for letting her hair down, joining in the spirit of the occasion. 'Sounds like my kind of woman,' I couldn't resist saying. 'The world would be a happier place for more like that. Are you complaining, it sounds like a bloody good fun evening. What do you want, a wife so inhibited she won't allow frank talk?'

In the Groove

'It went beyond talk,' Sam admitted wryly if unable to contain his pleasure at finding an appreciative audience. 'I went to the kitchen to get ice. Looking back into the lounge I saw 'em in a clinch on the couch, mouth to mouth and his hand inside her blouse feeling up her tit. I stood watching 'em snog like they wanted to eat each other, and you know something—?'

'It must have been the horniest sight you'd ever seen,' I reckoned. 'Your wife and this cock artist. I couldn't blame you for being turned on. I would have been—'

'You got it!' he exclaimed, delighted with my deliberate appraisal. 'I can't explain it – I *wanted* him to screw the arse off her with his big prick and see every inch go up her cunt. So I walked in on them and said, "Don't stop for me", and they didn't. Callum opened her blouse and she undid her bra and let her tits free so he could play with 'em and suck at her nipples. Then he unzipped and brought out his pride and joy, taking her hand to it. No wonder she gasped. It reared up over her grasp like a bloody great cucumber, long and thick and hard as iron. I heard her mumble she wanted it, then he was lowering her along the couch. "No," she said, "the bed, I want to do it on our bed." So she got up, leading him still clutching his dong.'

'Fuck me,' I said. 'You couldn't do much about it then.' I noted his glass had remained empty and he hadn't called for a refill. I rather hoped he had finished his tale and I could work around to suggesting I caretake his bungalow. I was wrong on both counts. More drinks were called for and he continued.

'I couldn't do a thing about it,' he said, his voice thick with drink and emotion. 'Of course I was well pissed,' he attempted to excuse himself, 'or I could have stopped it.

But Marje was all for it, the way she took him off to bed, desperate to have that monster dick. So I poured myself a stiff drink and went into the bedroom. Their clothes were strewn all over the floor, like they couldn't wait, and she was already on the bed, on her back and with her legs around his waist, hauling on his arse while he shagged her rotten—'

'Both naked and bellies slapping,' I encouraged him. 'That must have been some sight. I'd have liked to have seen it. Loving it, was she?' Sam must have savoured every moment for his recall was blow-for-blow. He had revelled in the spectacle.

'Loving it? The horny cow was rolling her eyes, grunting and crying out for more, thrusting up to him to get the lot. "Does it feel good, love?" I asked her, a bloody stupid question, with all that prick up her. And Callum, the boastful sod, pulled out his dong from her and said, "This is what she's taking." Jeez, it was glistening bright pink and looked foot long. And Marje cried out, "Put it back, never mind Sam, fuck me with it, don't stop, don't stop," bucking like a sex maniac out of her skull—'

It went on, how she had shamelessly sucked Callum's giant cock to get it up again; how she had ridden over him with her big tits swinging like bells, and couldn't get enough of it, Sam seeing it all until Callum was fucked useless and he had taken over, his wife seemingly insatiable that night.

As the waiters waited desiring to clean up and get finished, we adjourned to the bar. The story concluded while Sam drank. He admitted that Callum had visited his wife while he was at work, coming home to find her, no doubt, with a broad smile on her face. Before he collapsed at the bar, he said that his missis had suddenly expressed a desire to go home for a visit to England, where he was sure she was shacked up with the virile Callum.

Left with an unconscious drunk slumped in an armchair, the barman informed me Sam's house servant was waiting outside in case he needed help to get home – evidently this was a regular occurrence.

'Send him in, then,' I said. 'Between the two of us we can get him on his feet.' The servant who appeared was a comely African girl who introduced herself as his housemaid. Very nice too, I thought.

'Bwana Sam cannot drive in this state, sir,' she said. 'Perhaps you would drive him home if I show you the way.'

There seemed little else for it. We got Sam out of the chair, no easy task for such a bulky figure, and he came to somewhat. 'Ah, Bibi, the best girl in the world,' he said in a maudlin fashion, hugging her for support. It was not hard to figure out that Sam was more than just employer. She looked embarrassed when he tried to kiss her, so we dragged him off to his car, a splendidly lengthy Oldsmobile with acres of chrome grill at front and large flaring flanges at the rear. I fished the car keys from his pocket and, with the girl supporting him between us, I was directed down dark roads fringed with banana plantains until the headlights revealed a lone neat bungalow with verandah.

The girl and I undressed Sam while he lay slumped across a king-sized bed, the very one Callum had fucked the eager Marje on, I had no doubt. 'You will stay the night, sir,' the girl offered. 'No *mzungu* could walk back to the hotel at this time of night, you would be killed for your money and watch, even your shoes. There is a spare room ready.'

I decided that this was commonsense and, after the amount of booze I'd consumed keeping up with Sam, I fell into a deep sleep, exhausted by the day's travel and my energetic bouts with the eager Beverley Marchbanks. Awakening to bright sunlight on the curtains, I felt absolutely starving.

I arose, found a splendid tiled bathroom and showered, using Sam's razor to shave, and then investigated the house. In the corridor outside the main bedroom I paused to hear the bumping of a bed and the grunts and muffled moans of a fuck taking place. Sam had obviously recovered and was screwing his servant.

I sat on the verandah to take in the local scene. African women were passing by on their way to market with saleable produce balanced on their heads, and aircraft, both military and civil, took off at intervals from the airport beyond the trees. Eventually Sam appeared, yawning and stretching. He greeted me affably.

'Come on in, there's bacon and eggs on the go,' he said. 'Bibi cooks up a great breakfast, fried bread and all. You said you were needing a place to stay until you get fixed, I dimly recall. Why not stay here while I'm in the UK? It would be doing me a favour, this joint would be burgled for sure. The locals know when occupants are away – they know everything about everybody – they'll rob you blind because they ain't got much of anything. You want it?' He held out a bunch of keys. 'That goes for my car too, Tyler or whatever you call yourself. You get everything but Bibi. She's going home to see her mama so you'll have to find a servant for yourself.'

In the Groove

'Bloody good of you, Sam,' I thanked him, but he waved my thanks aside. At the breakfast table he considered me again, scratching his stubble. 'Looking for work too, eh?' he said. 'I can fix you up there. My clients feel safer on safari with another white man knowing the lingo and in charge of the boys. Speak Swahili and know the bush, do you? Drive a LandRover and know how to act with the hoipoloi, nobility and millionaires and film stars and the like?'

'To the manner born,' I assured him.

'I'll take you to the airport before I fly out today and show you my office and set-up,' he decided. 'You're my sort, I reckon. Joginder Singh is my manager at base, good bloke. He'll see you right. I'll pay you same as he gets.' He held out a huge hand. 'Have we a deal?'

'You got it,' I told him. Safari leader to rich tourists seemed promising. Lucky old Tyler Wight, I congratulated myself. As ever in my darkest moments, fortune had smiled on me. 'Hope your trip home works out,' I dared suggest. 'Getting your wife back. She seems worth the going after.'

'You'll see, if I can get her to come back,' he promised.

Chapter Four

Photo Safaris' office was in the main terminal building of Entebbe airport, handily placed to receive Sam Bishop's clients as they arrived from America, Europe or Japan. In those days, before package tours, people had to be rich to indulge themselves in the African scene. On the fringe of the airport itself, Sam had a workshop and garaging for his fleet of LandRovers, with African drivers, cooks and mechanics on hand. The office was modern and decorated with large photographs of all the main game of Uganda: lion, leopard, elephant and buffalo, well suited to give arrivals an idea of what they could see and photograph themselves.

It was all very professional, surprising me that rough-as-guts Sam Bishop could run such an operation. Not so, I was informed by the turbanned Sikh, Joginder Singh, who was the office manager. Mr Bishop and his wife Marjory were excellent business people, he said loyally, who could mix with the highest-born, the famous and the wealthy who took the safari holiday. It seemed it was no cheap-skate operation, either, gourmet meals and champagne being served even out in the bush. The Sikh looked hard at

In the Groove

me as if to say I must keep up the standard. We went outside to see Sam off on his afternoon flight.

No clients were expected for two days, so I made myself known to the boys at the garage workshop, and then drove back into Entebbe town to supply myself with groceries and drink, paid for by the advance I'd received as an employee of Photo Safaris. My work permit was already assured by Joginder making a phone call to some corrupt official. An Asian-owned store, a mini-supermarket stocked with European goods plus blankets and cooking pots for the locals, provided all I required. Going out with my box of supplies to the splendid Oldsmobile car, I saw Beverley Marchbanks drive by and do a double-take, pulling up sharply alongside in the deserted street.

'I take it you met Sam Bishop,' she smiled warmly. 'I'm so pleased for us. You're evidently caretaking his car as well as his house, then?'

'Yes, employed by his firm, at least while he's away too,' I said. 'Thanks to you, Bev—'

'And to the man Sam's wife ran off to be with, otherwise he wouldn't be going home to collect her.' She leaned out of the open car window, a wicked look on her attractive face. 'Can you imagine a good wife wanting to sleep with another man? Goodness, what the world is coming to—'

'Doesn't bear thinking about,' I agreed.

'I shall pop down to see if you are settled in Sam's bungalow soon,' she said meaningfully. 'Unfortunately for me, we're giving a dinner party and tonight I must do my perfect hostess bit for the British High Commissioner and others of that ilk. But don't think I won't be calling on your services before long, Tyler Wight. I've thought of

In the Groove

nothing else but what you did to me. I'd so enjoy a good romp right now.'

Though Sam's bungalow was off the beaten track I smelt trouble with Beverley so blatant about me fucking her regularly. At the same time, I did not want to miss out on such a well-upholstered lady, who obviously would welcome me trying out every sexual permutation on her lush body. 'Go easy, for Christ's sake,' I warned her. 'We don't want it getting out, do we?' As she leaned out, I could see down the neck of her dress and couldn't help admiring the big rounded mounds of her breasts.

'You're ogling my tits,' she taunted me. 'Do you still fancy – what did you call it – titty-fucking them? I've never experienced that. We must try it, darling. Be at home tomorrow night. I'll call by—'

I didn't like the 'darling' bit as she drove off, or her ordering me to be at home. Perhaps that was her way of addressing people, but I suspected she now regarded me as her lover, her sole property in a passionate affair. If it was kept entirely secret, I was happy to shag her rotten, but purely on a physical basis with no other strings attached. Resigning myself to to my fate as ever I envisaged it would all end in tears and wondered how long I would last in Uganda. I drove back to the cottage considering this fact, surprised to see waiting in the garden a dozen or so African men and women. They rushed around me as I got out of the car, waving papers at me that were references from previous employers as to their honesty and efficiency as cooks and house servants, all entreating me to choose.

Which one to pick was the question. All of them were dressed in their best and I hated to disappoint so many.

Then I saw the statuesque Jovial Nkutu who I'd seen feeding her child before joining me on the bus the day before. 'Oh, good.' I said, 'Mrs Nkutu, you came as promised.' Turning to the others, I apologised. 'I'm sorry to say, ladies and gents, I've already engaged a house servant. Thank you all for coming—'

The little throng melted away, leaving me with Jovial, the proud creature regarding me with her usual calm despite landing the job. She held out a previous reference for me to read. I didn't need to see it, having made up my mind it would be pleasant to have such a beauty around, but went through the motions as was expected. It was dated over two years before and began abruptly. 'Nkutu is clean and a good worker, a plain cook and honest. She has been with me several months and leaves my employ because of impending confinement. Recommended. Major John Marchbanks, OBE, 32 Ovango Drive, Entebbe.'

My first thought was of the coincidence, that the girl had worked for Marchbanks. And how like the pompous ass to put his wartime rank and his decoration with his signature. 'So you know the Marchbanks?' I ventured. 'How did you get on with the lady of the house?' I could foresee trouble if Beverley intended to call and Jovial knew her. Gossip about their white employers was a main topic of interest among servants, all of which became common knowledge in the whole community. Too late, I thought, Jovial would recognise my visitor.

It did not bode well, but the girl answered, 'I did not know the memsa'ab, Mrs Marchbanks. She was at home with her children in England while I worked for her

In the Groove

bwana.' That was a break, I decided, but I still intended to ensure that the two women did not meet. By evening, with Jovial settled with her belongings in one of three little houses in the garden that were the servants' quarters, she was busy in the kitchen making my evening meal. As she laid the table I admired the rounds of her arse, the movement of her breasts under the busuti gown. She served pork chops and chips which were perfectly cooked, then busied herself washing the dishes while I sat on the verandah enjoying the sunset. It seemed I had again stumbled on the good life.

She asked for a bucket of hot water to bathe herself as I was leaving to drive to the hotel, remembering I had to pay for the room I hadn't used. I had certainly got my money's worth fucking Beverley Marchbanks there. I also had my holdall to pick up which contained all my worldly possessions.

In the bar I got talking and drinking with two airline pilots, then drove back to the bungalow, feeling like a good jump after being in the company of the air hostesses who were with the pilots – three gorgeous young German girls all painted and scented, who aroused a lech in me. I would have to settle for my lonely bed, I considered. On entering the house, I was followed in by Jovial, who enquired if I required supper?

'No,' I thanked her, 'you finish every day after you've made dinner. If I need a sandwich I can make it myself. Your time off is for you, I won't expect anything else—'

'Do you want me to come to your bed, sir?' she asked almost matter-of-factly. 'I do not mind, if you would want me there—'

In the Groove

'Christ,' I said, amused and surprised. 'Is this the usual, what you called "all services" in the bus? Thanks for offering, but the pay we agreed on was for housegirl wages. What makes you think I'd expect you to sleep with me?' The thought was exceedingly tempting. But for the threatened visits by Beverley Marchbanks, I would not have hesitated.

'I have seen the way you look at me, sir,' Jovial said. 'You have no woman here for your bed. Take me there, if you would like that. I myself would like it also—'

Spoken like a properly brought-up African maid, I remembered from my time in Kenya, where the practice was instilled in girls to please men as a duty. I told myself if I refused her generous offer she would feel humiliated by the rebuff. A sudden thought struck me as well. 'What about when you were housegirl to old Marchbanks? Was that "all duties" too while his wife was away?'

'I went to his bed, yes, sir—'

'The fat old fraud,' I had to grin. All the same, he went up in my estimation somewhat, and I also felt I had something on the officious bastard if push came to shove one day. 'We'll have a drink on that,' I announced, knowing that African girls enjoyed a beer, going to the fridge to get out two frosty bottles of the locally brewed Nile Special. 'Let's take it through to bed—'

Life can be a bitch, as they say, but it does have its moments. One of them must surely be tilting a bottle of ice-cold beer to your mouth in a cosy bedroom while you watch a strapping wench take off her clothes and savour all that will follow. When Jovial was naked, her skin as black as ebony with a polished sheen that glowed in the bedside lamp, she stood still to let me look her over. I admired the merchandise: magnificent full breasts with nipples like thumbs, a narrow waist that flared out to rounded thighs with the plump wiry-haired bulge of a prominent cunt mound between and strong shapely legs.

'Do I please you, sir?' she asked.

No reply was necessary. I handed over the uncapped bottle and she drank several swallows before placing the bottle on a bedside cabinet. I began to undress, my dick already hard, noting the delightful way her big tits hung forward as she bent to place the beer bottle; the fat round uplifted teats swinging out to become elongated ones. Then, to my surprise, she opened the wardrobe door which had a long mirror fixed behind it, moving the door until the mirror reflected the bed. She then manually shifted the dressing table with its large mirror until that too allowed an image of the bed. Now as we fucked we could watch ourselves.

'You like to see what's going on,' I said amused.

'I thought all white men liked that,' she replied, getting on the bed and reaching again for her beer. 'Major Marchbanks always moved the furniture so that he could see himself—' She gave her beautiful perfect white-toothed grin, studying my erection. 'Perhaps you did not need it like he did—'

'No problem,' I assured her, joining her on the bed to have her free hand clasp my boner. 'Had trouble getting it up, did the dirty old major?' I could imagine the sight of his fat arse thrusting over the girl and getting his kicks watching his reflection. I made a mental note that I'd use the same trick when his wife called. Cool fingers now slowly and sensually stroked my shaft, bringing it to full iron-hard rigidity and length. I reached over to place her beer bottle on the bedside cabinet. 'Later,' I said.

She giggled, turning to me, still holding my prick. 'You are like African man,' she informed me, pleased. 'The major he was—'

'I know, I know,' I said, cupping a weighty tit, finding my palm sticky from a leaking nipple. I recalled how she had fed her child before leaving him. I kissed her full lips, my tongue probing a warm sweet mouth and she moaned, pressing her cushiony body against me drawing my hand down to the fork of her thighs. I covered the mound with my hand, curling my middle finger to insinuate it into a fat lipless cunt, the inside soft, receptively warm and moist. She moaned softly, gripping my finger like a vice with her cunt muscles, working her pelvis to my hand. The girl enjoyed kissing too, rolling her soft lips over my mouth and using her tongue to flick and curl against mine. If it was putting on an act to please me, it was an Academy Award performance.

I didn't think so as her agitation increased, and she threw her right leg across my waist. Her left leg was straight out, the other crooked from the knee over my middle, and in that position her cunt was directly over my prick. Holding it upright in her hand, she shuffled down until my knob pierced her split and then she thrust, taking my length to my balls. It was, for all my past experience, an entirely new way for me to fuck a woman; on my back, with her half-inclined on her back above me, both of us facing the ceiling. She then uttered little whimpering cries, rotating her smooth arse on my upper thighs, relishing the hard cylinder of flesh poking her. 'Oh, mama, *mama*,' she moaned. 'He is making me do this—'

Jovial was obviously a sexual animal, well-versed in fucking to gain the ultimate pleasure from a bout. Her cunt passage clenched, relaxed, clenched again over my shaft as if milking it, a sensation that had me writhing below her, my balls churning with liquid fire and the cock imprisoned up her on the verge of jetting its load deep within. It would have been a blessed relief except that I'd always prided myself on being a stayer, bringing my women off several times. I liked to have them jerking and mouthing wild utterances until they were sated, fucked ragged. In this instance I'd met my match. The African girl was firmly in control and determined to bring me off inside her. I clenched my teeth, held back from letting fly with determination, set upon lasting the course. It became a battle of wills, the girl bucking over my thighs ever more calculatingly, furiously.

Another reason I did not want to come in her was the fear of impregnating the girl. In my experience, to become pregnant during child-bearing age was almost a reason for existing so far as African women were concerned. They loved having babies, were proud of motherhood. And to have sons was an insurance for their old age in a land where state pensions or other sources of income were non-existent. 'You come, sir!' she shouted, thrusting against my loins, as if aware of my thoughts. 'Put your milk down there! Let it come into me now—'

But I won, she at last gurgling and undulating faster and crying out that she was done, *done*! Helplessly out of control, she juddered and gyrated, coming with loud

In the Groove

groans until her spasms subsided and she fell aside from me, just in time as my prick left her cunt and I jerked and my offering came in strong spurts over her thigh. We lay gasping from a great coupling, but when she spoke it was to complain. 'You did not finish inside me, sir,' she said disappointedly. She turned away from me, presenting her noble black backside to me with its two full moons. I could not resist fondling such opulence, going into the cleave. As if to show her annoyance, she clenched her buttocks, trapping my hand.

'I don't give out babies, Jove,' I told her kindly. 'It was a tremendous fuck and I loved what you did for me, but there will be no kids made when you come to my bed. What would your husband think if you went back to your village with a *mzungu* child in your belly—?'

'There is no husband,' she said, and I should have known. 'The father of my son is chief of my tribe who has many wives. I was taken to him by my father, who owed him a debt—'

'You didn't mind?' I asked. I noted that she had relaxed her backside, allowing me to continue fondling. She wriggled on my hand, sexy creature that she was, enjoying the touching up.

'I have my son,' she said, as if that was reason enough. 'And do not worry about making me with child. I am wombed again.' I knew that lovely African expression for being pregnant. 'This I found out when I was to leave the village to earn wages. It is the first weeks.'

'Your chief again?' I enquired, thinking I wouldn't have to refrain from spurting my lot into her in future couplings. There would be plenty more, she was such a good ride and

In the Groove

delightful with it, my cock was already reviving for the next session. Her cunt throbbed under my fingering as if willing me there. She turned to face me, kissing me lingeringly, reaching to hold my semi-erect prick.

'No,' she said. 'It was by a friend who is a schoolteacher in Kampala. So it will be a clever child. You wish to have me again, sir?'

'The thought crossed my mind, Jove,' I told her. 'Give it a chance to rise again and I'll be there. Rub it nicely and I've no doubt it will respond—'

'There is another way,' she said, wriggling down on the bed to face my dick. To my pleasure and surprise, the act not being common among Africans that I knew of, she held my prick and covered it with her soft lips, beginning a gentle suck. I moaned my delight and she paused, letting a saliva-glistening prick slip from her mouth while she looked up at me.

'You do not mind, sir? Doing this to you? You like—?'

'Feel free, Jove, I like,' I said, encouraging her to continue. 'Who taught you to do that to a man, your chief or the clever schoolteacher?'

'It was Major Marchbanks, he liked it too much,' she said giggling. Once again his stock went up in my estimation as her sucking on my dong resumed. Brought to full hardness again by her warm wet mouth, I resisted going the whole hog and fucking her face to a climax. I withdrew and had her kneel up on the bed. Her plump arse, I'd decided, would be an ideal buffer to bump against while shafting her from the rear. As I knelt up behind her, she lowered her shoulders to the bed, tilting her buttocks for me. Already fucked once and well lubricated, the cunt presented to me accepted full penetration first thrust.

It is always an added pleasure when one's partner is as keen to be put to the cock as the male is to supply it. Jovial scrunched her cushiony bottom back to meet my slidings, squealing her pleasure, once again calling out 'Mama, mama!' as if imploring help from her mother under such pleasurable duress. I fucked her with deep thrusts, deliberately withdrawing so that she begged, then ordered me to remain within her. Her cunt gripped me as if to imprison my cock. Her head rose on her neck, braying and crowing, urging me on in her native tongue. I had a good grip of her hips and as she climaxed I let my own release flood her, buffeting her arse in my final frenzy.

I slept deeply with the comely girl cuddled beside me, to be awakened in the dark of pre-dawn with her pulling my head to her breast. 'What is it, Jove?' I asked, barely out of sleep, realising she was cupping a large tit to my face, directing a nipple to my lips. Comfortably nursed in her crooked arm, I sucked and warm milk filled my mouth.

'My bosom, sir, my breasts, they are too full of milk and are hurting me,' she whispered. 'Please to drain them and take away the pain. You like—?'

What was there not to like about it, being fed one nipple and then the other? The soft yielding mound of a breast pressed to my face as I suckled each in turn. I felt the milk-taut rounds actually soften as I gulped hungrily, tremendously aroused by her feeding me. My prick responded, growing quite painfully erect and hard. Relieved of her milk, I got over her sturdy body, her legs parting and encircling my back, as eager as I to fuck, a hand urgently directing my knob to her cleft, buttocks lifting from the bed to meet my thrust. Quite rejuvenated by hours of deep sleep, aroused tremendously by the girl feeding her breasts to me, my prick was of that iron hardness that women love inside them.

'Oh, oh,' she groaned, rearing her body to me as every inch penetrated. 'It is too good, you will kill me, sir!' Her hand reached out to switch on the bedside lamp and glancing sideways I saw our reflection in both mirrors: my white body pistoning over her, strong black arms and legs wrapped around me urgently pulling down as she heaved up to meet my strokes. With a loud gasp she increased even that furious pace, hauling on my arse cheeks and climaxing in helpless spasms.

To show how good I was, I continued screwing her, bringing screams and taking her to what seemed a continuing series of violent orgasms, her body undulating wildly, pelvis thumping into me like a pile-driver until I could contain myself no longer and I let fly, spurt after spurt flooding her core. We rolled apart, unable to speak, utterly spent from a magnificent coupling. I dozed, slept again from the exertion, to be awakened in sunlight by Jovial, now dressed in her work dress to inform me that breakfast was on the table.

'I think an increase in salary is due,' I told her, 'for providing such excellent service.' After all, there are few freebies going in this world, and I never expect any. Besides, Jovial needed money to keep herself and send as much as possible home to help her mother and her son before the next baby was due. Doubling her meagre pay would hardly break me and she deserved it. I needed her friendship and loyalty too, with Beverley Marchbanks coming to call as she indicated. How Jovial would take to another woman being in my bed posed an intriguing problem. I wondered what Beverley would do if she discovered I was fucking my housegirl. Hell hath no fury like a woman in such a situation. Doubtless my goose was going to be cooked ...

Chapter Five

Uppermost in my mind that day was the impending visit of Beverley Marchbanks and what to do about it. I offered Jovial the whole day and night off, suggesting she could visit friends in the African township of Kitabi, which adjoined Entebbe and where she had headed when alighting from the bus. I gave her an advance in pay as a bribe, but she insisted that, after a visit to the post office to send the money home, she would be cleaning the bungalow, which she considered untidy, and would be there to cook my dinner and do *whatever else was required*. This last said with a sly grin. I decided that the best I could do when my white woman visitor called was to lock all doors and keep Jovial at bay.

I went in to the Photo Safaris office, taking the long route there and hoping to catch sight of Mrs Marchbanks on the road heading for tennis or golf. Had I spotted her, I'd have lied in my teeth, saying I had to work late as a safari party were due the following day. At the office I was briefed by Joginder Singh as to the group expected, going over the prepared map of where I'd be leading them upcountry to camp sites set up in the bush. Six people

In the Groove

were booked to arrive, a mixed bag. Two were an American millionaire and wife; a chap on his own was just as rich, his fortune made through jam doughnuts that sold in franchised outlets all over Europe and the United States under the Doughnut King trade name.

The other three people were using the trip for work on an assignment to provide photographs for the expensively produced prestige calendar for the following year, commissioned by an international firm of tyre manufacturers. Among the names listed to arrive I recognised Bettina, one of the world's top beauties and highest paid models. I gathered I must meet the group as they alighted from their flight, looking the part of a typical white hunter in bush hat with a leopard-skin hatband, safari suit with bandolier of ammunition and laced-up knee-high boots. It was evidently expected.

'You will also carry this weapon,' Joginder Singh informed me, handing over a high-powered rifle with telescopic sight, 'all the times you are out with the photographic parties. It reassures them when game is near. Of course, you will try to ensure they stay in their vehicles, but often they insist on going on foot. We have not lost a client yet—'

'I'll try to maintain your record,' I assured him, thinking wryly of all the odd situations I've found myself in during my life. I only wished we were all driving off on safari that afternoon to save me from the evening ahead. I went to the hotel Lake Victoria for my dinner, one less duty for my eager housegirl to perform, lingering until darkness in the bar before summoning up the courage to drive back to the bungalow. With a sinking feeling in my gut, my head-

In the Groove

lights illuminated Mrs Marchbank's car in the forecourt. I found her sitting in the house nursing a drink, looking annoyed. Jovial was in the kitchen.

'You didn't tell me you'd hired a servant,' she said in a furious whisper. 'You know how they talk—'

'I hadn't employed her when we last met,' I said. 'You'd better have your drink and leave. I'll tell her you are just a good friend, called to see that I've settled in. It would be for the best, for tonight at least—'

'No,' she said determinedly, 'I've been looking forward to seeing you again all day. Send the girl away, lock the doors and draw the curtains. What we do is none of her bloody business.' She looked at me distrustfully. 'Extremely handsome African girl, isn't she? Have you been up to something with her?'

'Of course not,' I lied. 'How could you think that—?'

'I know about men out here, taking advantage of their servants. There's something I want to know, Tyler. Have you fucked her?'

I was saved from answering that leading question by Jovial tapping on the door from the kitchen and appearing. 'Shall I prepare dinner for your guest as well, sir?' she enquired.

'No, we've both eaten, Jovial, thank you,' I told her. 'The memsa'ab and I have business to discuss about my job. You are finished for tonight. I'll see you in the morning.'

Alone with Beverley Marchbanks, she immediately came to me and put her arms about my neck. Her big pliant tits crushed against my chest; she pushed her plump cunt mound against my crotch, rotating it slow and sensuously over my prick. Our mouths clung, her tongue wetly probing. 'Much more of that,' I warned as our lips parted, 'and you'll make me come in my pants.'

'You'd better not,' she said aggressively, disengaging herself with a last thrust of her plump cunt against my responding dick, drawing her dress over her head and shaking her hair into place. She wore a brassiere absolutely overflowing with bulging tit and a matching brief lace panty that clearly showed the triangular outline of her lush bush on the mound. Kicking off her shoes, unclipping and discarding the bra with a shake of her magnificent tits, she drew the briefs over her feet and stood ready for action. I like my women keen, but this was brazen.

'You do need screwing,' I had to say, admiring the full figure flaunted before me, throwing off my few clothes, rock hard in anticipation. 'If that's all you want, let's fuck and then you can leave. That would be safest—'

'I'm not here for just a bloody quickie,' she swore, coming to me and circling my rigid dick with cool fingers. 'So get that out of your head, Tyler Wight. My husband is dining in Kampala so is well out of the way until after midnight. God, but I like the feel of this thing in my hand,' she added, stroking my shaft almost idly. 'And better still, up my cunt—'

'What about your mouth?' I ventured, my hands on her shoulders and gently applying pressure. She looked at me querulously for a moment before allowing herself to be lowered to her knees, lips level with my rearing cockstand. 'Suck,' I told her. 'Don't tell me that you've never.' If she intended to make a meal of our time together, no pun intended, I could but make the most of it.

In the Groove

'You are a foul creature,' she said but drew my prick down horizontally to her mouth and pressed a kiss to the bulbous knob before covering it with her lips. At first she sucked gently, then with ever-increasing suction as she found it to her liking, her lech getting the better of her reluctance. 'Oh, God,' she muttered, pausing for breath, 'to think I'm doing this, sucking a penis in my mouth and liking it. Do you intend to ejaculate there?'

I held her cheeks, steadying her face as I moved my hips sensuously to her sucking motions. 'The thought is tempting,' I admitted, 'and we will get around to that sometime. Right now I want to fuck you, Beverley, fuck you until you beg for mercy. Fuck you bloody rigid—'

'Yes, do,' she urged, my prick at her lips. 'On the couch, the floor, any place. I don't know what you've turned me into, damn you, with that huge thing between your legs. A raving sex maniac, I imagine—'

'You'll do until one comes along,' I grinned, drawing her up from her knees, tits bouncing enticingly. 'Let's go through to good old Sam Bishop's bed where his wife was screwed by big Callum. I've a little trick to show you, all done by mirrors—'

She followed me into the bedroom and stood watching while I adjusted the wardrobe and dressing table so that the mirrors reflected the bed. Beverley then laid herself across the covers, breasts splayed and legs parted to give prominence to her hairy split, shaking her head and giggling at the sight.

'Good God, we'll be able to see ourselves going at it,' she laughed. 'What a dirty beast you are. That's the product of a sick mind, young man.' She cupped her breasts in

In the Groove

her palms, holding them as if on offering. 'You threatened to fuck my cleavage, didn't you? Shall we try—?'

I joined her on the bed, straddling her body so that my prick guided itself until nestled comfortably in the tight warm valley of her tits. 'Press the sides and make a tunnel for my dong,' I instructed, sitting upright as she did so and moving my hips in a fucking motion. In the humid tropical night her cleavage was damp with perspiration, allowing a nice slow sliding. I was content to take my time, seeing how she would react, my right hand going behind me to finger her cunt. It was moist and receptive. I made contact with the taut stub of her clit.

'Aaaagh, yes,' she moaned. 'This is so depraved. I shall want to fuck all night, have your lovely big prick everywhere—between my breasts, in my mouth, deep within my cunt. You make me want to do things, try out all the disgusting ideas I've ever had—'

'And never did,' I said. 'Did your husband never fuck those lovely big tits, lick your cunt or make you suck him off? We'll do all that and more—'

'Yes, yes,' she agreed, her voice strained as if in torment. 'Did you do all those things to other women? Talk to me, my love, tell me! I want to hear. Every detail. I want you to do them to me. Tell me what you've done to women—'

It was patently evident that the long deprived Mrs Marchbanks craved vocal stimulation as well as the physical. That was fine by me, always having had a liking for crude pillow talk. 'All the cunt I ever had,' I assured her, 'I fucked front, back and sideways. Mouth, tits, cunt, up the arse, you name it, Bev. Same as I'll do with you – use and abuse your body and you'll love it. You're a natural, you

In the Groove

know? A whore's mind and can't get enough—'

Trapped below my sitting position, Beverley keened and whined, her body jerking from the hips, roused to insanity with the unstoppable surge of her climax. 'Fuck, fuck, fuck your prick into me!' she howled, pushing at me with her hands. I slid back on her until poised over the widely parted thighs and raised knees. My engorged dick slipped through the bush and into the waiting fanny.

'Yeah, YES!' Beverley screeched, taking me to the balls, hooking her heels into the small of my back, humping to me furiously. I was certain she could be heard beyond the house, but it was too late to worry about that. I fucked her with vigour, our bellies smacking, her wild undulations going on for a multiple orgasm. Cradled in her thighs, locked in the grip of her arms and legs, she was still bucking to me and grunting her lust when finally I shot my hot volley in a series of determined thrusts.

'How crude you are when making love', she muttered breathlessly. 'You have found that women like that—?'

'When encouraged to talk so, like you did,' I teased her. 'Actually that was one tremendous fuck, Mrs Marchbanks. I have to hand it to you—' I was still lying across her, my diminishing dick sheathed in her cunt, my balls in a hot slot in the cleave of her arse, a hairy pocket damp with exertion.

'The tremendous fuck one gets from a natural,' she teased in reply. 'From one with a whore's mind who can't get enough?' She stirred languidly. 'I wish I *could* stay the whole night, and I won't be satisfied until I do sometime. Now I suppose I'd better dress and leave you – reluctantly, I'm ashamed to admit. I've never been like this before, you know. I'm married to a responsible person and I'm the mother of teenage girls.' She sat up to hold me, naked breasts pressed to my chest, her stiffly pointed nipples hard to my flesh. 'I'm forty-six and should know better. Kiss me, kiss me nicely! Lord help me, I believe I'm in love with you—'

Anything but that, I grimly decided, but the kiss she pressed to my mouth was of an ardent woman to a lover. As her soft warm lips circled mine with her tongue deep in my mouth, her curved naked body made my cock stir and want her again. 'I do love you,' she affirmed. 'Blast you, Tyler Wight—' To make matters worse, I returned her kiss as enthusiastically before lowering my mouth to the deep cleave of her fullsome breasts, burying my face in the warmth of pillowy mounds uplifted for my pleasure. 'Suck my nipples,' she murmured, a hand directing my head. 'Do that for me, my love—'

Much as this fond canoodling aroused me, I braced myself to stop it. I couldn't afford to have a woman in love with me, more so a married one, the worst kind. 'It's my cock that you love, Bev,' I told her bluntly, taking her hand down to encompass its regained erection. 'That and nothing more. See what you do to it? Turn over and lift that magnificent arse of yours for another poking. Isn't that what it's all about between us? There can't be anything else—'

'Beast,' she muttered, but complied, rolling over to present wide and firmly rounded buttocks for my use. Then to my consternation she began to sob quietly into the pillow, her shoulders shaking, making me hesitate in the crouching position behind her with the engorged glans of my

In the Groove

prick nudging the outer lips of a rear-tilted cunt. 'Go on then, that's all there is between us, isn't there? You said it—' Beverley accused, her voice muffled in the pillow between sobs. 'Poke me, as you so crudely put it. How could I love you? Go on, never mind me.'

How could I not mind her, lying there bottom up so invitingly yet catching her breath between heartfelt sobs and tears? In all my experience I'd never fucked a crying woman apart from one crying out for more. All the same, my shaft slid up her to the hilt. Once so deeply embedded in the warm moist folds, I was lost to lust.

It felt so mind-bendingly good up there that I ignored her sobbing, could not have stopped my thrusting if her husband and kids had appeared in that room. I was on my knees, almost bolt upright, hands clutching the firm flesh of her ample bum cheeks and drawing them apart for deeper access to her core. It became one of those fucks when all reason flees and self-gratification rules. The woman's sobs were now intermingled with low moans, her bottom buffeting and rotating against my heaves. Strangled cries came from both our mouths. 'You lovely thing,' I heard my voice croak out to praise her. 'You are beautiful – such a great fuck! Oh, you heavenly darling—'

'Yes, yes!' Beverley agreed, sounding as wildly hoarse and lewd as myself. It had become a one-in-a-million type of fuck, brought about no doubt by her admission that she was in love with me and the tears that ensued. The subject was not closed, I learned, for even in her extreme arousal, climaxing repeatedly in helpless shudders and spasms, she cried out: 'Say that you love me, Tyler! Tell me, my darling! I want to hear—'

In the Groove

At that precise stage when cock rules the head, my hips almost a blur as I pistoned my prick up that receptive cunt, ready to unload my balls into her, I heard myself shouting back, 'Love you? Oh, I do love you—' and immediately knew I was in trouble. I certainly loved what I was doing to her, what she allowed me to do with her comfortable body, but in my rashness I had uttered the sacred words that she would hold me to, with consequences that boded ill. All through a mad moment's loss of reason while in the throes of coming!

Sated with sex, she rolled over onto her back, eyes brimming with tears as she regarded me fondly, long fingers reaching up to caress my face as I remained on my knees before her. 'My own darling,' she said, her hand going down to caress my chest and finally cup my balls and limp dick. 'And this lovely thing that pleases me so wonderfully. I'm mad about you both—'

Stretched out below me so magnificently naked with her big breasts quivering and cunt still parted, it would have been the easiest thing to have pressed kisses all over her beautiful body. 'Don't forget you've got a husband,' I reminded her. 'You'll be going home to him.' I was about to add that this was our bit on the side when she pressed her fingers to my lips, silencing me.

'Yes,' she said, 'and while he's with me I shall be thinking of you fucking me. I shall want you again tomorrow—'

'I'll be on safari for at least a week,' I told her, happy in the thought. 'Time's moving on too. You'd better shower and leave, Bev. No sense overdoing it.'

'Damn,' she said, sitting up, reaching out for her clothes. 'I shan't shower, I'll drive home with our sweat on me to remind of our lovely time together. Now I suppose I must go.'

I escorted her out to her car, the night air perfumed with the heavy scent of tropical flowers, the wide black sky freckled with bright stars. Africa was in my soul, and the last thing I wanted was to have to move on. In the corner of my eye I sensed a figure hovering in the shadows, Jovial no doubt.

Making the parting brief, almost to the point of bundling Beverley into her car, would have been favourite. Instead, as I held open the car door she flung her arms about my neck and gave me long lingering kisses. 'I meant what I said, Tyler,' she promised almost threateningly. 'I've never felt like this before about someone. You've had all there is of me and I will not allow you to discard me—'

'Let's not go overboard, for Christ's sake,' I said, trying to disengage myself. 'This could make deep trouble—'

'Then make sure you never let me down,' she warned, her meaning clear. I watched her headlights disappear along the road and then Jovial was beside me.

'You want me in your bed, sir?' she asked quietly. Gawd, I thought, why not? In for a penny, in for a bloody pound; famine or feast. Then I remembered the very rumpled bed that Beverley and I had used so vigorously.

'Thank you, Jove,' I said, 'but you don't need to—'

'I want to, sir,' she affirmed. 'Also my breasts are very hard and full tonight. They pain me. I would like you to do what you did for me before. I do not think you mind—' While I stood pondering this offer, I saw her white teeth shine in the dark as she smiled. 'Was the white memsa'ab good in your bed? I do not care about that, African men take many women. You take me now, sir. Let me come to your bed.'

'Lead the way,' I agreed almost wearily. The morrow's safari trip, I decided, would be as good as a rest for me. Or would it? Things had a nasty habit of happening to me.

Chapter Six

Dressed for the part, I met the arrivals off the aircraft and then led them off north upcountry towards the Murchison Falls area in a convoy of three LandRovers. Though our African drivers were well versed in the route, before we started out I'd made a big deal of gathering the party around the bonnet of one vehicle with an outstretched map and detailing the journey ahead. I thought it went down rather well, impressing the tourists with my imitation of a veritable Jungle Jim. It had our Ugandans grinning broadly as well.

En route I sat beside the driver and the so-called Doughnut King, who turned out to be a squat and friendly Englishman named Neal Shuttler. Ordinary as they come, he must have been a shrewd cookie all the same to have built up such a successful international chain of outlets. Quite frankly, with my sexual exertions of the previous night allied with the heat and motion of our vehicle, I could easily have nodded off to sleep. But the Doughnut King wanted to chat. Despite the expensive camera equipment slung about his neck, his main interest seemed centred on whether there was any spare nookie upcountry. A soul mate, it seemed.

In the Groove

He was greatly struck with the two female photographic models who were travelling in the second LandRover with their photographer, Ted Sutherland, and equipment. 'Nice work if you can get it,' reckoned Shuttler, who had insisted that everyone call him Shutty, as all his friends did. 'Imagine getting paid for taking pictures of beautiful birds. Did you cop a good look at the two models with him, that one called Bettina and the black bint named Yasmin? She's a Yank—'

I couldn't help but do so, both girls having lovely faces and figures that would knock your eyes out – perfect breasts, curved hips, pert bottoms and long legs. I agreed that Ted Sutherland had the goods to work with. 'Do you think he's knocking 'em off?' Shutty asked wistfully. 'He's pretty chummy with the white one. He calls her Bet and had his arm about her on the plane. I'll bet he's screwing her.' He gave me a knowing look. 'He's photographed her bollock naked before. I've seen his pics of her nude in magazines.'

I must admit that I had a strong lech for her myself. The trip augured well. 'What do you make of the two Americans, the married couple?' I asked. They rode in the third vehicle, an odd pair. He was short and fat, over middle-aged. His wife was a brassy blonde, her make-up heavy on the mascara and lipstick. She was curvaceous, verging on the ridiculous, with flaring pointed tits and an extravagant arse. A friendly type obviously, she was dressed in a safari suit with the top two buttons of the shirt undone to reveal a creamy cleavage. Her handshake was warm and lingering, her fingers covered with rings that were the real thing, as were the dangling earrings, incongruous with the safari outfit.

'Elmo and Laverne Zackall,' said my informant. 'I had a drink with them before we boarded the plane at Heathrow. They'd been doing London and staying at the Ritz. The old chap's loaded, no doubt, and proud as hell of his tarty missis. She can give him a few good years. Told me she'd been in the theatre. I reckon she looks a performer. Did you note the tits on her? Custom built, I reckon.'

The road had run out and we bumped along on a dirt track surrounded by scrubby plain and squat trees, sighting zebra and elephant before reaching the first prepared camp beside the Nkusi river in Mubende province. It looked a bloody dangerous place to me, with fierce-looking buffalo nearby and edgy gazelle grazing warily with lion about, reminding me that the safety of the party rested on my shoulders. I was glad to see a motley crew of cooks and servants awaiting our arrival, who did not seem unduly cautious. Watching us nearby, squatting on their heels, were a group of Acholi tribesmen with feathered headgear, and little else but their spears and shields. Sitting a little way behind them were their women, ebony black and bare-breasted, eyes trained on the party of wealthy whites landed in their midst. There was more to this safari-leading game than met the eye, I decided, slinging my rifle and wondering what the hell.

But all proceeded with me standing around just looking good. Tents were allocated to us and I discovered I was to share with Shutty and Ted Sutherland the photographer. Tables were being laid, food was cooking. Obviously Sam Bishop, absent in the UK after his errant wife, had things so well organised that the operation went so smoothly it ran itself. All the same, I nosed around as if to appear in charge, finding myself approached by a tall Muganda named Semmengo who introduced himself as head boy. I shook his hand, pleased to find an experienced ally. 'What's to do with that armed tribe out there, watching us like we were their next meal?' I asked, jerking a thumb in their direction. 'And just how safe are we from marauding animals at night? I don't want to lose any customers—'

Semmengo grinned. 'The Acholi men and women hope that they'll be paid to be photographed, bwana. There will be many fires built at night for warmth and to keep the animals away. Leave everything to me. Bwana Sam Bishop, he spends his time entertaining his guests. They expect that. If you want anything, sir, you send for head boy—'

I liked him. 'For starters I'll call you head *man*, and forget the bwana and sir stuff – call me Tyler,' I told him. He gave his wide friendly grin while shaking his head.

'I cannot do that, bwana,' he laughed. 'The tourists expect it. It's what they believe happens in Africa from seeing Tarzan films. Sam Bishop insists we give them the full treatment, just like in the cinema—'

I had to laugh with him. 'Where the hell did you come from?' I asked.

'London School of Economics,' Semmengo said. 'But my Uganda Government pay was not half of my present salary.'

I could see his point. Later I learned he had it pretty good, running an efficient staff, with four pretty brown wives for his comfort. And there was more. With his handsome, manly figure and proud bearing of over six feet, his duties had including fucking some of the wealthy white women tourists who longed to satisfy their curiosity about black men. The gold Rolex watch he wore was a gift from a satisfied customer, although money was more usual. His job obviously beat the hell out of being a poorly paid civil servant and I was glad to have Semmengo along.

Canvas shelters had been erected where the arrivals could shower. Deciding to look in the spacious tents to see my charges were settling in, I found the model girl, Bettina, fresh from her shower and wrapped solely in a fluffy towel that seemed to defy gravity, being held up by her nipples and showing the delightful swell of her perfect breasts, twin orbs that nestled together in ivory-white fullness. The towel barely reached her thighs below the fork of shapely legs, making one imagine the nest between. As I apologised for my intrusion, she laughed, offering me a drink from the selection on a folding table. The photographer, Ted Sutherland, sat on one of the two camp beds loading one of several cameras.

'Not shocked, I hope?' he said, inspecting his equipment. 'You'll have to get used to seeing all there is of my models on this trip. I specialise in the female form. Art studies. Do you think the others in our party might object? I intend to use my girls in various African backgrounds.'

I would like to use them myself I thought, feeling my cock stir in my khaki drill trousers as Bettina leaned forward to pour my drink, allowing me a good look at the deep valley of her fine tits. 'I don't think there'll be any objections from the others,' I said, my voice sounding strangely hoarse. 'Say what you want done and I'll see that it's arranged.' We were joined then by the black model Yasmin, who had entered the tent similarly towel-wrapped from her shower. A lovely slender creature, several shades of brown lighter than the African locals, she regarded me while lighting a cigarette, oblivious of the fact that in doing so the towel slipped down to reveal extravagantly pointed pear-shaped tits.

'Just you arrange to be around with that rifle of yours, Mr White Hunter,' she smiled beautifully at me. 'This little girl is from New York City, get it? I may look like I'm from Africa, but no damned lion is gonna eat me—'

'You've been eaten before now, Yas,' Sutherland laughed.

'Only by male animals,' the girl replied. She let the towel drop to the floor, standing gloriously naked, not in the least concerned. 'Get my drift, buddy?' she said. 'You stay close to me.'

'Every inch of the way,' I assured her, meaning it in every sense if the chance allowed. Bettina had dropped her towel as well, turning away and presenting a pertly rounded backside that made me want to fall to my knees and press kisses to each smooth moon. She got dressed, still facing away from us, while Sutherland fiddled with his cameras and Yasmin, still nude, poured herself a drink, adding ice. It was plain that being unclothed as a profession made propriety and inhibition unnecessary, at least with them. 'How in hell do you make ice out here in the wilds?' said the black girl.

'Paraffin fridge,' I said, unable to refrain from eyeing her charms: the sharp-pointed tits and flat belly that went down to a clean-shaven lipless cunt-prominence between brown thighs. 'The refrigerator runs on paraffin—'

'You never seen a naked girl before, buster?' she asked.

In the Groove

'Your eyes are popping.' She giggled. 'You the strong silent type or queer maybe?'

'Neither,' I rejoined. If they thought I didn't approve, noting that Bettina, now in well-filled lacy bra and brief matching panties, and the photographer were watching my reaction, I decided to enlighten them. 'You can fuck each other in front of the camera if you like—'

'Promises, promises,' teased the black girl. 'Would you care to join in—?'

'You've paid for this trip, I'm here to satisfy,' I said. The suggestive talk and the beauty of the two girls had now given me a cockstand that bulged my trouser front. It was time to leave, on all fives as the saying goes.

'Is that a pistol in your pants, or are you just pleased to see me?' Yasmin laughed. 'Our man's got a big boner on!'

'Cool it, Yas,' Ted Sutherland advised. He stood to offer his hand. 'Never mind her, she loves to torment all the guys—'

'Just a hot and horny black bitch, that's me,' Yasmin agreed pleasantly. She winked broadly at me, pursing her lips, as if threatening to seduce me at the first opportunity. That was fine by me, I decided, leaving the tent.

Dinner was served at a long table under lamplight, with the sounds of Africa all around. We were a friendly group with much animated talk. As leader of the party I was plied with questions about African lore, the tribes and animals that could be heard in the night. As most of my time in Africa had been spent flying out of Nairobi, living in an hotel, I lied brilliantly and impressed my audience. More to the point, Yasmin had seated herself beside me and throughout the meal fondled my upper thigh, giving

In the Groove

my dong an occasional squeeze and getting the inevitable response, a good erection that bulged my pants.

If she intended merely to tease me and put me off track while trying to converse normally with the others, she was messing with the wrong person. Later, when taking a last look around the camp, I found Yasmin, Bettina and Sutherland sitting in canvas chairs outside the girls' tent, drinks set up on a table. I was invited to join them. Camp fires burned out where the Acholi warriors were still sitting. 'I'd like to get pictures of the girls with some of that bunch,' Sutherland said. 'Do you think they'd let us?'

I knew they would gladly, for payment. 'I'll talk to their chief in their language tomorrow morning,' I said, putting on the old Africa hand bit casually. Ted Sutherland, I noted, had his arm along the back of Bettina's chair, a hand idly fondling her neck under her long dark hair. They were no doubt close and I envied him. I wished them goodnight, rising and slinging my rifle, one more stage prop in my act. The black girl Yasmin stood up with me, smoothing the loose dress she wore suggestively over her breasts and hips. She eyed me like a predator.

'I need to walk before I sleep,' she announced. She hooked an arm through mine, a soft tit pressing into me. 'Do your thing, Mr White Hunter, and escort me. I'll need a big hunk like you to protect me, won't I?'

'Who's going to protect him from you, Yas?' Bettina laughed. 'Don't do anything I wouldn't do—'

'I know what you two are going to do,' Yasmin returned, leading me off. We strolled to the edge of the camp. Alone and in near darkness, the girl huddled close with her scent and warm body arousing me. I decided to let her make the move she intended. 'Can we sit here?' she asked. 'I'm not likely to get my pretty black ass bitten by a snake, am I?'

'This snake would like to bite your ass,' I just stopped myself saying, sitting down beside her. 'How long do you intend to stay before you return to your tent?' I asked.

'Long enough to let Bettina and Ted fuck each other to a standstill,' she giggled. 'You can see they're an item. They'll marry and have kids when she's through with modelling—'

'Lucky old Ted,' I replied, feeling Yasmin's hand slide across to my lap. I lay back on my shoulders, legs slightly apart to facilitate her groping at my zip, my tool already stirring. 'She's a really beautiful girl—'

'Never mind her,' Yasmin said determinedly. 'I'm not exactly an old hag, am I? That thing in your pants, is it as big as it felt under the dinner table? I want to find out. You got any objections—?' Without waiting for an answer she unzipped me and delved in, fingers grasping my thickening stem. 'Christ, you were there when they dished them out! This I must see.'

My stander was drawn clear of my pants, balls as well, rearing proudly in her inquisitive fingers. 'You shouldn't, you know,' I mumbled, as if protesting in an agony of ecstasy, enjoying every moment. My delighted dong responded magnificently, throbbing in her hand. 'What will you think in the morning?'

'Fuck the morning,' she hissed. 'Right now I want this big dick.' She gave it a few tentative rubs. 'You married or something, buster? Are you queer?'

'Nothing like that—' I began, so she dipped her head, covering my knob with her mouth, sucking greedily. I'd

In the Groove

had enough of the passive stuff by then and was eager to get at her myself. As she withdrew her mouth, I lowered her beside me, covering her lips with mine, tongue probing a warm sweet mouth. I squeezed her tits and slid my hand under the loose dress, cupping a neat shaven cunt bulge and insinuating a finger between inrolling fat lips, finding soft moist folds and a button-like clitty. She wore no briefs to impede my progress and hefted her arse off the grass to thrust against my titillating. Yasmin, my girl, I told myself, you're going to get the whole treatment.

She had decided that for herself, moaning in her throes, now mumbling her words. 'Eat me!' she groaned. 'Lick my pussy! Tongue-fuck me, you honky bastard! Then screw me with that big dick!'

'I will,' I assured her. 'All in good time.' I began to draw the dress over her head and she helped me, throwing it aside. She was completely naked underneath. My hand went back to her cunt, my mouth seeking her nipples, drawing tit flesh into me while she arched her back. Then I lowered my lips over her smooth belly, palms pushing her thighs apart before delving into her tilted crotch. Her taste was sweetly musky as my tongue found her tight little nub. She bucked, grasping my head, on the verge of coming. 'Fuck me, fuck me, fuck me,' I heard her groan from above.

I was more than ready, moving up over her as she grasped my prick and directed it to her hairless cleft. As I went in to the balls, she gasped as if in great relief before gripping me with arms and legs, hauling on my arse and thrusting back wildly. 'Easy!' I told her sharply, smacking her thigh. I withdrew to my knob and she screamed.

In the Groove

I fucked her slow and fast, altering the angle of penetration, getting whines and moans from her as she climaxed and then worked up to the next come. I imagined with her lifestyle as a glamorous model she had known many lovers – studs both black and white – but out here in the bush, on the bare earth, I determined to give her a fucking she'd remember.

My hands cupped her cheeks and a finger entered to the second knuckle up a tight puckered arsehole, making her squeak as my prick pounded away. I decided I'd have that too before the safari was over, even as her spasms were lessening and her energy was drained. In her last throes I let my cock have its way and shot my wad deep up her cunt. I rolled off her, satisfied I'd done a good job.

'You're no fucking amateur, mister,' she said at last, sitting up to reach for her dress. 'Whew! You should hire yourself out. Take me back to that damn tent, will you? I've got to work tomorrow.'

At the tent she pressed herself to me, kissing me lightly on the cheek. 'That was one hell of a screw,' she said. 'We must do it again.'

I found Shutty and Ted Sutherland drinking together in my tent. They welcomed me with a bottle of beer. 'So what have you two been up to?' I asked, knowing full well that Sutherland had used the time shagging his gorgeous model. I hadn't done too badly myself.

Chapter Seven

Morning came with Semmengo shaking me from deep sleep to announce there was hot water in the shower tanks and breakfast would soon be served. I found the camp alive with activity, the smell of bacon and eggs on the go, the morning air fresh and Africa all around. Life was good and a nagging worry reminded me that a besotted Beverley Marchbanks could end it all if she persisted so blatantly with our affair. I was shaving myself when I was joined by an excited Neil Shuttler, just bursting to tell me of the evening he had spent after dinner.

'Old Elmo Zackall came across to invite us for drinks,' he said. 'Once we'd sunk a few, and that wife of his can knock them back, you know he as good as offered his missis to me? Kept saying he knew she was much younger than him and that females need satisfying. She was nodding and simpering away at me. I was sure he was hoping I'd start something and shag her in their tent. I wouldn't have minded, she's built for the job.'

'You should have tried your hand then, Shutty,' I told him. 'Maybe that's how the old boy gets his kicks, and his wife gets serviced. What stopped you?'

In the Groove

'You're never sure, are you?' he complained. 'They didn't exactly come right out and offer it on a plate. I reckon I missed out there. But next time I won't,' he vowed. 'I'd love to fuck her.'

I had the strong impression that Shutty would fuck any reasonable female. Walking past one of the shower cubicles, towels around our necks, Bettina stuck her head around the canvas flap. 'Good morning,' she said brightly. 'I can't get this thing to work.'

The apparatus was simple enough, an overhead tank released water when a chain was pulled. 'Give it a good wank, lass,' suggested Shutty, 'that's what I had to do. Would you like me to try for you?' I grinned at his cheek. Bettina, too, gave a mischievous smile, as if thinking she'd see how he accepted a challenge.

'How kind of you, a real gentleman offering so gallantly to come to my aid,' she said quite sincerely, her beautiful face set as if to stifle her amusement. 'How could a lady refuse—?' To our amazement, followed by our gasps and stares of helpless admiration, she pulled aside the canvas flap and stood before us naked as Eve, a vision of perfect young female loveliness. We two men did not move, rooted to the spot by the sight: the full uptilted breasts, flat stomach and shapely limbs, the well-forested thatch of dark hair covering the curved prominence between rounded thighs. 'Are you going to help—?' she said, stepping aside.

My companion shuffled into the cubicle beside her, hardly knowing where to look. He made a grab for the shower chain and pulled it with a jerk that tore it away from its mooring. He held it dumbly in his hand while water sprayed down, soaking him to the skin. Bettina laughed hilariously, her tits jiggling, pushing him out beside me. 'I can manage quite well now, thank you, Mr Shuttler,' she said sweetly. Then the canvas flap was replaced and the show over.

'That was worth all the money I paid for this trip,' I was informed as Shutty went back to our tent to change. No doubt it was.

Getting to know more of him later, I learned he'd left the navy as a ship's baker to start his first cake shop, specialising in the art of doughnut-making. He had gone on to become a rich man. As for Bettina, as a confirmed sun-worshipper, she had no inhibitions about going as nature intended. During the safari she improved her tan at times by sunbathing behind her tent in the altogether. Such were the comings and goings of the camp staff around her that though Semmengo rigged up a canvas shelter to give her some privacy, it didn't much concern her.

Following breakfast I further impressed my group by using my Swahili on the party of warriors of the Acholi who came into camp arrayed in leopard skins and spears and shields – as good an act as the one I was portraying. They all had eyes for our women, especially the sophisticated black New Yorker Yasmin in a bikini bra and skin-tight jeans. Semmengo had already paid them to pose for photographs from a fund Sam Bishop provided, no doubt skimming off a little for himself.

Camp would not be struck until the following day, I announced, there being so much to photograph in our present situation. In truth I needed the rest after a hectic

In the Groove

week since fleeing from Kenya and all that had happened since. Neither did I relish another day of bum-numbing jolting over dirt tracks. No one objected. There was an abundance of game to photograph from the LandRovers: lolloping giraffe, interested hyena I scared off with shots fired in the air, plenty of nervous gazelle, and the nearby river and bank busy with wallowing hippo and crocs lazing in the sun, jaws agape and allowing brightly feathered birds to pick their teeth.

At the camp of the Acholi, Ted Sutherland had his models posed in beads and little else among the warriors and their women. I noted Shutty was taken among them too, arrayed in borrowed leopard skin robe and weapons. The American couple snapped everything in sight. The ubiquitous Semmengo served up a cold buffet at lunchtime with chilled wine. I felt everything was splendidly under control until in the afternoon a lone and obviously bad-tempered old bull elephant appeared, annoyed at the sight of people. He scraped the ground with huge curved tusks and threw up dust with his trunk, trumpeting loudly.

The Acholi men rattled their spears on the shields, shouting defiance, which only angered our visitor more. I ordered my group back to the LandRovers, all of them piling in the uncovered back of the nearest one, snapping away and enjoying the thrill of a little danger, sure of my protection – which was more than I was. I ordered each of the African drivers to race off if the tusker looked like charging, all of them nodding most unconcernedly. Then I decided I'd better arm myself with the rifle which I'd left in the back of a nearby LandRover.

I stood up in the cab, rifle at the ready, getting waves

In the Groove

of encouragement from the others of my group, when a scrambling movement behind me made me turn. Yasmin had joined me, grinning wickedly, coming forward out of sight of everyone but me, on her knees. 'I want to suck cock,' she announced. 'I've been thinking of that big prick of yours all day. This heat has got me all worked up—'

I said nothing, concentrating on the big bull, with levelled rifle. I felt my belt being unbuckled, zip unzipped and my drill trousers drawn right down to my boots. Yasmin cupped my balls in one slim hand, the other almost languidly clasping my stirring dong. It responded to her gentle stroking, thickening and stretching stiffly. This is hardly the time or the place, I could have protested, but my shaft had a will of its own. 'Oh, yes,' the girl cooed naughtily. 'It's growing big for momma. Doesn't he just love what little Yassy can do for him? Mmm, he's good enough to eat—'

I gave a strangled groan as her mouth covered my now-engorged glans, her tongue probing in the slit. From nearby I noted that cameras were trained on me so I waved the rifle and tried to smile normally as Yasmin licked a warm wet tongue up the length of my stalk, pausing with her mouth at the bulbous knob. 'You know what deep throat is, honey?' she enquired in her taunting voice. 'Enjoy, you're just about to get it from an expert—' There was no doubt about that, for the next moment she was sucking avidly, bobbing her head, drawing in inches of my prick into her lovely mouth.

One hand squeezed my balls, the other went around to hold my arse while she sucked greedily, now drawing her mouth back and then engulfing my excited dick, all the time applying strong suction between her tongue and the roof of her mouth. My free hand grasped her hair, my hips jerked, all the while trying to make the visible top half of my body appear normal. Then it was impossible to resist the surge in my balls and hot liquid lava spurted down her throat.

She sucked on until my flaccid cock was allowed to slip from her lips. 'How was it for you, Mr White Hunter?' she teased. 'That was just for starters. Tonight I'll want the whole bit, suckin' and fuckin', so make yourself available.' The old elephant, losing interest, ambled off and I adjusted my dress quickly as the others came over to express their delight at the incident, as if I'd arranged it.

Following dinner back in camp after dark, I hung about, eager to meet the oversexed black model again. Ted Sutherland was in the tent with Bettina, enjoying her beautiful body, no doubt. Sure enough, Yasmin soon materialised out of the night. At that moment Neil Shuttler came up too, clasping several bottles. 'Party on in the Zackall's tent,' he said enthusiastically. 'This has been a great day and it ain't over yet. Come and join us, I got a feeling tonight's the night—'

I heard Yasmin giggle as she pressed her lissom body to mine. 'Am I right in supposing he fancies fucking Mrs Zackall?' she asked outright. 'That I'd like to see. If we can get her in the mood, why not? We can screw too, that's my scene—'

We trooped into the Zackalls' tent to be welcomed with open arms, filled glasses. Yasmin perched on my knee as if to show she was fair game; Shutty parked himself on a camp bed beside the voluptuous Laverne Zackall, squeezing her waist increasingly as the drink flowed. Her husband sat across from us nodding benignly. 'I met Laverne at Vegas,' he said proudly. 'She was a showgirl. Knocked my eye out the moment I saw her. Had to have her—'

'With his dough,' Yasmin whispered in my ear, 'I'll bet that wasn't hard.'

'I was a stripper,' Laverne announced, tipsy and proud. 'The best. You want to see how a pro does it? I had class, didn't I, Elmo dear?'

'Show 'em,' her husband beamed. 'Hell, this is one great safari and hell of a party. Laverne! Make with your act—'

'Yes,' we all chorused, Shutty loudest of all. To our amusement, Laverne rose unsteadily, stating that we wouldn't get the full benefit of her act, not having one of her special stripper dresses. All the same she began to sway, humming a slow sexy tune which her husband joined in. Off came her dress as she flounced around in the narrow space, leaving herself in flimsy undergarments of delicate bra and briefs, her body the colour of thick cream, upholstered extravagantly at tit and buttock. Suddenly she stopped, regarding the assembly with unsteady eyes. We waited expectantly.

'You folks appreciating this?' she asked boozily. 'You want I go on? I don't want to offend. Elmo, he likes me to do my act. A party piece, you know—'

I stamped my feet and clapped, in truth eager to see more of the act. Shutty raised his glass high, spilling most of the contents, shouting his approval. Yasmin nudged me, and indicated old Elmo with a jerk of her head. He was slumped in his canvas seat, glass in hand, head drooped forward with his chin on his chest. She reached over to

In the Groove

remove the glass from his hand but he was unmoving.

'You think he's really asleep or just kidding?' she said in my ear. Laverne carried on her stripping, draping her bra over Shutty's head while he crowed in delight, shimmying her broad backside at us while slipping down her briefs and kicking them. Naked, her ample curves bordered on the mature, but she was none the worse for that. She looked a very fuckable female. Shutty, naturally, reached out to clasp the formidable buttocks presented so enticingly inches from his perspiring face. On my lap, Yasmin squirmed her tight little bottom into my bone-hard projection. I noted her eyes widen at the sight of Laverne's shapely nakedness.

'You like?' I whispered connivingly.

'I could get to,' the black girl admitted, moving to adjust the cleave of her arse over my dong. 'You wanna watch or fuck?' she asked, observing that Shuttler had pulled Laverne across the camp bed and was feverishly kissing her mouth and breasts while the object of his lust pulled at his clothing. 'Watch or fuck?' Yasmin repeated.

'Both,' I said, envisaging a free-for-all and game for anything. 'Let's get out of these clothes—'

We divested ourselves in haste and fell across the other camp bed. Beneath me, Yasmin grasped my cock to direct it between her uptilted thighs. Both our heads turned to see how the action was proceeding mere feet away. Laverne now had the Doughnut King on his back and was hauling down his trousers. His dick thrust up proud, stubby but admirably thick, making Laverne 'Ooh' with pleasure as she draped her luscious tits over it, jerking her shoulders. Below me, feeling my attention was distracted,

In the Groove

Yasmin gave her arse a determined wiggle, lodging my dong further up her greedy quim. I gave a few thrusts to show willing, pubic whiskers nudging her shaven mound, making her crave more. Her ankles crossed high up my back, hands hauling my backside urgently, the camp bed threatening to collapse under us.

'Never mind them now, fuck *me*!' she hissed urgently, lifting her hips, only her head and shoulders now in contact with the mattress. 'Hold my ass, tickle my hole, put your finger up there like last night! Fuck—' To hear was to obey. As her nubile body heaved to mine, I rammed home my pulsating tool.

'Yes, yes!' Yasmin screamed, and across from us in his chair old Elmo stirred and grunted as if returning to life. For a moment we paused, her smooth flat belly to mine. On the other bed Laverne, impaled on the recumbent Shuttler, stopped moving, her big tits settling to a jiggle after bouncing with every determined thrust of her arse. Elmo blinked, bleary eyes drooping, then apparently nodded off obediently.

'I don't give a shit if the old bastard wakes up and joins in,' Yasmin declared, restarting her motor and squirming her cunt hard to my pubic bone.

She was a great fuck, no doubt about it, humping like a wild thing, muttering and murmuring as she came. Shuttler had evidently shot his bolt too, lying back gurgling his pleasure, leaving Laverne at a loose end so that she left him and came across on hands and knees to enjoy a close-up of Yasmin and I in mid-fuck. The girl below me, fully engaged as I thought she was, reached out an arm to draw Laverne to her. From my raised position, cock to the hilt

In the Groove

in a churning cunt and ready to unlease my jism in ever-increasing lunges, I was sent out of control by the lewd sight of the two females crushing their open mouths together as if desperate for each other. Yasmin, released from my diminishing dick, had found a new playmate, one as eager as herself.

She half-rolled from under me, her hands seeking Laverne's tits, hefting them, mouth searching for a nipple to fasten on. She was joined on the narrow bed by the other woman and I left them to it. I refreshed my glass, joining Shutty on the other bed where he leaned up on an elbow, engrossed by the sight of Yasmin and Laverne making out.

'I never thought I'd see that,' he said, impressed by the intensity with which the pair pleasured each other with mouths, tongues and hands.

Yasmin at last had Laverne on her back, legs wide and knees raised, sucking cunt avidly while Laverne croaked her delight, pert black bottom raised as she lapped and tongued. I arose, prick reviving at the lascivious lesbian loving so blatantly performed before us, wanting a piece of the action. From the foot of the camp bed Yasmin's smooth arse was uplifted waist-high to me as she knelt forward to tongue Laverne's pouting fig. I groped between the cheeks, feeling heat and juice, touching up the soft loose folds of a well-fucked cunt, drawing back a lubricated finger to the pucker of her arsehole.

'Yes, go on, fuck my ass,' Yasmin grunted, turning her face and getting it pulled back by Laverne at once, wishing the tonguing to continue. She's had this before, I decided, my knob forcing an entrance to the proffered anus, pushing steadily and finding the back passage cosily tight but accepting my girth. Yasmin moaned, raising her bottom, squirming it back into my lap, making me hold her narrow waist to steady myself, going on tip-toe to gain full depth. The three of us now were connected in a delightful combination of prick, arse, tongue and cunt, writhing and undulating, gasping out throaty cries, lewd in the extreme until the final hectic spasms left us slumped and drained of further effort. Later, dazed with drink and our excesses, I dimly remembered dressing and seeking my own tent and bed.

I was awakened at sunup by a smiling Semmengo holding a steaming cup of coffee under my nose, feeling wonderfully fit and ravenously hungry. It seemed a dead liberty to take Sam Bishop's pay for such a high time. I almost felt guilty.

Chapter Eight

Day followed day on the safari without a hitch, camp being struck and moved on without my having much to do with it. The paying guests were delighted with the organisation of the trip, for which I accepted the kudos due entirely to Semmengo and his crew. Each evening in the Zackalls' tent it was the accepted thing that, when Laverne's husband lapsed into what we imagined to be a weary and drink-induced sleep, the nightly orgy began. Yasmin always joined us, partners were swapped, and I had the pleasure of screwing both women as did a delighted Shutty. In between bouts the ladies entertained us doing their own thing.

Our last halt before returning to Entebbe was a stopover at Murchison Falls, where Chobe Lodge, an international class hotel built way out in the bush, provided a night's lodging with its comfort, excellent cuisine and native-dancing cabaret.

This meant being in touch with the outside world again, which I did not care to anticipate. I was called to the telephone soon after our arrival, expecting Beverley Marchbanks reminding me of her passion. Instead, I was

In the Groove

relieved to hear Sam Bishop's voice. Yes, he was back with his errant missis, all was ticketty-boo, whatever the hell that meant, and he was taking her off to the Kenya coast at Mombasa for a holiday, so the job and house were mine for a few weeks yet. He sounded chuffed with himself, and did not even enquire how the safari had succeeded. I went to my room and the phone rang there.

This time, to my dismay, it was the amorous Beverley. A week away from her had not cooled her ardour, as I'd hoped it might. A few good fucks were enlarged in her mind into a torrid love affair. 'Did you miss me, my darling?' her voice cooed. 'I thought of you, remembering all the naughty things you did to me. I can't wait for more of the same, how about you, my love?'

'I've been terribly busy,' I said, dodging her questions. 'Too busy to think of anything else—' I could sense her hurt and annoyance. 'Really, it's been one thing after another; on the go all the time—'

'You'll be back by tomorrow, I know,' she stated firmly. 'Wait for me at home. Jumbo is in Nairobi, we can spend the whole night together. Must I say it, Tyler? I want to sleep with you. Be fucked by you—'

'I don't know. I'll be busy seeing off my safari party on their night flight,' I lied. 'Let's leave it for some other time. I'm pretty bushed after this trip—'

I heard her voice harden. 'Be there for me. It can't be that you're tired of me already. I will not accept that. Until tomorrow evening then—'

It could only get worse, I thought gloomily as she banged down her phone to show she would stand no nonsense from me. Her claws were well and truly dug in, and

In the Groove

she was no doubt livid at my coolness with her. Any further thoughts on the matter were shelved by the arrival of Yasmin, announcing that old moneybags Elmo Zackall was throwing the biggest farewell party that evening in the dining hall. After which, she added wickedly, no doubt the night would end with a bang.

'Have that big dick of yours standing by,' she commanded. For once I had other things on my mind: the fact that in a week or two I'd again be out of a job and with no place to stay. Worse still was the fact I soon would have to face a married women with an obsessive infatuation of the kind that boded a full-scale scandal and a vindictive husband set on seeing me off. That's if I wasn't already long gone.

Mulling over these thoughts, I went out onto the balcony of my room, overlooking a wide River Nile with its varied species of wild game wallowing or drinking its flow in the heat of late afternoon: elephant on the far bank, an abundance of hippo standing nostril-deep in the water, sluggish crocs basking and the more timid types of antelope warily filling up before nightfall.

'Isn't that a wonderful sight?' said a voice from the next balcony and there was the gorgeous Bettina, standing at the concrete balustrade in a silken dressing gown that clung to the sweep of her back and swelled out over her luscious arse cheeks. 'What are those lovely animals there?'

'Tommies. Thompson's Gazelles,' I was able to answer, seeing as they were common enough. 'The bigger ones are wildebeest,' I guessed, though they might well have been hartebeest. She didn't know, turning to me with her lovely

In the Groove

smile, impressed. 'Africa gets to you, doesn't it?' I said, rueful of my future.

'It must be wonderful to live here like you do,' she said wistfully. 'In my work we never stop for more than a few days in any place. Tell me more. This is the River Nile that goes up to Egypt, isn't it?'

'All the way, thousands of miles,' I assured her, taking the liberty to climb over the narrow space of her balcony and join her. Standing deliberately close, my hip to hers, I pointed out how nervous the antelopes were. 'It's not unknown for a crocodile to drag one in for supper. Look, zebra are coming now,' I added, edging closer. 'Wild, isn't it?'

'In more ways than that,' she said teasingly, not moving the contact with her leg. 'Yasmin tells me that some pretty wild goings on take place at night in the Zackalls' tent. She's full of praise for you. Does that come under the heading of keeping your guests satisfied—?'

'It's a job,' I threw in, matching her amusement. 'Someone has to do it.' My right hand slid down her back to rest on her shapely buttocks, enjoying the feel of the smooth curves. 'I'd love to do it to you,' I dared add.

'Right here and now?' she laughed, but I detected a catch in her voice, both my hopes and my prick rising. Neither did she attempt to remove my hand which was now idly caressing both soft bum cheeks. 'Are you trying to seduce me? I think this had better stop—'

'Better continue, please,' I urged, my voice hoarse as I detected the slightest movement of her lovely arse under my fondling. 'Where's Ted right now—?'

'I don't know. Checking his equipment—' she began.

In the Groove

'Check mine,' I offered, unzipping with my free hand to draw out a rampant prick before taking one of her hands down to clasp it. To my delight she held on to the rigid shaft, even giving it a tentative jiggle.

'My goodness,' she announced. 'Yasmin did not exaggerate. Put it away—' Her gaze was imploring. 'Do put it away—'

'Yes, right up her cunt, fuck her good with it,' said an eager voice behind us, Yasmin approaching with a wicked grin. 'I want to see her fucked, Tyler. Little goodie-goodie Bettina the one-man girl. Don't stop now, I've been watching from the verandah door. She's tempted, I can tell. So give it to her!' The black girl laughed lewdly. 'I've longed to see her let her hair down for once. Screw the bitch!'

'Yasmin!' screeched Bettina. 'How dare you!' But when Yasmin went to her and put an arm around her shoulders, their faces close, she seemed to relax and accept the situation. 'This shouldn't be happening,' she protested meekly. 'Damn both of you lecherous beasts. As you're so determined, get on with it if you must—'

Yasmin winked slyly at me, holding Bettina's shoulders as I went behind them to do the deed. I rucked up the hem of the silky robe and tucked it into the belt of the same material, uncovering her cheeky bottom completely. My hand sought between the divide, fingers outstretched and meeting the downward hang of her split mound, hearing a strained 'Oh' as I parted the lips and found moist warmth inside.

'Drenched,' I informed the interested Yasmin, making Bettina groan in embarrassment, arching her back as I

In the Groove

found a hard nubby clitoris and tormented it. Eager as I was to put my cock into the enticing cunt recess I fingered so deliberately, I wanted to hear her beg for it. I gauged her reaction as her body twisted, legs parting, arse rotating and cunt starting to churn to my titillation. Then she let out a hollow groan of defeat, bucking buttocks against my hand.

'Go on then!' she ground out through clenched teeth. 'Put it in for God's sake. Do me—'

'Make her say it,' Yasmin demanded. 'Make her say "Fuck me"! Don't give it to her until she does—'

Before I could insist Bettina was gabbling away, 'Fuck me then, fuck me, fuck me, fuck me!' with arse raised and cunt tilted to accept the wanted penetration. My knob was eager to be in there. It slid up inch by inch until embedded to the hilt, nudging deeply and bringing forth a satisfied *Aaaargh* from her before my thrusting began in earnest. My hands ventured up under her robe to grip her firm heavy breasts and pull her hard to me.

So commenced a magnificent fuck, finesse abandoned lustfully in the sheer pleasure now overtaking all else. Suddenly Bettina cried out that she was coming, jerking wildly, then I could hold back no longer. Our climaxes coincided beautifully, rising and gradually losing pace until the spasms ceased and we drew apart, breathless and sated.

'I couldn't help it, help it—' I heard Bettina moan, excusing herself.

Whatever fate awaited me on our arrival back at the Entebbe base the following evening, I consoled myself it had been good while it lasted. I saw my group safely off on

In the Groove

the flight, Shutty shaking my hand and swearing it had been his best time ever, Elmo Zackall pressing two hundred-dollar bills into my hand as his wife stood by smiling. Ted Sutherland thanked me for my efforts, little knowing just what that had entailed. Yasmin gave me a lingering kiss and a sly wink. Last to board the aircraft was Bettina, who shook my hand, looking directly into my face. 'What must you think of me?' she said. 'I'm not like that at all, really.'

You could have fooled me, I might have replied, remembering the wild gyrations of her lovely arse with a rampant cock well up her. How many women claim the same after a hectic love-bout, as if it were something to be ashamed of? It reminded me too I had yet to face Beverley.

As I drove off, I considered my options. If she wouldn't be let down gently, I'd throw her out manually, I decided. We'd have to see what a vengeful woman would do about that. To my determination I added liquid courage, stopping off at the Lake Victoria Hotel to down several double whiskies with beer chasers. Even bolstered thus, it was with relief that on arriving at the bungalow there was no sign of Beverley's car parked in front. I went inside through the kitchen door to find Jovial there. Jovial the faithful, who fucked for the joy of it with no emotional strings attached.

In my mood I decided that was my kind of woman, the kind I should stick to, and I was genuinely pleased to see her again. I hugged her, enjoying the comfortable give of her abundant curves against my body. For once she seemed uneasy, trying to hold me off. 'Come on, Jove,' I encouraged her. 'Aren't you glad to see me back? Give us a kiss and then we'll get beer out the fridge and make a night of it—' I fastened my mouth to hers, pulling her to me. Stifled as she was, she made protesting noises. Never one to force things, I drew back my face. Her eyes were wide, the handsome black features containing wicked amusement.

'Your memsa'ab is here,' she giggled slyly. 'Your white lady friend. She parked behind the house hours ago to await you. Now she is drunk, I think, for I have been serving her from Bwana Bishop's cabinet all evening – gin, and when that was finished, vodka. She is in the lounge—'

But she wasn't, approaching unsteadily with a glass in her hand even as I stood holding Jovial. 'I might have known, you bastard,' she said, but more with acceptance in her tone than fury. 'It's my own fault, of course, imagining a fling with the likes of you could be the great love affair.' She paused as if about to throw her drink in my face but thought better of it, draining her glass. 'Don't worry, I'm coming to my senses. It must be the drink. I can see clearly now—'

My surprise, mixed with relief, was such that I still held on to the comely servant girl. 'I'd better get you home, Bev,' I offered. 'Or do you want coffee and drive yourself later—?'

'I want what I came here for,' she said, steadying her eyes on Jovial and sounding determined. 'If all I can expect from you is sexual satisfaction, so be it, you swine. All I've meant to you is a good fuck, isn't it? What if I agree to settle for that—?'

Beside me, Jovial disengaged herself. 'I will leave now,' she said, smiling. Beverley held her arm, stilling her.

'No, stay. I watched you kissing, it was nice. I like to see it, for some unexplainable reason. Go on, Tyler, kiss her again.'

Her unexplainable reason, I ascertained with private glee, was because the sight of me kissing the black girl had been highly arousing to her. Beverley, I knew from past romps, was a highly sexual creature, the more so for being an erotically imaginative woman obviously unfulfilled and frustrated all her girlhood and adult life. Hence her fastening on to me so romantically. Now she was hooked on illicit sex. I considered it a duty and obligation to bring her out completely, besides being tremendously pleasurable. Jovial, too, knew the score, locking her strong arms about my neck and moaning as if in ecstasy as I pulled her to me, our mouths fusing, tongues meeting, roving and probing in a long wracking kiss while Beverley surveyed the performance.

When I paused to gain breath I drew her to me, noting the flushed face and bright eyes of an aroused woman, my arms around the shoulders of both females, forming a close circle, our faces almost touching.

'Now it's your turn, Beverley,' I said, kissing her long and lewdly, getting the response of her lips crushing mine, the grunt of approval and her tongue eager to thrust into my mouth. I felt the tremble of her body, the lift as she pressed her cunt mound to my thigh.

'Now kiss Jovial,' I ordered, chancing that in her lewd state she would respond wantonly. Jovial glanced at me knowingly, sensing my objective, that the aroused white woman could be seduced into discovering the pleasures of female loving. She pushed her face closer to Beverley, her plump-lipped mouth pouted with the red tip of her tongue peeping. I pulled Beverley harder into our circle of faces, rubbing my thigh into her cunt mound, watching with a nod of satisfied approval as she muttered 'Oh, yes, I want to,' and locked mouth to mouth with the black girl, urgent in her surge of desire. Their lips met in a feverish kiss as their passion mounted.

I imagined the bedroom romp to follow, with mirrors placed to reflect the action, having both women in turn and watching them have each other between times. 'Through to the bedroom with you two,' I said, now standing apart from them while they clung and kissed as if desperate to eat each other's mouths. 'I'll see to locking up the house and join you right away.'

All my worst fears as so often had come to naught, I decided happily as Jovial led off Beverley, still kissing and clinging. It promised to be a night to remember. So it was to prove.

Chapter Nine

Making sure all windows and doors were secured and locked, I almost literally rubbed my hands in anticipation as I hurried to join the women in the bedroom. This was exactly my kind of scene, consenting adults doing what comes naturally, and I congratulated myself that the luck of Tyler Wight had once again arrived on cue. But I saw only Jovial beside the bed and wondered if Beverley had lost the urge as the servant girl came out into the passageway to me. 'Don't tell me,' I said, disappointedly. 'Where has she got to—?'

'Only the toilet, it was all the drink,' Jovial said enjoying my anxious query. 'It will be all right, sir. I think your friend likes me. Has she been with other women before?'

'I wouldn't know, Jove,' I said. 'Don't think so, but she certainly took to smooching you. What about yourself? If you don't mind, give her the treatment. I'll see you get paid for it.'

'You want to see it?' she grinned.

'I wouldn't mind,' I admitted, 'besides which it will get her off my back, give her someone else to get sex with. Do you know what to do with another woman?'

'With African girls at school, when there were no men for us,' she answered in her straightforward way. 'There was also a white woman later, a nun who loved me, taught me—'

'I'll just bet she did,' I said as Beverley appeared from the bathroom adjoining the bedroom. She swayed slightly, knickers in hand.

'Leave this to me, sir,' I was told. 'You come in later. It is better if I do this thing alone to start with—'

I wasn't too sure about that, having my own ideas how the threesome should proceed, my prick responding at full stretch as I indulged in my mind in all the lewd permutations a trio would allow. I'd have both kneeling on the edge of the bed, two magnificent black and white bottoms tilted for my inspection. Standing behind and between the raised rumps, I'd use both hands to touch them simultaneously, bringing forth little squeaks and moans of pleasure from the women, getting their arses to churn on my wrists. Then I'd fuck each in turn, inserting my stalk in one cunt and then the second, switching ploughed furrows regularly and hearing muttered complaints from the one left bereft. But Jovial's hands on my chest kept me beyond the door. Beverley tossed the knickers she held in my direction, landing at my feet. 'I won't be needing these, will I?' she said laconically.

'Stay outside, sir,' Jovial ordered and it struck me that she wanted to have the white woman to herself for her own sake or even to work her will on the supposedly superior memsa'ab. I could watch that.

Withdrawing slightly beyond the partly opened door, my view unimpeded, I saw Jovial go to Beverley and with-

In the Groove

out attempting to hold her stand face to face. Some words of Kipling from my schooldays came to me as the women looked deeply into each other's eyes without moving. Something about the colonel's lady and Rosie O'Grady being the same under the skin – only in this case it was a major's lady. Jovial ran a hand slowly and sensuously up one of Beverley's arms. 'Oh, madam,' she said in a strangled sigh. 'Your kisses were too sweet. I want to kiss you again too much. Never mind him—'

'Yes, yes,' I heard Beverley murmur, going into the black girl's arms readily. 'Let the bastard wait—' As their mouths crushed together hungrily, the bastard in the passageway did a little jig with glee. 'Let me look at you,' Beverley mumbled, between feverish kisses, and the pair began pulling at each other's dresses. I saw Jovial unclip Beverley's bra and free the big white breasts, rubbing her face across both globes, mouth open to seek the nipples. Jovial's curved black back and jiggling arse was towards me as she guided Beverley to the bed.

They lay side by side in a close embrace, continuing their avid kissing, hands wandering and fondling, cupping and squeezing tit, groping between parted thighs, backs arching. Tempting as it was to join in, my prick straining at the sight of nubile black and white naked female bodies squirming in their throes, it was too good an exhibition to interrupt. To be prepared for my grand entrance later, I took off my clothes, noting with interest that Jovial was gaining the upper hand.

She it was who adopted the superior role, with Beverley allowing it and increasingly passive as they sucked and nibbled at mouths and breasts. I saw Jovial nurse Beverley's head to her tit, pressing it to an eager mouth, directing the taut nipple beyond the lips and forcibly feeding each swollen orb in turn while Beverley gulped her milk. Satisfied, she pushed the other woman down on the bed and mounted her like a man, tit to tit, cunt to cunt, her arse working in strong thrusts as she rubbed her mound hard against Beverley's. As the buffeting continued, both groaned and whimpered in the pleasure produced, the woman below curling her legs about Jovial's waist, pulling on the firm buttocks. I judged their hectic climaxes came together and they rolled apart, gasping. I entered, clapping my hands to show my appreciation.

'Yes, you'd enjoy that,' Beverley charged me with. 'I can imagine. I can see it did,' she added, noting my rampant dick.

'You two girls weren't exactly faking it, Bev,' I rejoined. 'Going at it to the manner born. I wondered if there would be any left for me. Not for the first time with another female, either, I suspect. No secrets here—'

Beverley rose on an elbow, her fine tits drooping seductively, shaking her head at my insolence. 'God, what you've brought me to, you beast. Does it matter now? Yes, at my Swiss finishing school it was not unknown. Quite regular, in fact. Your very sweet housegirl is the first since then—' She smiled at Jovial who sat up beside her. 'I'd forgotten how good it can be.'

'The night is young,' I reminded them, holding out my prick on offer. 'Do something about this.' Lying before me as she was, legs parted, I stroked Beverley's cunt, scratching the bristly hair and inserting a finger into the warm wet folds. I was delighted to discover she was still in rut, working her pelvis to my toying. She lolled back, squirming her arse, glancing at Jovial who had reached out to grasp my boner, eager that I should do something with it.

'Does the girl suck?' Beverley enquired. I could have said yes, your husband taught her. 'I'd like to see that. Will she do it?' Jovial, taking in every word, nodded and smiled, bending forward with lips parted. My prick poked straight out in her hand, throbbing with anticipation as the knob was drawn into the cradle of her mouth, then sucked in inch after inch until I was at the back of her throat. Long moments of delightful suction made my knees quiver and then Jovial drew back her face. I reached out to pull her mouth back to the glistening stalk.

'You suck now, madam,' Jovial invited. 'Both together.' I thought that a good idea and so did Beverley, scrambling forward to get at me. 'Yes, it looks inviting,' she said, head to head with Jovial. My knob, bulbous and inflamed with the attention was now shared between their lapping mouths. Then they turned faces and kissed deeply before applying themselves to the task. 'I want to climb on him,' Beverley announced suddenly, shuffling her body forward to the edge of the bed.

I felt her cunt pressed to my groin and it was Jovial who directed my dick to part the lips, Beverley doing the rest by thrusting forward and being entered. Her legs encircled my waist as she fell back, only her shoulders in contact with the bed as she humped, desperate for relief. Standing before her, I clutched at her raised arse cheeks, thrusting back lunge for lunge in a wild fuck that could not last. With a series of chesty grunts, Beverley bucked to a sapping climax, sagging away from me moments after I had

In the Groove

drained my balls deep inside her. Only then did we hear it, a loud banging on the verandah door, even the shouts of someone enraged.

All three of us were naked, sweating with our exertions, and obviously not up to receiving a visitor – an irate one from the sound of it. The two women looked anxiously at me so I pulled on my trousers and padded barefoot to the front door, a glass affair with the protecting bars that were usual in ex-colonial type bungalows. I put on the light that illuminated the verandah and saw Jumbo Marchbanks standing there glaring in at me with a look that could have killed a lesser mortal.

'Piss off,' I shouted through the glass door, 'I was fast asleep.' I was intending to brazen it out, despite realising the reason for his presence. Supposed to be staying overnight in Nairobi, wasn't he? You really could trust no one.

'I know my wife is in there with you, Wight,' he hollered back. 'I flew back early because I suspected something of the sort. Open this door or I shall kick it in, blast you—'

Beverley's furious husband would not go away. Sam Bishop wouldn't go a bundle on his ornate verandah door being kicked in either, I decided, so I reluctantly unlocked to let the seething Marchbanks enter. 'You should be horsewhipped,' he hissed at me dramatically. 'Where is my wife? In your bedroom? I'll see you suffer for this. I have influence. You'll be thrown out for the lecherous swine you are—'

'Flattery will get you nowhere, Jumbo, old chap,' I said as he made to stride past me, halting him with a hand to his chest. I had one trump card to play. 'Your wife is here,' I admitted, 'but so is someone else you know, rather intimately too. A girl you weren't above having it off with yourself, you fat fraud. Does the name Jovial Nkutu ring a bell, Jumbo?'

It stopped him in his tracks. He stared at me with disbelief and shock mixed on his florid face. He trembled visibly. 'What – what – what the devil are you getting at?' he muttered.

'Only that it wouldn't go down well in your club if it got about you'd been screwing your ex-housegirl,' I reasoned, almost tut-tutting at his indiscretion. 'Really, old man, it's not on, don't you know, quite scandalous. With your loving wife absent you were doing naughty things with the servant now in my employ—'

'What did she tell you—?' he asked aghast.

'Everything. Alone in your house with her you did the lot. I particularly admired you for arranging the mirrors to watch yourself fucking her. Your friends and colleagues would love hearing about that quirk. I think our lapses and private affairs might be called quits now, don't you? So that they stay that way – private?'

'You unscrupulous bastard,' Marchbanks swore, calming down nonetheless. 'I do believe you'd use that information.' He mopped his brow, considering the situation. 'Have you a drink?' he enquired. 'I could use a stiff whisky—'

I gladly poured him one from Sam Bishop's drinks cabinet and joined him. I wondered what the two women in the bedroom were doing; waiting the outcome apprehensively, I supposed. 'You liked the idea of placing the mirrors, did you?' Jumbo asked thoughtfully. 'I never tried that on with my wife. Our sex life wasn't like that. My fault, I suppose, thinking she was too refined or something, so I went elsewhere to vent my lust—'

'She's a magnificent fuck,' I told him. 'You've been missing out. It's entirely your fault if she went elsewhere, Jumbo. Make up for lost time. Come on through to the bedroom and screw her now. We'll show her there's no hard feelings—'

'You say what you like, don't you?' Jumbo said, shaking his head at my directness. 'I should have done so years ago, it seems. You know what I'd really like to do, what I've always wanted to do when Beverley comes the madam and puts me down? Take her across my knee and show her who's master, spank her arse properly—'

'Do it then,' I encouraged him, wanting to witness the act. 'Let's join the ladies. I'm sure they're wondering what's going on.'

On entering the bedroom both females were still naked, sitting up on the bed together. Jovial was wearing her amused look and Beverley appeared openly defiant. Two beauties they were, with their contrast of colours, fine big breasts and rounded bodies. What a waste, I decided, if we didn't make full use of such lush beauty.

'Think what you damned well like, Jumbo,' Beverley snapped, getting the first word in. 'If you had half of what I've found a real lover can do for a woman, this wouldn't have happened—'

'Then I'll have to try harder in future, my dear, won't I?' Jumbo replied, icily calm. 'Right away, in fact.' He began pulling off his shirt and lowering his trousers before his wife's surprised eyes. 'As this seems a jolly free-for-all and undress uniform the order, I intend to do a husband's duty to you as soon as I've accomplished one other task. Namely to teach you a lesson for being an errant wife. You'll come to me, madam, now!'

Good on you, Jumbo, I voiced silently, kicking off my trousers beside him. 'Whatever do you mean—?' Beverley screeched as she was grabbed by her spouse and turned across his knees as he plonked himself down on the bed. 'Don't you dare!' she hollered, aware of his intention, looking especially spankable with her fine broad bottom raised and big rounded tits elongating in her face-down position. Her legs kicked wildly as she struggled. He held her fast and warned her it would be the worse for her if she didn't cease.

Jumbo's first smack across the plump cheeks sounded like a thunderclap, followed by several more that changed her howls of protest to pleas for mercy. I reckoned a good dozen hearty blows were delivered slap on target before he stood up and pushed her determinedly across the bed on elbows and knees.

I could guess what was coming next. Jumbo ordered her sharply to lie still, a thick erection poised before the deep cleave of magnificent buttock cheeks. 'Fuck her!' I said eagerly, unnecessarily too as he lunged forward, belly hard to her arse, and penetrated her to the balls as Beverley cried out in pleasure.

As erect as I was with the nude Jovial by my side, we made no move towards each other – such was the salacious sight. With each thrust at her, Beverley's head sunk lower and her proffered bottom rose higher, buffeting back to meet her husband's shaft. Face turned on a cheek against the bedcover, she gasped and grunted, lost in their lustful coupling. That she had climaxed once and wanted more was evident, as spasms shook her and she slowed before recommencing the movements of her arse. Jumbo seemed set to run a second course, looking across at me pleased with himself as he fucked his wife expertly, at times slowing his strokes, almost withdrawing, then ramming home again at full stretch.

Beverley was by now gabbling like a demented soul, urging her stallion on with guttural cries, hands back to pull her arse cheeks apart for full access to her cunt. Such arousal required an added extra, I considered, and Jovial obviously thought in similar vein, my prick being massaged in her hand as I stood admiring Jumbo's shafting. 'Her mouth,' Jovial suggested, agitated by the scene, frigging herself with her free hand openly. 'Use her mouth to suck you while she is so happy. She will like it. I want to see that myself—'

You horny bitch, Jovial, I thought, but was not averse to that suggestion in any way. It was an anything-goes situation by now, with Jumbo too engrossed in shagging his lewd partner to disapprove, I hoped as I got on the bed and knelt in position before his wife's face. She looked up wild-eyed, seeing my engorged dick. Jovial directed it to her parted lips and rubbed the rounded knob against them. With a low moan she covered several inches with her warm mouth, at once sucking avidly while her arse rotated and bucked at her other end, lost to all but the churning arousal surging up to yet another climax. I felt my gorge rise, unable to contain my coming emission, jetting strong spurts into her throat as her convulsions grew wilder then subsided, shoulders heaving and her brow resting on my thigh. Jumbo, I noted, had disengaged from her, standing with a limp dick to review the situation.

'So she sucks cock too, does she?' he announced agreeably. 'Well, well, my wife has hidden talents I'm pleased to know about. I shall take her home with me now and know what to do in future. This visit has been most enlightening.'

Beverley had to be helped to dress, then was led off by Jumbo – whom I had grossly underestimated. Placed in his car, she slumped back, still in a daze from her exertions while he turned to me, once more the officious diplomat. 'I take it then all this remains our secret,' he stated. 'Including the fact that you've had my wife and I've had Miss Nkutu—' He paused a moment, chuckling. 'Great fuck, isn't she, that girl? No doubt you'll be going back in to mount her—'

'It's more than possible,' I said, offering my hand. 'No hard feelings, I hope?' He clasped my hand warmly.

'None whatsoever. Now we know each other, I think we may well arrange such a get-together again. I shall look forward to it.'

Chapter Ten

Whether it came under the heading of marriage guidance, my advice that Jumbo stop treating his frustrated wife so genteely certainly worked. Now they had discovered each other's randy natures, all seemed well. I was happy for them both and relieved Beverley had more to satisfy the constant itch in her cunt at home, leaving me off the hook. When I bumped into Marchbanks a few days later he looked a new man, his usual frowning florid features relaxed and he greeted me with a broad smile. It just goes to show how vital good clean uninhibited sex is to a marriage.

'Just the chap I wanted to see, Wight,' he began, and I knew that's how he'd always address me. 'I've put your name up for membership of the club. You can't live here without becoming a member. Excellent facilities. Mere formality your joining now, of course, with my recommendation—'

I thanked him. 'How's your wife?' I asked carefully.

'Marvellous woman,' he enthused. 'Didn't know I had such a jewel. Fucks like a wanton. Thanks to you bringing her out, I suppose. She even suggested herself that we use the mirrors.' He allowed himself a wicked grin. 'I wonder who started that idea—?'

Invited to dine with them a few nights later, Beverley showed she could more than keep up with both of us. She was fucked in turn and together by Jumbo and myself, revelling in the two cocks, two mouths and four hands pleasuring her to delirious repeated climaxes, while her breasts, cunt and rear entrance received our full attention until our three bodies lay sated and dawn approached. I used their shower, fortified myself with bacon and eggs cooked by Beverley in a loosely tied dressing-gown that revealed the deep cleave of her gorgeous tits, then had to report right away to the Photo Safaris' office. The next trip was due that morning – just when I felt more like sleeping off the orgy.

At least I could go upcountry with a free mind now. I completed the next two safaris without a hitch with Semmengo and his crew doing the real work. Both parties on the photographic jaunts were composed of elderly Japanese industrialists and their wives so propriety was observed, and there was not half the fun of my first outing. Reporting to the office after seeing the second party off on their flight, I found Sam Bishop there with Joginder Singh, going over the account books. He was looking more leathery than ever from the Mombasa sun and sea but with a pleased look caused either by the success of his business or the reunion with his wife.

'You did all right, chum,' he greeted me. 'I see from the visitors' book my clients were full of praise for you as safari boss. Pity I've got to pay you off now that I'm back. I note you weren't at home when my missis and me arrived last night. Out getting the leg over somewhere, were you?

In the Groove

Found another place to stay, I hope?'

'I'm staying at your place, aren't I?' I said. Actually I had arrived back in the late hours with the safari party, seen them accommodated in the Lake Vic hotel for the night and then, because of a total lack of sexual activity over more than two weeks, had telephoned the Marchbanks' residence to make up for lost time. With little sleep from the resultant threesome with Jumbo and his wife, I was there to see off the Japanese on their early take-off. Now I watched apprehensively as Sam ducked below the counter and placed my holdall with all my worldly possessions before me. 'Christ, you're turfing me out,' I complained. 'I've no other place right now. I thought I could stay for a bit—'

'Yeah, a bit of the other with my missis maybe,' Sam scoffed. 'I'm taking no chances with her back and a bloke like you around the house.' He counted out notes on the counter. 'This is what you're due, minus an amount for the booze I see missing from my cabinet. Were you holding parties there?'

'I would have replaced it,' I said, picking up my pay, about enough for a night's stay in the hotel. 'And fuck you too, Sam, you're full of shit. So throw me out, okay, I'll survive. But what about the girl I employed? Where's she—?'

'I paid her off,' he said. 'That's deducted from your wages too. No hard feelings, mate, I like you, you did a good job. If I get an aircraft for my safari parties, I'll let you know.' He let out a loud guffaw at my consternation. 'I have got one job I could offer you right now. How are you on the Highway Code?'

'I'm a fully qualified pilot,' I said. 'I haven't seen a Highway Code since I passed my driving test in England years ago. What the hell's that to do with it—?'

'Another little business I run is a driving school,' Sam said succinctly. 'I need an instructor to fill in for a spell, until my regular chap gets out of hospital—'

'My brother Amrit Singh,' Joginder chipped in. 'He was in a very bad crash while instructing, now in intensive care in Mulago General. African drivers,' he spat out, 'they are madmen, going at such speeds, on the wrong side of the roads—'

'It sounds more dangerous than flying,' I considered. 'Stuff that. I'll try the airport to see if there's any pilot's jobs.'

'Don't knock it,' Sam advised. 'It's a great number for meeting young white cunt. They arrive out here as secretaries for the embassies or United Nations posts, they're stuck without a car and half of 'em can't drive. They need lessons to pass their test for a Uganda driving licence. I run the driving school from an office in the foyer of the Lake Vic hotel—'

'My wife Ranji is the booking receptionist,' Joginder put in. 'There are European girls waiting to start driving lessons—'

'Sure,' Sam Bishop agreed. 'You'd get paid commission on every pupil and there's a room in the hotel annexe for the instructor to stay in. You could kip there, and eat at the hotel on me too. What do you say?'

'I'll try the airport,' I said, and spent the rest of the day there fruitlessly selling myself to airline offices. The only glimmer of hope to get back into flying was at Lake Airways, an outfit with three Cessna aircraft and enough

In the Groove

pilots to manage at that moment. The boss was a Wing Commander Dove, ex-RAF, who was sympathetic and kept my name for the future.

'I like what I see,' he said, inspecting my papers. 'DFC and Mentioned in Despatches. Bombing Germany?'

'Till I was shot down. I've flown regularly since the war.'

'I see that from your log books. Awarded an Air Force Cross too. Were you a test pilot?'

'Berlin Blockade,' I said. 'It must have been the number of flights I made there with supplies. I can't wait to get back into flying. Do call me if you need a pilot anytime—'

'If you are desperate,' he said, 'there's always the Uganda Police Air Wing. They could use you. Most of the pilots are European and paid well. If you join I must advise that some of the work you'll be doing might prove unsavoury—'

'Such as what?'

'Bombing rebels in their villages; flying the army or Prime Minister Obote's secret police to knock off people they want out of the way,' he stated. 'There's always a threat of a coup, real or just suspected, to be put down. They don't ask questions, they shoot first. Uganda is a dictatorship and things will get worse. I smell trouble.'

'I just want to keep my nose clean,' I said. 'I don't think the Police Air Wing is for me yet. Only if I'm really stuck.'

Carless, I had to take a taxi back to the Photo Safaris' office, wondering how I'd do as a driving instructor without official status, though that didn't seem to matter much in a developing nation. I consoled myself that at least I'd have a place to stay, use of a car and commission for each pupil, exclusively young female secretaries according to

Bishop. On the road back in the taxi I spotted Jovial, erect as ever with her bundle of possessions balanced on her head as she proceeded on her way. I ordered the driver to stop and called out to her.

I commiserated with her on losing her employment, but she merely shrugged and gave her wicked grin in reply. 'I have another job to start tomorrow,' I was informed. 'Major Marchbanks is taking me as housegirl again. While you were away his memsa'ab came to see me. She said she would like me to work for them—'

'I bet she would,' I said and we both grinned, remembering how well Beverley and the black girl had made out. 'How did that visit go – apart from offering you a job?'

'She likes kissing me very much, I think, and holding my titties and sucking them. Also,' she added slyly, 'sucking on another part of me, like her husband has done. That is good, so I let her. Then I had to get on top of her, as we did before.'

I could imagine it – a steamy tropical afternoon and two sweaty women naked and cunt to cunt, humping to each other. In my aroused mind, picturing the scene, a hand inside Jovial's loose busuti dress at the neck enjoying fondling the firm rounds of her breasts, I determined to obtain a suitable dildo, preferably of the V-shaped double-ended variety, to present to them to increase their pleasure. I'm like that, always considering others, the more so because I relished seeing the women rogering each other with a dummy prick on future romps. 'You're in for a busy time when you work there, Jove,' I laughed. 'Does Beverley Marchbanks know that her husband has had you too—?'

The girl laughed with me. 'No, but while she was with

In the Groove

me, on the bed together, she said she would like to watch the major fuck me very much. She said she would make him—'

'Old Jumbo won't be sorry to learn that,' I said, thinking just how wanton Beverley had become. 'I'll come along and fuck you before her as well, give her an added eyeful. I feel like a fuck right now.'

The taxi turned into the African township straddled on the outskirts of Entebbe, a varied collection of bars, bungalows of the better off like army officers or in-favour government officials, even mud huts with thatched roofs. Jovial directed the driver along a winding dirt road, thronged with locals, armed soldiers, market stalls, ordering him at last to stop outside a shanty made of packing cases and a corrugated tin roof. I went inside with her, eager for a ride, finding it cosy and curtained off into two bedrooms, with double beds and old car seats for sitting on, all as clean and tidy as could be. Two young African maids rose as we entered, both in their teens and as alike as two peas, pretty brown things the most identical identical twins I'd ever clapped eyes on.

'My sisters, Juma and Nite,' Jovial introduced them, adding unnecessarily that they were twins. 'They want to start school here when they have money for the school fees. It is fifty Ugandan shillings a term—'

'I could manage that for this term,' I said, taking the hint. The two girls giggled at having a *mzungu* in their presence. Jovial watched as I brought out my slender bankroll and counted out notes to the value of fifty shillings.

'Each,' the mercenary Jovial added. I handed over the

amount, left with very little. 'They will go for beer if you send them,' she suggested, so I gave them the rest of my money. They returned with ice-cold litre bottles of Tusker lager, a local favourite, and we sat drinking, the girls eyeing me and giggling behind their hands. I wished that they'd leave, so that I could fuck their big sister. They made no move.

Pleasant as it was, sitting seeing off bottles of beer with the girls, I had to face the fact I had no job at that moment, no place to sleep that night, and I'd better seek out Sam Bishop and offer my services as driving instructor before the job went. As I got up to leave, the giggly twins went to their sister and whispered in her ear with much glancing at me as they did so. Jovial nodded and giggled with them at whatever they were saying. The two girls went back to their seats, holding hands and waiting expectantly.

'They say they have had men,' Jovial announced, 'but never a white one. They want to try. Take them to their bed behind the curtain. I do not mind. I go to buy maize and a chicken.'

Left alone with the two girls, seeing them awaiting my move with the naughtiest expressions on their duplicated features, I took their hands and led them behind the curtain. Their bed looked lumpy and it sagged, covered with a clean patchwork quilt, and they pulled off their school gymslips to reveal nothing but themselves underneath. Both were slender and nubile, but filling out with the promise of the large breasts and curves of their older sister. Their brown skins were smooth and shiny. I noted that at the forks of their rounded thighs plump little cunts bulged provocatively with few wiry hairs and lipless slits.

In the Groove

'Oh, yes,' I murmured, and the girls squealed with mirth as I threw off my clothes. Without being told, both got on the bed, lying back for my pleasure.

I got between them, hugging them to me, kissing each of their lips in turn. They readily accepted my tongue, cuddling close with their warm bodies, tits and cunts rubbing into me. Two small hands gripped my dong, by now a fully rampant pole revelling in the attention. As one both girls sat up, squeaking in admiration at the size and girth of the object they handled. I decided to let them have their head, so to speak, lying back at full stretch to observe their actions. Kneeling up on either side of me, facing away as they bent over, first one and then the other giving a trial suck to my knob, I had two neat little rounded brown arses over me. Reaching up with both hands, index fingers of each extended, I touched up both of their plump fig-like quims. The minxes uttered pleasurable noises, pushing and squirming their matching bottoms hard against my hands.

I suspected they were no novices at the art, as my fingers were gripped by the soft slippery wall muscles of their cunts as they worked themselves up to a frenzy. Then one, whether Juma or Nite I knew not, twisted around to straddle me, poised while her twin held my prick upright to ease down upon. My knob forced the lipless entrance with her pressure, then inch after inch was covered as her cunt lowered over the stalk until, sitting bolt upright before me, I felt she must be penetrated to the belly. The girl groaned, jogged her pelvis and set her uptilted tits bobbing, then worked with a will towards her climax. When it came with a series of furious undulations and squawks of joy, bucking ever wilder until a lessening of the pace, her impatient sister thrust her aside and clambered over me to take her place.

For the few moments my prick was free it reared glistening with cunt juice, an angry red and still rigid, leaving the cunt it had been engulfed by with an audible plop. Already gripped, the second twin impaled herself on it, made lewd with watching her sister, making me determined to control my surge until my second mount was made to convulse helplessly in climax. I lay back relaxed in every part of my being except for the bar of bloated flesh she thrust down upon, enjoying the reaction. The girl's eyes were wide, mouth agape and head tilted, tits flying, her pelvis working ever faster. She came with a screech and a few last delirious jerks. In good time too, for as she fell off beside her sister, my prick bobbing free of cunt, I'd run my course. Pearls of spunk arced up as I spasmed saturating my belly.

The two nymphs slumped on either side of me with heaving breasts and parted legs. What a sight our three naked bodies must have presented to Beverley Marchbanks – the last person I would have expected to see in the native quarter. She stood with the curtained partition partly drawn aside, her flushed face witness to the fact that watching the romp had been arousing. 'I might have known,' she said, trying to steady the quaver in her voice. 'Who won't you screw? Schoolgirls now, is it?'

'Very naughty schoolgirls,' I excused myself as the two in question squealed and darted from the rumpled bed to grab their dresses before the white woman. 'If they're big enough, they're old enough, and it wasn't my idea—'

'That I can't believe,' I was informed icily. 'How could I have thought the visits my husband and I allow you to

In the Groove

make to our home would satisfy *you*? Now I find this. Is Jovial aware what you've been doing with her sisters? Where is she, anyway? I've come to arrange that she start work for us—'

'I can imagine what her duties will include, Bev,' I said, rising from the bed as one of the twins reappeared with a basin of water and a towel for me to clean up. 'Don't come the old acid with me. Once I've dressed, I've an appointment to keep, so I'll be on my way.' She watched me putting on my clothes and I was forced to the conclusion by her displeased demeanour that she resented my screwing anyone else. She was such a good ride herself that I had no wish to antagonise her. 'A fuck is a fuck and not the end of the world, Beverley,' I tried to explain in passing her. 'It's not as if we weren't all at it. I hope this doesn't mean another jump at you is out of the question in future—?'

'Bastard,' she hissed. 'Smooth bastard. You say the nicest things. I hate you. Wasn't I enough for you—?'

'For any man,' I told her sincerely, 'but you've got your husband and Jovial besides me. Am I forgiven?'

She pursed her lips and shook her head as if in disbelief as I left, making me fairly certain in time she could not resist accepting my length again.

Now to the business in hand. My visit to Jovial's shack had left me penniless. I had to walk the mile or so to the Photo Safaris' office. I arrived to find Sam nowhere to be seen and a smiling white woman seated at the desk behind the counter who greeted me affably.

'You must be Tyler Wight,' she said, rising to offer a lingering handshake. 'It's so nice to see new faces here. I hope you've decided to work again for us. My hubby's at his driving school office and you're to go there if you want the job.'

Chapter Eleven

So I met Marjory, Sam Bishop's straying spouse, his pride and joy, seeing for myself why he enthused over her and accepted the occasional lapse in her morals. Such a woman was made to fuck, no doubt about it, and there was more than enough of her to go round. She was blonde and brassy, the ideal barmaid or pub landlady, bedecked in necklaces and rings, voluptuously endowed and the figure-hugging print dress she wore showed she was proud of her generous curves. Despite her time in the tropics her skin was creamy white and the low, square-cut neck of the dress allowed an admirable expanse of swelling bosom and nestling cleavage to be viewed. She was, I could tell, a woman who enjoyed male eyes upon her breasts.

From the lingering handclasp and the way her saucy eyes took me in, it was obvious she had a fondness for well-built handsome men, if I may describe myself so. So I gave her a flattering smile, squeezing the soft hand I held, laying the groundwork for some hopeful future liaison. One must have an eye for the main chance always. We were thus engaged in sizing each other up when Sam returned and bustled me out to his car, driving me to the Lake Victoria hotel and his driving school office in the foyer.

'Like what you saw, did you?' he said on the way. 'Well, eyes off and keep it in your trousers where she's concerned. I've just brought her back from one like you. When she spots a good-looking bloke you can hear her ovaries rattle—'

'Sam, you misjudge me sadly,' I pleaded, thinking what a fine cushiony ride his wife's ample body would make. 'She is a beauty, however. I can see why big Callum liked to give her one. You enjoyed seeing that yourself. Who wouldn't—?'

'Don't get ideas,' he warned. 'I must have been pissed when I told you that.' But once a wife-watcher, I considered, there was always a lech there for a repeat performance, determining it would be me if the occasion arose. Sam switched the subject, telling me of my duties as a temporary driving instructor. 'There's a back-log of clients awaiting lessons. In fact, there's one waiting for you this evening. Give 'em the rudiments and prolong the sessions to at least ten lessons. It means more dough for both of us. Take 'em around Entebbe first, then a few drives in Kampala where they have to pass the test. Don't worry, we've a hundred-percent pass rate.'

'That's very good. I hope I maintain that record—'

'No sweat,' he grinned. 'The testing officer is a brother of the Minister of Transport. Two hundred Ugandan shillings in his mitt and he'd pass a blind man. You have to tell your students that on the day they take the test, otherwise no driving licence—'

'Sounds par for the course,' I agreed. In a corner of the

hotel foyer was a reception desk with a telephone, a rack with British Highway Code booklets and leaflets on safe driving. A large sign hanging overhead informed the world that here was the *L Passo Driving Academy*. There was a letter L coloured red with a boxed border around it. Also there was a beautiful Asian girl in an amber sari with gold edging, who was introduced as Nanji, the wife of Joginder Singh, plus a white female in her thirties, a slender creature with large round spectacles and slightly buck teeth – my first customer, nervously awaiting driving instruction. This was being thrown in at the deep end, I decided, as Sam led me off with the woman to the rear carpark where his garden boy, Kidogo, was engaged in polishing a 1950's Morris Minor car with an 'L' sign attached front and rear. On the roof was affixed a board proclaiming the *L Passo Driving Academy*.

'You get it?' Sam said proudly. 'L Passo, like the place in California. It was my idea.'

'Texas,' I said. Kidogo, whom I'd known at Sam's bungalow, grinned at me knowingly. He was a strapping youth who had been well aware during my stay that I'd been fucking Jovial. Then I was left with the car keys in my hand and the nervous client.

'Tyler Wight,' I made the introduction. 'Do you want me to take the car out and find a quiet road, or have you done some driving before?' Kidogo hovered nearby. 'You want a lift to Bwana Sam's bungalow? Hop in the back seat and I'll take you there. It's a good area for a beginner.'

Dropping off Kidogo, I then ordered my client to get into the driving seat. She told me she'd never driven before, was a Miss Vera Steedman, and had arrived in

In the Groove

Uganda recently to be private secretary to the Minister of Defence. We drove for a good hour on an almost deserted road, clashing gears, driving painfully slowly, revving too much or stalling in turn. I made her drive back to the bungalow she'd been allotted, sweating in fear. She stopped the car, to our mutual relief, and invited me in for a drink.

Miss Steedman was hardly my type so I turned down her offer and drove back to the hotel, where I touched Sam for an advance while he showed me to a cubby-hole of a room I was to occupy. It had a bed and a slim wardrobe like an upright coffin, but it was more than adequate for the few clothes I owned. I sat on the one chair, determined that I must do better. Then, while showering in the cubicle partitioned off in a corner with a toilet and washbasin, I remembered Beverley and her reaction to me fucking the twins. I donned my one clean shirt and trousers, went to the hotel bar and called her number. I was hopeful that, if all was forgiven, she and Jumbo might fancy another threesome.

It was Jumbo who came to the phone. 'Wight, is it?' he answered, sounding like the old officious buffoon of yore. 'You're definitely *persona non grata* here, I've been ordered to tell you. I say, she's taking the phone from me—'

'We don't want anything more to do with you,' her voice hissed down the line. I was about to plead my case when she added, 'Do us the courtesy of not calling here again,' and slammed the receiver down.

So for the following week I had a thin time of it sexually. I gave driving lessons to a mixed bag of Russians and young African clerks, all of whom were excited about

In the Groove

owning their first cars but none came under the heading of 'young white cunt' as promised by Sam Bishop. I continued twice-a-week lessons with Vera Steedman, and, in the circumstances, began to eye her as a prospective fuck. I tried a bit of tentative chatting up to see how it would be received, giving her extra time in tutoring and praised her improving driving skill. All of this she accepted with her wan smile until I began to suspect I had a lesbian or a virgin on my hands. Which only goes to show how wrong one can be.

One lunchtime I sat with a glass of beer beside the hotel pool under the shade of the tall palms, thinking again what a paradise Africa was, when Vera appeared, dripping wet from a swim. She pulled off a frilly bathing cap and her thick dark hair, usually tied up in a bun over her neck, fell about her shoulders. Nice shoulders they were too and her small but shapely breasts encased by her bikini bra were separated by a deep enticing valley. Below, the briefs she wore revealed a smooth flat belly with an indented navel, the thin wet material clinging to a noticeable cunt bulge. She seemed in high spirits and not averse to being admired. She sat beside me and I ordered an iced lager for her from a passing waiter.

'I'm settling in now,' she enthused, 'and really enjoying the life. At first Africa terrified me, I'd never been away from home before, but now I'm getting used to it.' She held her arms apart. 'My first bikini too. Why not? Every one else is wearing them—'

'And you look lovely in it,' I said honestly, topping up her glass from the bottle. 'If you hang on I'll get my trunks and join you for a swim.'

We swam and splashed about together. I found she was

In the Groove

a more confident young woman than I had imagined as we conversed later, lying on sunbeds by the poolside. Her father had been a solicitor and she'd been a secretary in the family business. Her mother had died young and her old man had been struck down by illness years ago, so she had nursed him and worked at home as well, rarely going out. When he had died she had applied for the overseas post and it was the best thing she'd ever done.

'It's time I started to live,' she said. 'I'm thirty-six so I've a lot to make up. There's a dinner dance at this hotel tonight that I'd love to go to. Would you mind if I asked you to take me—?'

'I'd be honoured,' I replied. 'I'll pick you up in the car and you can drive.'

When I called at her bungalow that evening she opened the door in a housecoat, ushering me in and pouring me a drink. I noted her face and hair was made up nicely. She disappeared into her bedroom to return holding up two dresses, flushed with excitement.

'Which one do you prefer?' she asked. 'You choose—'

Faint heart, it is true, never makes the first move, and the moment seemed propitious. 'I keep thinking of you in your bikini, Vera,' I said forcefully, rising to go to her, one hand taking the top button of the loose housecoat, fingers unbuttoning and proceeding to the one below. 'Thinking of your lovely figure, how I'd like to see all of it. Don't think badly of me,' I added cunningly, 'I'm just a man, and you are so enticing.'

What a load of bull, I thought, but it seemed appropriate. I noted her face drained of colour but she did not

In the Groove

stop me as I went on right down to the buttons below her knees.

'Do you think you should?' she said. 'Can I stop you?'

'No,' I answered firmly. I opened the loosened housecoat and pushed it from her shoulders while she stood stock still. I saw the firm uptilted breasts with their nipples prominent and inviting a sucking; the flat belly again with the curved mound at the fork of her thighs, well furred with a thick triangle of dark hair.

'You're quite a beauty,' I told her, picking up her slim form in my arms as the housecoat slid off her to the floor. I pushed open her bedroom door with my foot and laid her across the bed, seeing her eyes watching me without alarm. It was not her first time, I concluded, and was glad of it. Bereft of cunt for too long a time, I wanted it badly and preferably with a cooperative partner.

Her legs were parted, hanging over the bed from the knees. While I got out of my clothes I admired her: breasts packed with firmly rounded flesh that remained upright and did not loll on her chest; an inviting cunt with the butterfly outer lips slightly parted, separating the thick growth of hair that continued on down between the neat buttock cheeks. I went on my knees before her, kissing the inside of her thighs, savouring the milky-white warmth. I had the scent of her in my nostrils, sweetly musky and acrid, irresistible. My tongue licked the length of the split lips bringing a murmured response, the first squirms and a hand on my head. 'Go on,' she said. 'Do. Kiss me there. Lick me out, dear. Don't stop!' she called, growing more urgent. 'Tongue fuck me! Ream my cunt—'

The quiet Vera had enjoyed this before, I decided, curling my tongue and probing her furrow, already a drenched trench, grasping her bottom cheeks to steady her quivering. Vera moaned loudly, bucking her hips hard, too far out of control for me to apply the tongue without getting buffetted by her thrusting cunt. I slapped at her thigh, held her fast, digging in my face with determination. She gasped, struggled as if to contain herself while I sought the clitoris with my tongue-tip, the pink pearl grown tautly to fingertip length as I tormented it. My tongue, even my lips and teeth were sodden with her love syrup. Then she was squealing, throwing up her pelvis, in the helpless throes of coming off against my face.

So far more than good, I complimented myself, eager now to reach my goal. Rising, I saw her laid back grasping her breasts tightly, eyes on me as I stood with a brute of a hard-on that positively reared up, thick and at full stretch.

'What a lovely one', she sighed, showing her willingness and desire to take it by hoisting her knees. 'Yes, fuck me now, Tyler. I went on the pill before I came out, hoping I'd meet someone – someone who would want me—'

I moved forward, cradled in her thighs and went in to the hilt, guided there by her hand. Legs locked behind my back, buttocks pulled in her urgency, Vera humped to me matching thrust for thrust, clamping her pubic bone to mine and clinging like a limpet. I was in a comfortable cunt, tight yet allowing my sliding, knob nudging way back to her cervix, getting her responses in pleasurable little groans. 'Please, please,' I heard her utter, as if the ecstasy was unbearable. 'How greedy I am. Oh yes, yes, fuck me there, don't come yet, it's too good to finish. Aaaagh – oh, I'm coming, coming again! I can't stop, thrust it up! Shove it all up, my darling—'

I came with her, the simultaneous climaxes making for wild thrustings and the smack of belly on belly. We uttered loud gutteral cries and she clutched me tightly even as our spasms subsided, my juice now mingled with hers.

Only when we rolled apart and recovered somewhat did I find the breath to speak. Vera had proved voracious on the job, she was no amateur and as good a reciprocal fuck as one could want. I wondered who had taught her to like it so uninhibitedly, and was keen to listen to her past sex history. 'You were right,' I told her, fondling a heaving breast. 'You are a greedy little thing. Such a good fuck, and I thought you a quiet mouse. For one who claims she seldom got out of the house, I think Vera is a dark horse with a lurid past. Come on, confess, girl.'

I leaned up on an elbow and regarded her naked body, pink with exertion. Was that a blush on her face? Without the big spectacles and with the look of a woman who had just been well fucked, she was quite attractive. She *was* blushing, for her flushed features went a deeper shade and her eyes lowered in embarrassment. 'I know I'm rather fond of it,' she admitted quietly. 'Too fond, I think at times, and it shocks me; the things I think about too, what I would like men and even women to do to me—'

'They are perfectly natural desires you shouldn't be ashamed to have,' I advised, acting the wise counsellor and sympathetic ear, while congratulating myself on such a find. Whatever Vera had fantasised having done to her, Vera would get. I'd enjoy worming her secrets out of her.

'Who was the lucky chap? Someone was good at it to get you going so. I'm in his debt.'

'It was just the one man,' she admitted self-consciously, as if apologetic for the lewd nature thus instilled in her by

In the Groove

the liaison. 'I suppose he was very good, very experienced. Oh dear, I don't want to talk about it—'

'But you will,' I told her. 'Confession is good for the soul.' Also, of course, it makes erotically arousing pillow-talk, the more so with a woman still hesitant to admit to past immodesties. As if to make me forget the subject she cuddled her warm nakedness into me, kissing my eyes and neck and lingering on my mouth, her sharp nipples to my chest. Her hand sought and cradled my balls and limp dick, squeezing gently as if to evoke further life there. Then she fell back on the bed, still holding me and parting her thighs.

'What an awful woman I am,' she muttered, face turned so as not to look up at me. 'I want it again, want you to make love to me. Make love to me like you did before—'

'Fuck,' I said sternly, enjoying my part as the dominant partner. 'You want me to fuck you again, Vera, so say that. Ask me to fuck you like your other lover did, and so expertly as to permanently wake the itch in your cunt. Say, "fuck me!" I bet he made you say it—'

Poor Vera was positively squirming with embarrassment beneath me, but I was sure that only increased her arousal. There's a sweet piquancy in having one's way with a woman reluctant to accept her fondness for vocal and physical sex. 'Fuck me, if you insist,' her voice quavered. 'Only do it, Tyler dear. Now I've said it. You will fuck me, won't you? Whatever will you think of me – begging you like a slut?'

'I like sluts,' I said, my hands squeezing her firm little tits. 'Women enjoy thinking of themselves as such at times like this and why not? It greatly increases the pleasure for both of us. Cows, whores, bitches – I've had women order me to call them all sorts of names while fucking them. Didn't your previous partner say you were those things while screwing you—?'

'Please, please,' Vera moaned. 'What if he did? He made me like that. He took me as a young virgin—' The prick in her grasp had stiffened up enough to make her try to insert it between her cunt lips. I drew back, cruelly wanting to hear more, to have her confess to all before plugging her as she so craved. Pulling her across my knees I laid a splayed hand across the cheeks of her pert bottom. 'What – what are you doing now?' she gasped.

'A little game of truth and consequences,' I said, my free hand holding her neck lightly to stop her wriggling. 'You speak the truth or pay a forfeit. Like this,' I added, giving her upraised bum a tentative smack. She squirmed and protested, so I gave her a smarter one, making her settle down. 'First of all, who was the guy? And how many times did he have you? This is for your own good, girl. It will get it off your pretty little tits and let you face what you are without any bloody silly pretence. Speak, or get your backside warmed—'

'He was a family friend,' Vera admitted, her voice choking with emotion. 'He visited my parents over the years and made advances to me. It was always at home. I told you I rarely went out—'

'Your parents weren't suspicious? A young man calling—?'

'He was middle-aged,' Vera continued in her strangled tone. The way she shifted to rub her cunt mound to one of my knees indicated her mounting arousal. 'Derek was the family doctor. He first came when mother was ill in her bedroom. Father was at his office so when Doctor Merrill came downstairs we were alone. I trusted him. I was seventeen then and too embarrassed to resist his, his—'

'Trying it on,' I finished for her. 'How did he begin—?'

'It was just kisses at first,' Vera recalled in a subdued voice. 'I knew nothing, I just liked him putting his tongue in my mouth. Then he would feel my breasts, take them out and fondle them. Suck them too. It made me go faint. Then he showed me his penis and made me stroke it while his hand was – was – under my skirt. He'd ask if it excited me, and he knew it did because he'd make me come – climax on his hand. I was so embarrassed—'

'I bet naughty little Vera couldn't wait for his next visit,' I taunted her. 'So the dirty doc kept you going until he took your cherry, eh? Where did that occur?'

'On the big couch in my parents' lounge. I suppose being a doctor he knew what parts inside me brought on such sensations. He always made me have an orgasm, sometimes more than one when we did it. Just like you. Mother died and then father got ill, so the visits continued—'

'For how long?' I demanded.

'From seventeen until I was thirty-two. Then he passed away. At his funeral I felt awful, with his wife there crying and me thinking of what we'd been doing all those years—'

'And not just fucking either, I'll bet,' I said as her face turned to me to see if I was satisfied. I parted the cheeks of her bottom, looking on the darker skin tone of her furrow with the wisps of hair surrounding the down-hang of her quim, the lips thickened with tumescence and the entrance pouting from her excitement and our previous fuck. I looked at the tight little puckered asterisk of her anus and wondered if the good doctor had enjoyed that passage too. Drawing two fingers along her cunt lips, I heard her draw in breath as I reached her back entrance, clenching her cheeks on my hand.

'Did he have you front and back?' I demanded. 'No doubt such a man would.'

She turned her face again to me as if imploring.

'If you mean different positions, yes,' she said. 'He was very experienced with women – there was gossip that he had affairs with his patients. He made me do all sorts of things—'

'And this?' I asked, my finger inserting the merest tip in her arsehole, feeling it gripped and making her squirm most sensuously and utter little moans and sighs. 'He wouldn't pass this up, would he?' I pressed my invading finger up to the second knuckle, increasing her agitation and embarrassment.

She turned her face to me, blushing furiously.

'I'll bet you liked that too, once you'd got the feel of it. Say it!'

'Yes, yes, he did, he did!' she howled, her arse now churning wildly under my titillating. 'He buggered me frequently, he enjoyed humiliating me so. God, I shall come, I can't help it,' she cried out, thrusting her cunt against my kneecap while her bottom rotated ever faster. 'He made me suck him too. What else do you want to know of me? Aaaagh, ohhh – I'm there, there, COMING—'

The pleasure was as much mine as hers, to get a woman

In the Groove

so worked up through talk and a little touching up.

'You must think me a fine example of womanhood,' she complained as I laid her back on the bed to recover. I told her that was exactly what I did think of her. Some kind words and flattery made her feel better about herself, enough for me to have her shortly afterwards in a long slow coupling that brought her to climax again before I let fly my wad of jism into her receptive cunt. Then we showered, dressed, and drove off to the dinner-dance as I'd promised, knowing we'd return later to Vera's bungalow to share her bed.

With this in mind I particularly enjoyed the dance. Beverley Marchbanks glared at me from her table as I was grabbed to quick-step with Sam Bishop's Marje. She jammed her cushiony breasts against my chest and invited me to visit whenever I felt like it – the 'it' being said with a gleam in her eye while Sam sat drinking steadily at their table.

'I might just take you up on that,' I told her and was hugged tighter with her cunt pressed to my crotch.

Later I took the chance to ask Beverley to dance. She rose as if reluctant to accept, but after a few turns around the floor seemed to melt into my arms.

'You bastard,' she said. 'I should have nothing more to do with you, but you're the kind of rogue that women forgive. Will we see more of you if I permit you to call on us again?'

'All of me,' I promised, 'like before.' One could not have too many irons in the fire, I decided, or good available cunt.

Chapter Twelve

Mail was not delivered house to house in Entebbe, the routine being that it was collected personally each morning at the ramshackle post office, a wooden structure with a definite lean and a sloping verandah. I had no reason to call there, expecting no letters from anyone, so I was surprised to be handed a large square envelope from America addressed to me at Photo Safaris. Nanji had collected the mail and her handsome dark eyes gleamed as I opened the package. Unaware of the contents, I drew out a selection of large glossy photographs of the models Bettina and Yasmin posed gloriously nude, recalling memories of their lovely black and white bodies. The Asian girl smiled wickedly as I stuffed the photos back out of sight.

The letter with it was from Yasmin, saying the pictures were souvenirs of our happy safari together. If ever I was in the United States, I was to call her number, she said. A postscript, added with a long line of exclamation marks, said that Bettina was now pregnant and she and Ted Sutherland were delighted and getting married at last. 'If it's a boy Bettina should call it Tyler,' Yasmin ended, with more exclamation marks writ large in purple ink. While engaged

In the Groove

in reading this, Nanji leaned her light brown elbows on the counter before me, eyeing my reaction with suspicious interest. I had the gut feeling she had read my mail, the envelope being merely sealed with a metal clasp, the kind easily bent straight to allow access.

'Very beautiful girls,' Nanji remarked, with the ghost of a smile on her full lips. 'You must have given them a nice time on safari to remember you. There are no pupils for you until this afternoon, so would you do *me* a kind favour—?'

'Name it,' I said, thinking Nanji showed promise and that we could get more than friendly in time. 'I can never refuse any beautiful girl. You look lovely today – every day, in fact. Are you considering taking driving lessons?'

She dropped her dark mascara-lidded eyes as if she found my flattery unwelcome, but still retained the smile. 'Lessons for my mother,' she said teasingly. 'My husband will not allow me to take lessons with anyone but himself. He is very jealous, like all Sikhs. You will teach my mother?'

For you, Nanji, yes,' I said. 'I take it this is a freebie, not on the books. I'd rather teach you, of course, but trot on your ma. Does she look as good as you?' Looking her over – she filled out her colourful sari so well with her rounded shape – I did not notice the presence of her mother until she was beside me. I turned to see her regarding me closely, my lech for her daughter not passing unnoticed by the older Asian woman. Nanji giggled at my being caught out.

'My mother, Dulip Kaur Singh,' she introduced us. 'She has decided to learn to drive. Now she is a widow she says she does not want to call on her family for lifts every time she wants to go to the market or visit friends—' I nodded my agreement, turning to give a reassuring smile and offering my hand.

It was accepted with the slightest touch and her hand immediately withdrawn. I had the feeling Dulip Singh, widow, did not trust or like me. I liked the look of her, however. She was in her early forties I judged, a solid well-built woman in a black sari trimmed with silver, handsome of face with jet hair parted in the middle and a thick plaited strand down her curved back. Her posture was erect and I could not help noticing her bust, firm full rounds which filled out her costume, and her hips and thighs which swelled out splendidly from a narrow waist.

'My morning is free, Mrs Singh,' I told her politely, hoping to ingratiate myself with such a fine woman. 'We can take our time and have a good session.' A good session of another kind was just what I could go with her, I thought, fancying her greatly. 'Follow me out to the car and we'll get started—'

'Will you be near Mr Bishop's bungalow?' asked Nanji, holding up a letter, the wicked smile on her lips again. 'This has come for his wife. I think perhaps she would not like her husband to see it.'

'From England,' I agreed, grinning back to her. 'I think I understand. I'll see she gets it personally. It's a quiet road I use for beginners anyway.' The letter's address was typed and I guessed Callum was keeping in touch. It also gave me the excuse to call on the voluptuous Marje Bishop, which I'd intended to do. In the car with Mrs Singh I explained the use of gears, clutch and brakes and she drove off confidently for a beginner. Her smell intrigued me, sitting there as I was, helping with the gear changes and leaning close, a warm musky scent like no other I'd known from a woman.

I murmured *good, good* as she negotiated the busy airport road and directed her to the under-used stretch near the Bishops' place. A fast learner, not nervous and obviously intelligent, within a couple of hours she had got the hang of the rudiments of driving, speeding up and growing in confidence. She said little, remaining serious of face and acting upon my guidance and instructions first time.

'Time for a break,' I suggested when we tried an emergency stop in the road outside Sam's bungalow. I handed over a copy of the Highway Code to keep her busy, hoping to spend a little time with Marjory of the splendid tits while delivering her letter. 'Study that, Mrs Singh,' I said. 'We have copies in Urdu or Punjabi if you prefer—'

'I read English,' she said in her lilting accent. 'My husband and I had a newsagent's shop in London for six years until he died. Do not try to catch my daughter, Nanji. She has a good husband in Joginder Singh but is too free with other men – Europeans especially. It was our time in England that makes her so—'

'I can assure you I've no intention of catching your daughter, as you put it. The thought never entered my head, madam,' I lied, watching her handsome face express a cool look of disbelief. Walking up Sam Bishop's drive, the place seemed deserted. The gardening tools abandoned near the central flower bed as if Kidogo the garden boy had been called to other work. I noted the empty wicker chairs on the verandah, the half-finished drink on a

In the Groove

table, the bottle of vodka beside it and a woman's large straw hat. As I approached the front door, I saw it was slightly ajar so I walked into the lounge, finding that deserted also.

I was wondering where the hell everybody was when sounds that were a dead giveaway echoed from the passageway leading to the bedrooms. They were the unmistakable squeals and whimpers of a woman helplessly embroiled in the throes of fucking to climax. Was it Sam shafting his ample wife? I considered, or maybe his housegirl, Bibi, if Marje was safely out of the way? Curiosity aroused, I ventured soundlessly along the passage and found the bedroom door left open the few inches necessary to give me a full view of the inside. Marje was being screwed right enough and very well, too, judging by the gasps and gurgles produced by the cock in her. But it wasn't her husband pleasuring her so nobly – Kidogo the garden boy was on her.

I saw it all from the side: the ivory-pale Marje on elbows and knees across the juddering bed, neck bent and head lowered, while the ebony body of Kidogo was curled over her arched back, thrusting manfully against her bottom. What a plush bottom it was too! Broad and rounded, tilted up to her fucker to take every inch of penis. Kidogo was on his knees between hers, now over her to the shoulders as he plunged in, now bolt upright behind her, grasping and forcing apart the cheeky moons of a voluptuous arse. I plainly saw his jet black stalk glistening with her cunt juice – a goodly thick and lengthy prick – emerge momentarily from the clasped lips of her rear-presented quim before being shunted home to her loud squeal of delight.

In the Groove

Such a sight could arouse a corpse. My own unruly dick rose to the occasion and I envied the garden boy his task, in the much favoured 'doggie-position' on such a splendid mount.

Marje's big tits hung below her as the pounding at her comfortable bottom continued – outsize rounded udders, elongated in shape, that swung like bells as she thrust back and rotated her arse to the cock. I doubted if it were the first time, noting the confidence with which Kidogo fucked his mistress, making her plead and beg for more as he withdrew his cock to the knob and paused before piercing her once again to his balls. He nestled in the cleave of her broad buttocks, slapping flesh as he jerked in flurries at her cleft.

Nor was Marje backward in voicing her appreciation of his effort. 'Oh, yes, yes, – there, *there*! Harder there—' I heard her mutter as if in an agony as he rammed in. 'God, yes, do, DO IT! Fuck me faster, don't you dare stop, I tell you! Oh, it's so bloody good, your black cock up my cunt. It's heaven, heaven—' and her arse bucked to match each thrust. From her throaty utterances unintelligible to the ear and her wild undulations, I judged she had reached orgasm and was demanding more. Then Kidogo withdrew completely, prick in hand, guiding the swollen organ upwards the inch or so to the puckered ring of her bottom hole, placing the plum-shaped helmet to the entrance. Marje turned her face to him, nodding. 'Yes, that too,' she muttered. 'I do like it there. Go on, go on – fuck my arse—'

One is not often privileged to witness such a sight. This was not a set-up but the real thing – the spectacle of an

In the Groove

eager and highly aroused woman encouraging her partner to bugger her. I plainly saw Kidogo apply pressure and Marje's serrated arsehole 'give' as the knob entered. She expelled a loud breath, then dipped her back to raise her behind, holding her rear still as Kidogo eased inch after inch up the back passage. His well-lubricated shaft disappeared to the root and for a long moment both were still. Marje grunted softly, moving her bottom slightly as she sought to get comfortable with the rude intruder embedded up her bum. Then, as Kidogo began his first tentative thrusts, she uttered little squeaks and squirmed her arse back to meet his rocking motions, her lust increasing as he quickened his pace.

I could hear his sliding in and out, saw from Marje's raised head and twisted features just what sensual feelings the thickness filling her rear portal was giving her. All else of no consequence, both went at it like a dog and bitch. Kidogo's flanks pistoned at her upraised bum and Marje braced herself on her elbows, meeting every stroke. The climax was simultaneous, Kidogo jerking madly and crying out tribal shouts, as Marje's ample bottom slapped against his belly, her gyrations beyond all control. I could imagine the spurtings drenching her innards as Kidogo finally shot his bolt. The boy's deflated prick slipped from his mistress as he got off the bed to stand beside it. Marje fell flat on the bed, legs apart and with a seeping trail of Kidogo's spunk trickling down from her bumhole.

'Get dressed and leave me, Kidogo,' I heard her say.

Thinking it was time to leave myself, I felt a hand clutch at my sleeve. I was astonished to see Mrs Dulip Singh behind me, gesturing that we get out quick. In the midst of the hectic fucking, I had not been aware of her approach or knew how much she had witnessed. More than enough, I reckoned, for her eyes were bright with excitement.

I too had a large and obvious bulge at the crotch of my drill trousers as we slunk back to the car. It did not go unnoticed for once in our seats it still reared and my Asian companion sat with a mocking smile on her face.

'You Europeans,' Mrs Singh declared, 'are so fond of sexual matters. That woman has already run off with another man. Now she is back and using her shamba boy to amuse her. What did you think of what she allowed him to do to her—?'

'It's entirely her business,' I said, 'and none of ours. Maybe her husband doesn't give her all she needs.' I could have added that Marje Bishop was the kind of woman I liked, she was not ashamed to enjoy a good romp with whoever could do the business.

'Then you won't tell others of what you saw?' she asked thoughtfully. 'Spread it round to other Europeans that she takes her garden boy to her bed?'

'No. What good would that do me? Good luck to her—'

'I believe you,' she said, smiling again and making me think what an attractive woman she was. 'You were not able to deliver her letter—'

'Hardly the time, was it, Mrs Singh?' I agreed, laughing. 'I'll see she gets it later. Now let's drive—'

'You may call me Dulip if you wish,' she said. 'Would you mind now if I drive to my house. I wish my lunch.'

At her pink-painted stucco house in an area of Entebbe composed mainly of Asian residences, she regarded me as if deliberating something. 'Do you like curry?' she asked.

In the Groove

'I have plenty, hot Madras curry. You may have lunch with me if you wish.'

I did wish, liking a good curry as well as having a lech for the lady and wondering what her intentions were. Inside the house, the walls were garlanded with coloured streamers decked around large garish portraits of Sikh deities, including a turbanned Guru Nanik. We ate at a low table and I complimented her on the best curry I'd ever eaten, accompanied by ice-cold beer from her fridge. She talked of her life in England, her long widowhood, her quiet life as a dowager woman. 'Once we are widowed, you know,' she said, her eyes upon me, gauging my reaction, 'Asian women are expected to live still faithful to dead husbands. It can be difficult.'

'I'm very sure it is, Dulip,' I said, using her name and, in my most sympathetic tone, thinking what a waste this was of a splendid woman in the prime of female maturity if she wasn't getting fucked.

'Europeans do not understand,' she said almost wistfully, gathering the plates. 'The disgrace for the family if such a respected widowed mother took a lover—' adding as she stared meaningfully at me— 'if such became known.'

I ardently hoped I was getting the gist of her meaning correct. 'There's no reason why it should,' I said conspiratorially. 'I mean if the lady has a trustworthy partner. What kind of man would let it become known? Not I—' My hand reached out to stop her clearing the table and she sat again. The air in the room, the whole atmosphere, had become charged with sexuality. Her hand trembled under mine before she withdrew it. In my pants I felt a lightness

In the Groove

in my balls as my cock stretched. With craft and luck I would have this fine woman, I deliberated, my first Asian and what a beauty!

'When you did not return to the car this morning,' she said with a downcast look in her dark eyes, 'I thought you were having that Bishop woman. It excited me strangely. I know she has other lovers, married as she is. So I went into that house to see for myself. I could not help it—'

I enjoyed her admitting as much, reaching out to clasp her hand again. 'Were you shocked by what you saw?'

'It aroused me,' she confessed shyly, 'to see such a sight. It has been so long for me. Did you mean what you told me – that it was her business and no word of it would be said by you?'

'Absolutely,' I assured her. 'Europeans here would love the scandal. I wouldn't give them the pleasure, nor hurt the lady—'

Dulip had not withdrawn her hand. 'Have you no wife or woman?' she asked. 'No one for you here—?'

'No one,' I said sadly. 'It can be difficult for me too—'

For a long moment she did not speak. Then she braced her nicely rounded shoulders and drew in breath, as if preparing herself to say her piece. 'Then if you like, if you want—' she began in a low whisper. 'I would not mind—'

'It would be an honour and a pleasure,' I declared, trying to keep the lech out of my voice. I stood, lifting her with me, clasping her and feeling her big pliant breasts flatten against my chest. My root was already fully primed, iron-hard, an upright thick cylinder of flesh ready to explore the plump cunt mound it nestled against. My hands went down to clutch firm contoured buttocks, pulling her tighter to me as my mouth and tongue forced her lips apart.

After a brief moment she responded eagerly, her arms around my neck, mouth open and rolling about mine. I sensed the slow, sensuous movements of her pelvis grinding her bulge to my stiffness. 'I will show you my bed,' she offered, sounding breathless as we broke apart for air. 'Will you come—?'

Not before I've made you writhe on my dong, you beauty, I could have said. But I merely nodded as I was led through to a room with red-painted walls, a fine ornately carved bed with a red bedspread and even red pillows. Before me Dulip unwound her sari – with steady hands I noted, as if the die were cast and now it was down to business.

Such was the splendid body she uncovered that I stood still to admire the sight. She had breasts like melons, round and full, with brown smooth skin and thick jutting nipples of a darker hue, almost deep purple. At the fork of strong thighs a thatch of jet black hair forested her prominent bulge, the thickest growth I'd ever encountered, curling around the cunt lips that peeped through the bush. She turned to lay hair-pins on her dressing table and let her hair tumble over shoulders, down a delightful curved back that narrowed at the waist and swept out to the full orbs of firm buttock cheeks.

'Do you not undress too?' she said, settling herself on the bed, tits spreading, legs parted, her knees drawn up in invitation. Whoever was due a driving lesson that afternoon, I decided, would miss out, for certainly I was not going to. The lady had laid herself on the line for me and bravely admitted she required sex. I was not about to disappoint her or hurry it. Her hand idled at her cunt as I undressed slowly in front of her.

I saw her eyes widen as I stood beside the bed with my erection at full stretch, rearing before my belly like a pole. 'No secrets between us now, Dulip,' I told her. 'We must say what we think and do what pleases each other. Tell me what you like and I'll do it. I see your hand on your pussy. Did you do that to yourself when there was nothing else—?'

I saw her frown, look away, but she answered. 'There were nights, in this bed alone . . . yes, yes, a woman must!' In her excitement she stroked her mound, slipped in a finger and squirmed her fine arse. 'Men like to see this, do they not? A woman satisfying herself. My husband used to make me do it, so that he could watch me and make us aroused—'

Under her fingering the cunt lips had parted allowing me a glimpse of the inner folds, glistening with her lubrication. I drew her hand aside, kneeling before her, and lowered my mouth, directed to cover the outer lips and suck, my tongue probing as she moaned and tilted her hairy fig to my face. My palms clasped both firm buttock cheeks, drawing her to me as I tongue-fucked her, feeling an urgent up-and-down movement of her pelvis against my bobbing head, which was now gripped in her hands. She tasted strong and sweet, her juices drenching my nose and chin.

A loud gasp and furious undulations of her pelvis told me I had her, making her come and cry out helplessly. Then she was pulling me over her, legs circling my back,

In the Groove

ankles locking, hands hauling me into the cradle of her thighs, as she urged me to penetrate her.

What a magnificent fuck she was, bucking, thrusting, lifting, desperate to take every inch of my prick and more, jerking from one climax to another. What she garbled in her native tongue when in those throes I'd have loved to have known. Urging me, pleading me, ordering me, I had no doubt. In return I grunted out my contribution in plain English, saying what a lovely fuck she was, what a hungry cunt she had, what tits she had to mouth and kiss. Finally I lost control and ended in a belly-slapping finale as I shot my hot load deep into her crevice.

We fell apart gasping, sated, glad of the respite. When she arose it was to leave the room and return with a tall glass of ice-cold beer. She sat on the bed in her glorious nakedness while I drained it. 'You wish to leave now?' she asked. 'There is work for you—?'

'Not such nice work as this,' I said, fondling a big breast, finding it as smooth as marble. She held it out to me and I sucked the nipple, first one and then the other, feeling the first stirring of a reviving prick as her free hand went down to massage it gently. 'Suck it,' I asked quietly. 'Do you do that, Dulip?'

'Of course,' she said. 'My husband liked that very much,' and her head dipped to the semi-stiff prick she grasped, a tongue tip to the crown then a licking up the stalk that had me groaning my pleasure. Her warm wet mouth then covered an inch or two of it, sucking gently on the growing length as her hand continued stroking. This was expert cocksucking. No wonder her husband died, I thought. He'd been shagged out.

Fully erect, she withdrew her mouth and my dong, silvered with her saliva, sprang up like a coiled spring. I would have been content to fill her throat, but she held the shaft and looked at me slyly. 'You said we were to say what would we like. Do what we saw the garden boy doing to his madam—'

'Dog-fashion?' I said, glad to oblige. 'From behind, you want it that way—?'

'Behind, yes,' Dulip said. '*My* behind. You have—?'

'It's been known,' I admitted cheerfully. If ever a bottom was made for tailing, hers was. 'Your husband again?' I teased her. 'He was quite a lad in his day. If you insist, bend over. I'm here to please—'

But first she went to a drawer and handed me a small pot with a label picturing a tiger and Chinese lettering. 'Use it,' she instructed, getting up on hands and knees before me, presenting her magnificent buttocks. 'On yourself, please, and then me. You are big and must use it. Then it is good.'

I uncapped the pot, smearing a greyish ointment up the length of my shaft, finding its immediate effect was a strange warmth that permeated right through my shaft and down to the balls. My cock seemed to set like stone in a permanent hard-on. Before me, on hands and knees with turned head, Dulip watched and then waggled her bottom. 'Now for me,' she directed, head lowered to the pillows, reaching back to draw apart the twin cheeks of her arse for my access. I was faced with a darker-skinned divide, the heavy hang of her cunt, and the tight puckered entrance to her rear orifice. Too tight, I thought.

'Are you sure about this?' I asked, reckoning as a widow

In the Groove

that entrance had not probably been breached for some years and my efforts might prove painful. I felt her cunt to see if that would change her mind, but she waggled her bottom at me as if in annoyance, telling me to use the ointment. I was still rock hard, wondering what the stuff was, but obediently greased her ring with it. I ventured in a fingertip and got a low moan of pleasure. She urged me on again, so I crouched behind her, directing the knob of my cock to the watertight hole, pushing tentatively. At first there was resistance then it gave, swallowing my glans, gripping me in a vice.

'I'll hurt you,' I warned. 'It's too tight. I'm in far enough.'

'*Not* far enough,' Dulip argued. 'Please, push, and I will push to you. It will be all right. It has been there many times—'

Push I did as she squirmed her bottom back to me. Inch after inch I forced a passage, lodging home with my balls hard against the cleft of her fine arse. 'Yes,' she grunted, beginning a see-saw motion with back dipped and her bottom rotating. I was clamped fast but able to slide up and down the narrow passage. Getting the feel of it, my lust reared. As I thrust deep into her warmth, she began to whinny and whimper. Her head tossed and her backside pummelled my curved belly as the pleasure took over. My hands went below her to squeeze and fondle her hanging breasts and my pace increased. Then her whimpers became loud howls and we increased our wanton thrustings. I came inside her with a growl, quite out of my mind.

I fell away from her, my dick drained and lay prone across the bed. After some moments Dulip got up to leave the room again and I admired the firm curves of her rolling buttock cheeks. I ruminated that the day had turned out well – a private view of Marje Bishop on the job and a glorious no-holds-barred romp with a full-bodied uninhibited Asian woman. She returned still naked and offered me a fresh bath towel and soap, saying we should wash. I took a cold shower while she knelt at a bowl and sponged her magnificent tits and thick hairy nest between her legs. After we had dressed, she brought me tea and sweet cakes. She sat at the table, watching me thoughtfully.

'What's on your mind, Dulip?' I said. 'You've no worries about me divulging what we did today. I want more—'

She waved a hand as if dismissing any anxiety she felt. 'My daughter has talked of you. She likes you. Now that you have the mother, do not be so friendly with the daughter. Nanji is too English, not like a good Sikh girl. I do not trust her—'

This only further aroused my interest, since I found the thought of having both mother and daughter stimulating in the extreme. I laughed as if dismissing the possibility. 'You are more than enough to be going on with,' I assured her. At that moment the subject of our conversation breezed in, looking young and succulent in a yellow sari and expressing pleasure to see me. Her mother rose to take dishes to the kitchen, throwing me a warning glance.

'So here you are,' she smiled. 'I've looked everywhere—'

'Your mother kindly asked me to lunch after her driving lesson,' I explained, rising. 'She makes a great curry.'

'There's a client waiting at the office,' she said, going with me outside and joining me in the car. 'A very pretty white girl too,' she added with her mocking smile. 'You will like her, I know. Big here—' and she cupped her hands before her own pouting breasts, giggling at her forwardness. 'I made her wait for you. How did you get on with my mother?'

'She's remarkable. Best first-time session I've known—'

'She's done it before with my father,' Nanji said, as if we were talking of the same thing. 'He gave her driving lessons when we lived in London. Didn't she tell you—?'

'No, but she's obviously had experience,' I said, tongue in cheek. 'The way she went at it. She's good.'

I put the car in gear and we drove off with Nanji's mother watching from outside her house. 'She is so suspicious of me,' the girl remarked, her scent in my nostrils. 'Don't wear jeans, don't do this or that, you're not in England now, you're a married woman. She thinks I'm too friendly with you—'

'Your ma did say I was not to catch you,' I ventured. 'That was the very word she used.'

'She meant fuck me,' the high-spirited girl laughed, bubbling over at her daring use of the forbidden word. 'You wouldn't do that, would you, Tyler—?'

I pulled up before the hotel, leaning across to open the car door for her, my arm brushing her breasts. 'The thought never crossed my mind,' I said in mock innocence.

She slipped from the car, turning as she made to walk away, her face a picture of wicked delight. 'Why not?' she giggled as she skipped away. I had little time to ponder on that open invitation before a girl with a remarkably pretty face screwed up in annoyance looked through the open window of the car. She was young, in her early twenties, a

In the Groove

little on the plump side but with a lovely curvaceous figure. Nanji had not lied about the size of her breasts. They were level with my eyes as she accosted me angrily.

'I'm Anne Gregory, United Nations,' she said haughtily. 'You have kept me waiting here for over an hour for my lesson. It's not good enough, whoever you are.'

'Something urgent came up, Miss Gregory,' I apologised, which was not so far from the truth. 'Hop in now and I'll give you extra time to make up for the delay.' I watched as she settled her comfortably rounded bum in the driving seat as I shifted over for her. 'I'm Tyler Wight, by the way. I take it you are a beginner?'

'I wouldn't be sitting here otherwise, would I?' she replied impatiently, ignoring my proferred hand. 'I've read all the manuals, so proceed with your instruction. One must have a car to get about in this awful place. I was quite happily settled at the U.N. headquarters in New York with a nice apartment until I was ordered here. Now I've got to live in some horrible little cottage out on a God-forsaken road surrounded by bush. Show me how to start up and operate this thing. How I hate it here in Africa.'

Chapter Thirteen

Bushed from an exhausting day, not the least of which was the hour or so spent tutoring the short-tempered Anne Gregory, I fell on my bed in the box-like room in the hotel annexe and decided that, for once, an early night was in order. Getting across the rudiments of driving to the United Nations girl had proved an ordeal. Despite honours degrees in law and economics, and fluency in several languages, I had a job on my hands getting her to understand the simplest instructions. Not that she considered it her fault as she clashed gears, stalled and almost drove into a roadside market stall sending the natives fleeing for their lives.

So I fell on my bed, sweat-streaked and uncaring, and slept deeply until I awoke in darkness and my watch told me it was after seven in the evening. I showered and once again felt invigorated and ready for the world, hungry as a wolf. The dining room beckoned and I went through every course at dinner, courtesy of Sam Bishop, which made me recall that I still had the letter for his wife in my pocket. Wined and dined, I went through to the bar to see what talent might be available.

I was pleasantly surprised to find Marje Bishop herself,

In the Groove

well in her cups it seemed. She had settled with her plush bottom overflowing a barstool and was engaged in ribaldry with the male members of the crew of a Boeing jet. All were in high spirits as they gathered around her at the bar, no doubt priming her up for later, their intention obvious.

She spotted me and waved a glass tipsily in my direction, telling me to join the party. 'Sam is off on safari,' she hiccupped, 'I'm a loose woman, I mean I'm on the loose tonight,' she blearily corrected herself. 'Meet my friends—'

Some friends, I considered, seeing the way they were smirking and ogling down the neck of her dress at her big tits. My hand was shaken heartily as I was welcomed to the group. 'Do you know the lady?' one fellow asked me furtively. 'We think she fucks. We're taking her to a room to find out. Join us, it should be good, if you don't mind—'

Why should I mind? I thought. Marje didn't seem to be complaining as hands pinched her bottom, giving squeals of laughter and waggling her cheeks in reply. Guests in the bar were starting to frown and the barman looked worried, so I suggested we'd better adjourn to a room right away. Marje was helped along a corridor, up a flight of stairs, and we entered a spacious room as different from my poor abode as a room can get. I envisaged a wild time ahead, glasses filled with generous pourings of champagne, Sam's wife being hugged and kissed by all the men in turn as she revelled in being the centre of attraction.

What others do, especially consenting adults, has never been any of my business, but Marje was pissed out of her skull and not in control. I feared the worst for her with this lot, the more so as I watched them strip off, surrounding her with bobbing erections. She was hoisted up and pushed flat across the bed and her dress pulled over her head. Rough hands drew off her stockings and briefs. It was no doubt the uncouth manner in which they stripped her so blatantly that sobered her somewhat and she howled out a protest as she floundered naked. As her breasts were grabbed and a prick directed to her mouth, I saw her struggles were genuine. She tried to rise but was held down. She rolled over, presenting her fine arse and two pairs of hands smacked at it smartly before one of the men got in position to mount her with his prick guided to the divide.

'Bastards!' she yelled. 'I say who fucks me and when! Let me up, you pigs,' and she drew her arse forward as the prick was nudging to enter her cunt. I felt it was high time to intervene, unpopular as that would be with the drunken rabble eager to have their way with her.

Marje was held down more firmly, their hands gripping her arms and pulling her legs apart to combat her endeavours to break free. A strapping woman, she took some holding, rolling her backside around so that the splendid downward hang of her wispy-haired split mound was no easy target. I heard one shouting to hold the bitch. He took his belt from his trousers and thwacked Marje's twisting posterior. Her face pressed into the pillow with the pressure of being pinioned and her protests continued muffled and inarticulate as she was belted.

I grabbed at the arm wielding the belt, getting the man to turn in surprise and ordered him to lay off. 'We have bought this woman drinks all evening,' he complained. 'Now she pays—'

'Fucking hard luck, mate,' I told him, feeling my arms

pulled behind my back and gripped by someone while the belter raised the strap again. I was mobile enough to lunge forward and give him a 'Glasgow Kiss', nutting him smartly across his nose with my brow. He yelled and dropped the belt, bending over and holding his face, blood on his fingers. My turn was next. I took a glancing blow between the nose and mouth and I kicked out viciously at the crotch of my attacker.

Suddenly all was still, my arms were released and the men stood back. In the doorway stood a man I took to be the aircraft's captain. He strode in looking furious, his crew backing away. Marje sat up, naked, her big tits jiggling, mascara running down her cheeks and mixing with her tears.

'Let's get out of here,' I said, gathering up her clothes and holding out a helping hand. I had expected her to dress, but she lurched out of the door in to the carpeted corridor with as much dignity as a well-proportioned nude woman can command. There, who should we meet as I supported Marje and led her to the back stairs out to the car park, but my driving student, Anne Gregory. She stood at the door of her room, key in hand, about to enter. Seeing me holding up a completely naked woman made her purse her lips in disdain.

'Good evening,' was all I could think to say, while Marje slumped against the wall.

'So it would seem for you,' she said acidly. 'Do you know your nose is dripping with blood? It's staining those clothes you're clutching. That person will need them later, I presume?'

'I want to go home,' Marje suddenly announced, trying

In the Groove

to straighten up. 'Who is this bloody girl, anyway? One of your spare fucks? Take me home, Tyler—'

'Charming,' Anne Gregory declared. 'I was going to allow you to use my bathroom to clean up, but now you can get on with it. This is quite usual for Africa, I imagine—'

'Every night,' I assured her. 'I thought you'd been given a cottage—?'

'I'm not moving in until it's been repainted and better furniture put in,' she said. I could imagine that. 'Will you be fit to give me my driving instruction tomorrow?'

'On the dot,' I said.

I got Marje down the stairway, padding barefoot beside me to the old Morris. There she snuggled up to me with her head on my shoulder, a pliant tit on my arm as I tried to start up. It was as well Sam Bishop was on safari, I thought, with his naked wife nestling up to me so comfortably. I tried to disengage her hand from my crotch, but my dong was responding to her touch.

'Kiss me,' she moaned, almost climbing in my lap. 'I want to kiss you. Not those bastards back there. You saved me—'

Her arm dragged my head sideways and soft wet lips were crushed against mine. Her mouth tasted of vodka. The kiss lingered and the feel of her body affected me. I cupped one of her bared breasts. She sighed, pulling at my zip to delve inside and clasp the girth of my big boner.

'I want to be fucked, fucked by *that*,' she muttered against my mouth. 'I want you to fuck me. Here!'

'Home first,' I promised. At her bungalow I wondered if she'd be up to it, stumbling behind me as I almost dragged her through the garden. She fell once and when I lifted her she clung to me, pushing her tits and cunt hard against my body, seeking my mouth greedily. I got her inside and dumped her on the bed. For anyone in her condition, I decided, hot black coffee was the prescription. I made a pot, going back to the bedroom with two brimming mugs, expecting to find her already sleeping it off.

Instead, she was awake, sitting up in all her ample nakedness, obviously unable to relax until something was done about the itch in her lower region. Propped on one elbow, she accepted the coffee and sipped while making a face. 'You do intend to fuck me?' she enquired. 'I'm a little pissed, but that has always made me randy. Take off your clothes, let me see if that prick I felt in the car is as big as I think—'

Personally, I had no wish to disappoint her, having a cockstand that almost made me walk with a limp. The lady was all for fucking, looking extremely desirable with her big tits lolling and showing the hairy nest at the plump fork of her parted legs. I got out of my clothes, going to the side of the bed, proud of the upright dick I presented. She admired it, pressed it between her tits and then kissed it.

'I could suck that lovely prick all night,' she said ardently, flicking the head of it with her tongue. 'I think I shall eat it!'

She really tried, taking so much of its length in her mouth that I thought it would choke her. Nevertheless she gobbled on it greedily, bobbing her head and sucking energetically and sensuously, rolling her tongue around the stalk so expertly that I knew it would be soft and drained by the time it came out. Marje's nose was buried in my pubic whiskers as she increased the suction, made lewd with the pleasure, a hand behind me drawing my arse in. 'Fuck my face,' she managed to gurgle through a mouthful of dick. 'Go on, fuck my mouth, imagine it's my cunt—'

'Yes,' I agreed throatily, pushing Marje's hair back to her neck, keeping my hands there to hold her, jerking my hips to fuck her mouth as ordered. I sensed, as I shunted into her surrounding lips, her hungry sucking, my slidings, her free hand at her cunt, a finger squelching noisily as it worked its magic. My knees buckled and I croaked, thrusting ever faster, feeling that she aimed to suck my balls in as well as its contents. I came sending what seemed like never-ending spurts of scalding jism deep into her gullet, her jaw and throat muscles working as she swallowed the stream. Still she did not seem fully satisfied, sucking on furiously after draining me until with loud grunts and helpless spasms, she fell back, bringing herself off on her fingers.

I got on the bed beside her, content to revive somewhat, but Marje had other ideas, rubbing her bush against my thigh to show she was still horny. 'Give it time,' I told her, remembering the letter I had in my pocket and rose to get it. She studied the postmark and frowned.

'Bastard,' she swore vehemently, 'the big bastard, and his little bitch of a whore too!' She ripped the envelope apart and tossed it over her head, making me surmise that her former lover Callum was not her flavour of the month. 'That's what I think of him. You're nicer anyway with that big thing of yours. I want it again, I want to be fucked. Don't just lie there, do something—'

In the Groove

She was obviously randier than ever, worked up and impatient to get a cock up her cunt. Shuffling on her bum, she moved sideways until the hairy bulge of her sex was within an inch or two of my face, dragging a pillow with her to bolster her rear higher for my inspection. Her split fig was well parted and pouting, exuding the strong smell of aroused pussy, glistening and tilted for my mouth. 'Suck my cunt,' she demanded. 'You will, won't you? Do that until you are hard again—'

I licked her thighs, sticky with her juice, then I was deep in her undergrowth from nose to chin. 'Lick!' I heard her command from above. As she rotated her arse in my face, my tongue probed among the soft wet folds, finding a curled finger already in place as Marje diddled away at herself. Her wanton behaviour soon had the desired effect of raising my limp tool. My probing tongue, her squelching finger and hoarse cries, the very lewdness of our actions made me stiff again. I pulled away to mount her, getting an urgent 'Yes!' as I positioned myself. Marje was more than ready, eager to be fucked. She clutched at my swollen cock, lunging at it.

Her forward thrust took me in her to the balls and almost beyond. She was a big mature lady with flesh on her bones. I was comfortably ensconced between supporting thighs to enjoy a fuck in a million with a cunt so hot it burned. Her arms and legs hooked about me, her striving arse barely touching the bed, she howled her joy as I dug into her, my knob nudging her inner works in varying angles of penetration.

'Fuck! Fuck!' she screamed. 'Hold my bum – get a finger up it!' I cupped her bouncing cheeks in my palms, getting a digit to the second knuckle up her bottom. Its effect was to make her work her arse even more furiously, going at it like she had been deprived of a good fucking for weeks. It was more than human nature can stand and soon the friction of my shafting reached boiling point as I inundated her with long spurts of come.

Even in my diminishing throes Marje clung like a limpet, as if reluctant to lose the fullness that had filled her, thrusting her bushy mound against my lower belly as I lay across her, spent. Such a horny bitch I'd rarely encountered. As I rolled aside to separate our clammy, sweat-glistening bodies she leaned over me giggling, offering her big tits for me to suck. No wonder Sam Bishop called in reinforcements at times. I sympathised with him as a thick nipple was pressed to my lips.

While it was pleasant enough to lie there being fed her teats, I could see from the gleam in her eyes that she would require fucking again before the night was through. She dandled my dick, hoping for signs of revival. 'What a lovely thing,' she cooed.

Lovely or not, it would take time to respond. I could wait, stretched out as I was on a comfortable bed with a comfortable woman. I asked if she had a beer, and she paddled away naked to return with a frosted bottle which she held between her tits as if to cool them. She curled up beside me as I drank and her hand went back to my prick as if unable to leave it alone. One half of the letter she had ripped apart had become stuck to my hip. I picked it off, interested to know the reason for her angry reaction to my giving it to her.

'It's from a man I once knew,' she said haughtily. 'Fuck

In the Groove

him, I don't want to know what he has to say. That's all over—'

'Name of Callum?' I enquired. 'I know Sam dashed off to get you back from him. So he's had it, has he—?'

'I caught him fucking my step-daughter,' Marje recalled jealously. 'I was out of the house for ten minutes and I found the pair of them at it. Sam's daughter from his first marriage. I brought the little slut up and this is how she repays me. She did it just to spite me, of course.'

Even more intriguing, I thought, hoping to hear more. 'Does Sam know?' I asked. 'How would he take that—?'

She took the bottle of beer from me and drank deeply, sitting up with her large tits level with my eyes. 'He'd go bloody spare,' she said. 'It was bad enough that the big sod was having me, let alone his darling daughter. The way they were going at it, it wasn't the first time, little cow. She was squatting over him, loving it. Sixteen and riding away like a whore. Bitch! And as for Callum—'

Lucky him, I thought, suppressing a grin. A man after my own heart, no doubt. 'What about Callum?' I prompted.

'You would think that with me, a grown woman, giving him everything he wanted,' Marje said spitefully, 'that that would be enough. But no, he has to fuck a slip of a girl with tiny tits and hardly a hair on her cunt, not that she objected. Why am I telling you this? Kiss me. Cuddle me. I don't want to talk about them—'

'The things that go on between people in this wicked world,' I told her. 'Isn't it too much? Who can you trust?' I indicated that she roll over so that I might admire her broad round buttock cheeks, recalling that she had wanted me to finger her anus. After watching Kidogo up her, I had a strong lech to have her there too. She turned on her belly, rump raised as if knowing my intention, glancing back over her shoulder.

'I certainly won't trust Christine again, the tart,' she said emphatically. 'She's coming out to stay with us during her summer holidays. No doubt she'll be smirking all over her face thinking how she took Callum from me. I'm not looking forward to it. And don't you get any ideas—'

'As if I would,' I vowed, my hands caressing the soft mounds of her bottom, parting the cleft, kissing the sweet flesh. I moistened my index finger in her well-juiced cunt and probed her arsehole, watching it pucker up and quiver. 'When does your step-daughter arrive, by the way—?'

'Never mind that,' Marje groaned, wriggling her hips as I fingered her deeply. 'Just keep on doing what you are doing. God, god, it does something to me. Do you intend to bugger me?'

'It had crossed my mind. You've got a lovely bottom to screw,' I admitted. 'The thought's got me going again—'

'Then put it up there,' Marje insisted. 'Do it, please.'

'You've had it there before?' I said, wanting to hear her admit to it, my knob now replacing my finger and nudging her hole, poised to press into the tight ring. I'd seen Kidogo the garden boy there, of course, but there's nothing like hearing a woman in the throes confess what she's done. 'Did big Callum have your bottom at times?'

'Yes, yes,' she conceded impatiently. 'You want to know everything. Fuck my bum, I want it—'

I eased in, finding as usual a delightfully warm and tight

passage in which to lodge a stiff cock. Marje groaned an 'Aaaagh' of satisfaction, clenching and unclenching her anus to allow my entrance and tilting up her behind. I went in to the hilt, balls nestled snugly to her cleave, taking my time to relish the corking. I took hold of her tits as I crouched behind her, getting a fine response as she writhed her arse, balling it back hard to my belly.

'You sod,' I heard her mumble. 'You're up my bottom, you dirty sod. Heaven, oh heaven—' and I could imagine the fullness she felt with my tool lodged all the way in her. She pulled one of my hands from her breasts to direct it to her cunt, jerking away to match my pistoning.

Yet even while I was so delightfully engaged, my mind recalled her step-daughter's imminent arrival. She sounded like a young lady worth getting to know.

Chapter Fourteen

All was well with my world, it seemed, over the following weeks. I had a job that was not too demanding, apart from time spent giving driving instructions to the snooty Anne Gregory, a girl with a real chip on her shoulder. I had a place to lay my head if necessary, free meals and pay, plus a stable of ever-ready women. With Sam on safari, the buxom Marje had received several visits. Each weekly driving session with Dulip ended with a session of a different kind. I'd been invited by Jumbo Marchbanks to wine and dine at his table again, following which the expected bedroom romp ensued, he and I taking it in turns to fuck Beverley and Jovial. And in between bouts his white wife and the black servant girl entertained us with wholehearted lesbian scenes. Riding so high, I might have anticipated a fall.

As if to dampen my spirits, an out-of-season tropical downpour lashed down that morning. It drummed on the roof of the Morris as Vera Steedman drove me back from Kampala, the proud professor of a Ugandan driving licence, even though it had meant slipping two hundred shillings to the test inspector. That was obligatory but did not lessen her joy.

In the Groove

'Let's swim when we get to the hotel,' she said in her exuberance. 'I've always wanted to bathe when it's lashing down. Then you can have me on your bed, Tyler. It's a day to celebrate, I've already ordered a new car for myself. It's all happening—'

Something certainly was going to happen, although I had no idea of it then. Like a teenager on the loose, she threw off her few clothes to reveal her slim body, her little pointy tits and wispy lipless cunt. I had stripped off myself and the inviting sight made me reach for her. 'Later, later,' she giggled naughtily. 'If you're very good now I'll show you something later we haven't done before. Something quite rude—'

'Something your doctor friend did to you?' I enquired.

'No, what I did to him,' she confessed, laughing. 'Aren't I awful? You make me want to tell you these things, and I know you like it. Let's be daring. Let's swim nude—'

'It's a stroll through the hotel to the pool,' I laughed, admiring her daring. 'The two of us in the buff might cause a stir. Otherwise I'd be all for it.'

'We've got towels, big bath towels,' she said, still excited. 'If we wrap them about us, whoever we meet will think we've got bathing costumes underneath. Do let's, come on—'

It was bucketing down hard, like a sheet of glass. The poolside was deserted as we discarded the towels and leapt in. There is a good feeling about swimming free as nature intended, balls and chopper floating as if defying gravity. Vera was truly on heat, putting her arms around my neck and clinging to me as we trod water at the deep end, pushing her sharp nipples into my chest and rubbing her mound up-and-down against my dong. The rain hit the water like pellets, plastering hair to our faces as she kissed me lewdly. Of course my cock rose stiffly and she grasped it in her hand.

'Put it in and fuck me,' she urged as our heads submerged, and the horny secretary directed my prick to her cunt and wrapped her legs around my waist. It was a good way to drown, I considered, as my prick lodged up her twat and her arse began to jerk. Our feet touched bottom as I gripped hers, thrusting now to her thrusts, shafting strongly as she held on tight, breaking surface to gasp air and lewd grunts. From the quickening contractions of her pelvis it was obvious she was coming off, pulling me under in her eagerness, her body on top of me as I sank. All the same, half-drowned or not, my prick tensed, nerve ends tingling, the surge driving up from my balls to flush her innards. She thrashed about as if wishing never to stop as I clung to the pool's steps, half-immersed, choking up chlorinated water, pelted by stinging rain.

We wrapped ourselves in the sodden towels and dashed back to my room, drying ourselves with fresh ones, standing close and laughing about our watery coupling. 'What was the something quite rude you promised to do to me?' I reminded her. I glanced down at my shrivelled dick. 'See what you've done to him?'

'It's special to make him stand up again,' Vera predicted solemnly. 'When I did it for Doctor Merrill he could always get another erection after – after—'

'Fucking your hot little cunt,' I finished for her, chuckling at her seriousness. 'I was going to suggest lunch before we had it again, but you've got me intrigued. Show me,

Vera. I think you've got the itch for it, whatever it is. Just what do I have to do?'

'Don't make it sound so perverted,' Vera said, blushing but stifling a giggle too. 'Even if it is disgusting that a girl should want to do it. Get up on the bed with you, kneeling up, with your knees wide apart. Turn, face the pillows, that's right. Now stay like that, Tyler—'

On my knees, upright and facing the headboard and wall, I waited. I felt the weight of Vera getting on the bed, a shuffling movement ensued, then her face appeared between my legs. She was on her back, looking up, her nose and mouth directly under my balls. I could just see her forehead, eyes and one free hand. Then she was gently clasping my flaccid dick, lifting it as a wet tongue lapped at my bottom hole, licked along the frenum, the stretch of skin separating anus from scrotum, making me moan and mutter 'Oooh, yes, yes,' and going as weak as a kitten under her ministrations. She licked under my balls and all around them like a cat cleaning a saucer of milk, then took one of my downhanging eggs in her mouth, sucking gently, and all the time, with fingers closed lightly about my dick, stroking it to tumescence.

Of course my cock responded, thickening and stretching in her hand. She had somehow managed to get both balls in her mouth; now flicking her tongue at them, now sucking as if to draw them down her throat. I was uttering unintelligible noises, mouth agape and chin lifted in the agony of ecstasy, unable to stop my arse churning until she used the free hand behind me to slap hard at my left buttock to warn me to stay still. I had to tense myself to give only the tiniest squirms as she noisily slurped my bollocks.

In the Groove

I had to hand it to her for doing an expert job. The prick she had massaged so delightfully was now rearing rock-hard like a poker. I owed a debt to her dubious doctor tutor too, who had instilled such lewdness in her on his corrupting house calls. No doubt the salacious medic had studied anatomy and taught her the parts he enjoyed being titillated. I was the fortunate heir to his training of the teenage Vera. Her mouth widened to release my balls, soggy with saliva, then she tilted her head as she drew down my stander to lave it with her tongue, going up the underside of the stiff stalk until nibbling the head with her lips.

'Suck, suck, you horny bitch,' I ordered as she covered my first few inches with her mouth and applied suction. Then she drew her slim body forward on the bed until first her tits, then her belly, and finally her neat split bulge came into view, resting directly under my crotch. 'Don't you swallow?' I asked in my hugely aroused state. 'I was for giving you a mouthful—'

'No, no,' Vera returned. 'I do swallow, he made me do that all the time, but I want your prick. I want you to fuck me – put it in, put it in! Go up my cunt with it.'

'Roll over then,' I told her in my urgency. 'Cock up your bum, Vera—'

'We're so crude, aren't we?' she said, complying and turning to hoist her boyish bum. 'But it's lovely, isn't it, saying what you like? Please don't come too soon, give me one of your long slow fucks, please. Make me come and come. I've never felt more like it. Do you want me to part my cheeks for you? I want it to slide right into me, all the way—'

All the way she got it, till my balls nestled deep in the

valley of her raised arse and I clasped both firm cheeks and commenced rogering her. 'Oh, heaven,' she gasped, wriggling her backside and balling back to my belly. 'Have you ever had a black girl, Ty?' she asked throatily. 'Are they as good as this? They say Africans are very sexy. One of the young officers at the Ministry of Defence where I work has asked me out—'

Engaged as I was in shafting her tight but juicy lubricated cunt, I could not suppress a short laugh. 'So you fancy being screwed by a black dick, do you? Why not. Don't die wondering, he'd be one lucky guy.' I felt her flanks quiver and jerk, going berserk as she accomplished her first climax, then settling down at a slightly reduced pace as I pounded away. 'You showed me your party piece with your head between my legs,' I told her, 'now I'll show you one of mine.' I withdrew from her, despite her protest, raised the bulbous crest of my weapon to her compact rear hole and pressed it in. She groaned, turned her face enquiringly to me and clenched her buttock muscles. I eased up an inch or two, remaining still to let her get the feel of it. At least she did not attempt to pull away, containing the intruder and squirming her bottom gingerly.

'Do you know where that is, Tyler?' she asked as if afraid to draw breath. 'Is that possible? I mean your size—'

'It will stretch, I've corked ones as tight before,' I enjoyed informing her. 'I take it old Doc Merrill has been there. Relax your bottom and you'll get to enjoy the feel of it again. There, a few more inches and it's buried its snout. That's great! You're so tight, it's a perfect arse to poke. This must be like old times for you—?'

'I've never had it there,' Vera groaned, but I took pleasure in noting her hindquarters were beginning to move gently as I worked in my stalk. 'I said I did when you questioned me at my cottage because I thought that's what you wanted to hear. But he never did, not that. Oh, aaagh, it feels so big up there! It's so hard! Oh God, you're pushing it up and down now. It's burning inside me! Aah, yes, it's right up—'

'And you're getting to like it,' I said, shunting harder, withdrawing the stalk an inch or two then sliding in, gazing with salacious gratification at the now definite motions of her rear end as I pumped flesh up her back passage. It was erotically arousing seeing the ridged anal orifice stretch to accommodate my girth, stretching like an elastic band to permit my in-and-out thrusting.

'Tell me what it's like now,' I commanded. 'How is it for you—?' It was marvellous from my end, I could have told her.

'Lord, lord,' croaked Vera, getting her first introduction to a cock up her bottom. 'It's – it's – not nice but it's very nice, isn't it? Oh dear, what a thing to do! making me feel so funny. Push more, Tyler, I'm sure I'm going to come with you there. Aaaagh, what's happening inside me? My stomach is doing somersaults. I shall want this again—' and her arse worked like fury at the coming explosion, making my own hectic climax gush its outpouring into the dark recess of her bum.

She fell flat on her stomach, legs splayed, with me still over her and gripped by her hole's final twitches. I kissed her neck to show my gratitude.

'That's the second test I've passed today,' she said quite

proudly. 'I've thought of doing it that way, of course. Fantasising.'

'Now you've had the real thing,' I told her, rolling aside and patting her bottom in appreciation. 'Let's dress and go for lunch now. This afternoon won't be so much fun. I've got to take the uppitty Miss Gregory for her lesson. I'd gladly fork out the two hundred bob myself to get her a driving licence and off my back.'

'I think she's quite beautiful,' Vera said ungrudgingly, rising to shower. 'She's everything that I'm not.' She looked at me with eyes aglow, taunting me. 'I'll bet you'd like to do to her what you just did to me—'

'That haughty bitch would be ice cold,' I said, sitting up.

Suddenly, through my door, came two huge black Ugandan Army officers, entering without the courtesy of knocking. Vera screamed and bolted to the cramped shower cubicle, her arse cheeks flying. One of the intruders was flat of face with four tribal scars cut deep to decorate his cheeks. He looked as mean as they come, a hand resting on the holstered revolver on his webbing belt, staring expressionless after the fleeing Vera. His companion was just as menacing despite the broad smile on his gleaming ebony round face, his bulk towering over his fellow officer. I had met him before as Sergeant Idi Amin. Now I noted he wore a major's insignia on his shoulders, a further step on the ladder that would lead upwards to Field Marshal. In a few years he would be his nation's President.

'Don't bother to knock,' I thought acidly, not daring to voice the actual words. Instead, I hastily drew the bedsheet around my nakedness, saying, 'What is it you gentlemen want?' Idi Amin's great body shook as he laughed uproariously and he extended a ham-like hand to shake mine.

'This is the *mzungu* pilot?' questioned the expressionless thug beside him, cold eyes giving me an immediate feeling of dread. 'In such a cheap room? Major Amin informs me you can fly. Is that correct—?'

'You must answer Colonel Wasswa,' Amin said, a warning note in his voice. 'We have very important business to discuss, top secret, very important. Do not lie for we will know—'

'Why should I lie?' I asked, my feeling of unease increasing by the second, a thought flashing through my agitated brain of poor Vera cowering naked in the shower cubicle with her clothes strewn over the floor. 'Of course I fly, just about everything but the latest jetliners. May I ask how you got onto me, knew where to find me, I mean—?'

'We know everything,' the icy Wasswa said simply. I'd heard of him. He had a reputation as a torturer and mass murderer. 'A staff car will pick you up at the hotel main entrance at two this afternoon. Good day to you—'

I very much doubted if it would be as he turned and left the room, leaving Amin to resume his cheery manner. He clasped my hand again. 'We came at a very bad time for you, I think, old friend,' he said with his deep laugh. 'Please, carry on with the lady—'

'I don't think the mood will be quite the same,' I said, chancing his joviality to risk a direct question. 'Just what is it I'm supposed to fly and where?'

'Very top secret,' he repeated inanely. 'Now I must go—'

'I was booked to give someone a driving lesson this

In the Groove

afternoon,' I said feebly, shutting up as his dark eyes cautioned me.

'Do not disappoint Colonel Wasswa,' Amin advised. 'Very bad man. He went to your Sandhurst, don't you know?'

A fucking lot of good it did the bastard, I thought, feeling my safe and comfortable world crumbling about me by the second. Vera appeared timidly when I said our visitors had left, trembling and muttering what a frightening pair they had been. I could not have agreed more.

I skipped lunch and went straight to the driving-school office, where Nanji regarded me with a look of horror in her eyes and Sam Bishop shook his head at my approach.

'You're in deep shit, lad, when people like those two want to get hold of you,' he sympathised. 'They came here to ask for your room number. What did they want—?'

'Very top secret,' I imitated Amin's poor English. 'They want me flying something somewhere. Today. You'll have to tell Miss Gregory I'm otherwise engaged. For once I'd welcome instructing her.'

'I bet,' Sam agreed. 'What a fine pair of tits she's got. She'll be mad as hell, you know—'

'Tough,' I said. 'You saw that Colonel Wasswa, never mind his pet gorilla. Too bad if Miss Gregory misses her lesson. Do you want to go and explain to Wasswa—?'

'I'm just thinking,' Sam said, stroking his moustache. 'If you don't go, they'll undoubtedly knock you off. So you go, delivering surplus army weapons upcountry to guerrillas, I reckon, a nice little earner for Wasswa and Amin—'

'Tell me more, Sam,' I said miserably. 'You're cheering me up by the second.'

In the Groove

'They might kill you anyway, once the guns and ammo are delivered, to save paying you. Then again they might let you come back, to get further deliveries. You are getting paid to do this?'

'I was too shit scared to ask,' I admitted.

'That's another point,' Sam reckoned. 'They may make you vanish because of what you know. Again, they may let you live so they can use you time and again. It ain't good, is it?'

'Let me have a car, Sam,' I begged. 'I'll make a quick exit to the Kenyan border—'

'No can do, lad,' he said, indicating with his eyes an armed soldier sitting across the foyer. 'I'll give your apologies to Miss Gregory—'

'Fuck Miss Gregory,' I retorted in my anguish. 'The cold bitch probably does fuck herself, the way she regards me. With a bloody great dildo too—'

'That I'd like to see,' Sam allowed. 'Let's adjourn to the bar. You could probably use a drink.'

'That is the understatement of all time, Samuel,' I said. 'So what if I'm pissed and crash the aircraft. I think I'm a goner anyway.'

'A dead duck,' Sam agreed, and that did not in any way help to relieve my wretchedness.

Chapter Fifteen

Two o'clock on the dot saw me at the hotel entrance and, typically, the car coming for me was half an hour late. It was no sand-coloured open jeep but a long black gleaming Merc, as befits loyal, newly promoted officers. Amin sat grinning in the driver's seat. He roared off, burning rubber and setting civilians diving for cover.

'You missed *him*,' I pointed out, referring to a bent old man at the side of the road, standing and staring at such grandeur flashing by. By now I didn't care. 'Where's your sidekick, the warlike Wasswa? He's a laugh a minute, that character.'

'You did not like him,' Amin decided after thought, then laughing almost gleefully. 'No one does. He was a private in the old Uganda Rifles when the British ruled. One day I will kill him—'

I had no doubt, the company I was keeping. 'Then you'd be colonel,' I said, which made Amin roar again. 'General?' I asked. 'Should you be telling me this? Not that I'm likely to get chummy with the guy. Won't he mind—?'

'He would kill me first if I allow him,' Amin said casually. 'That will not happen. He is above himself, from a poor tribe, the Aru. He does not use a knife and fork.'

'He must have gone down a bundle in the mess at Sandhurst,' I said.

We drove to Bombo, some miles north of Kampala, a village of mean huts beside a dried-up river bed with pools of stagnant water where ragged hopefuls fished. A dirt runway had been created at one time, but now it was overgrown with clumps of bushes and knee-high elephant grass along its length. There was a forlorn hut flying a limp windsock and a waiting Cessna aircraft looking the worse for wear with battered fuselage sides. Inside the hut was a white man in the filthiest overalls I'd ever seen, along with two young African girls with blossoming tits bare to the waist. A single unmade bed in the corner made me suspect the dirty engineer had been fucking the girls in turn. The aircraft was loaded with its cargo, fuelled, I was informed, and ready for take-off.

Amin disappeared in a cloud of dust after yet another handshake. 'You're a brave bastard,' the engineer told me when we were alone, offering me a bottle of whisky. I'd had a few in the hotel with Sam, but such was my apprehension that the drink had had no effect. 'You wouldn't catch me going up there. Those bastards call themselves freedom fighters. Knocking off priests and nuns is what they do best, and terrorising unarmed civilians. Like it is in the Congo now.'

'Never mind that,' I said, studying the map before me on his workbench. 'Christ, my destination is the south of bloody Sudan. I haven't got permission to land there—'

'Stuff permission,' said the engineer cheerfully. 'This crowd have their bases in Sudan and raid into Uganda. It's

In the Groove

safer that way. You do know what you're taking them—?'

'It ain't fucking scripts of Noel Coward's play,' I opined cynically. 'More like a bloody arsenal. Just my horrible luck.'

'I don't know how you are on navigation,' he said, 'but the country up there is all the same, baked dirt. Fly around and they'll light fires for you. Bloody great columns of smoke, you can't very well miss.' He took the whisky bottle from my hand as I took a deep swallow. 'I suppose you're now Colonel Wasswa's private pilot, in case the bastard has to bolt with his loot. Christ, he's sold enough army equipment up there to start a coup. Maybe that's what he's got in mind, they're his tribe mostly. You'd be for it if it got out you'd been supplying arms to rebels, mate. The way they execute someone here—'

'Thanks a bunch,' I said. 'If there's nothing else, I'll get this over with.'

'You could have a fuck at one of the girls for luck,' he suggested. 'Both of 'em if you're up to it.' The girls grinned at me, wobbling their tits, but for once I did not think it possible to raise a hard or even have a sexual thought.

The aircraft handled well and around six in the evening, the red sun a huge ball lowering to the horizon, I saw not one but three columns of smoke miles apart below me. I also saw what I considered a ground-to-air missile making a trail in my direction before it curled over and fell earthward. Keen to land, I throttled back and began my descent to the nearest grey pillar of smoke.

On landing, I was surrounded by wild-looking women and girls, all dirty yellow with dust: faces, arms, legs and ragged uniforms that I imagined had once been jungle green but were now more suited to the terrain. They whooped, waving a selection of weapons from Kalishnikovs to bolt-action rifles, all swathed in ammo belts and looking fierce.

'Fucka me mucho,' was my reaction, amazed by the female warrior band. The circle of faces around me fell back as a big Nubian-type woman approached, automatic rifle in hand and escorted by a group of what would now be called minders. The bodyguard was composed of strapping women, in better uniforms than the rank and file. On their caps they wore red metallic stars to denote their political allegiance. The leader came forward, clasping me to her like a comrade, then stepping back a pace to consider me proudly. She raised a clenched fist in salute and I decided it politic to return it. I'm easy.

'Commandant Gulu Knosi, First Marxist Women's Brigade,' she introduced herself. 'You will come to my tent and eat with me while your cargo is unloaded. How is my husband?' Her English was surprisingly fluent, but I was to learn she had been a schoolteacher trained by nuns and later was instructed in a guerrilla warfare camp in Russia. I was about to say do I know your husband when she added, 'Colonel Wasswa. I am his chief wife.'

'Oh, he's fine. What a delightful chap,' I said. 'If it's all the same with you, I'd be glad to help unload and fly back. Report to your husband, you know, tell him you are—'

'We will eat,' she said, walking off, her large buttocks swaying in her tight trousers. 'Soon it will be dark so you will stay the night, take a woman if you wish.' We passed several girls cooking over open fires, the slabs of meat they fed to the pots so swarming with flies that they covered the

In the Groove

flesh until the last moment before it went into the boiling water. 'Tonight there is meat. We killed a goat for you.'

'Gourmet fare,' I felt bound to say in appreciation, while swallowing hard. If the sun roasted one's backside, inside her dirt-grimed tent it was like a furnace. Crouched close to each other in the corner were two terrified white girls, once blonde but now streaked with dust. They wore rags that I took to have once been tailored safari suits. Seeing another white face, their eyes searched mine appealingly. I squatted beside the guerrilla leader as indicated on a rush mat. Soon the cooked meat was brought in, nestling among watery grey rice in a huge shallow pan. 'Eat,' I was told curtly.

'Most hospitable of you, comrade,' I said, picking out the tiniest scrap of meat while Commandant Gulu dug in with her fingers, drawing her wrist across her mouth to wipe off the grease. She was large and threatening, with a fuzzy mop of hair, swathed in ammo bandoliers and with her automatic rifle across her lap.

'Who are the two women in that corner?' I asked. 'Prisoners?' I feared the worst for them, but then my own situation was not too secure. 'I could fly them out with me tomorrow,' I ventured tentatively. 'With the cargo unloaded there'll be room for them—'

'Hostages,' I was told. 'Held for ransom from their country. Eat more!' She turned to look at the petrified young women, throwing across to them the piece of meat she'd been chewing. 'They are what is left of a Swedish television crew who came here. As for tomorrow, you will fly me to other camps like this one to confer with my comrades. You will not leave until I say so—'

In the Groove

Fucking great, I thought. But then rifle fire and a loud explosion like a mortar bomb landing made her leap to her feet, gun in hand. There were shouts outside, automatic weapons rapping a response. 'Shifta bandits,' announced Gulu. 'They know that you have brought us weapons and they want to steal them. Stay here while we drive them away.'

What else could I do? Hoping against hope that the aircraft remained undamaged, my one hope was of getting out of this hellhole. A pitched battle took place outside until darkness, when I was given a blanket and joined the two women hostages in their corner. It was obvious they considered me their enemy too, but I tried to console them. I looked the part, unshaven and filthy. 'I'll do all I can to get you out,' I promised. 'My own situation is pretty hairy with this crowd.' I wondered where the ghastly Gulu had vanished to. I hoped she was dead. I settled in my blanket.

'Help us,' one of the Swedish girls said quietly, touching my shoulder, 'and you can have one of us now. Whichever you choose. Fuck is the English word, isn't it? We are desperate—'

Not for a fuck, I knew, but desperately willing to offer any inducement. I shook my head. Both girls were no doubt pretty and shapely females in normal times, but to take advantage of their present fear was hardly on, even if I was in the mood for a ride. We huddled down and then were rudely disturbed by three of the Commandant's guard entering the hut with lanterns. One prodded me with her boot roughly.

'Sit up, *mzungu*,' she ordered while her mates stood

over me, tee-heeing like schoolgirls. 'We want to see what a white man has got between his legs. Very little, we have heard. You will show us. Pull off his trousers, Yoti. Let us see.' I had a rifle muzzle in my face as my belt was loosened and my trousers dragged down.

'Your Commandant will hear of this,' I shouted, the Swedish girls beside me sitting up in alarm as the guerrilla named Yoti pulled both pants and underpants over my boots. Bared from the waist down, my prick hung limply curled over my balls. Even at rest my dong is thick and of appreciable length, a fact not unnoticed by the laughing African girls. One reached over to hold it upright.

'Like Nubian man,' she giggled, which was said in Swahili. 'I shall make him stand for us. Who will be first—?' She stroked my shaft with a long up-and-down motion of her wrist, getting little response. The apparent leader of the group pulled the girl's hand away, taking over with a quicker movement, rubbing vigorously. My unruly dick liked the treatment. Twitching, it thickened whether I wanted it to or not, growing long under her fingers. I was about to be raped, I conceded, a new experience for me. As a last protest I warned them that Gulu would hear of my treatment.

'Gulu is busy tonight,' I was told. 'Tomorrow sees us march and fight in Uganda. Tonight we will have you. See, it is now big! Big!' It was indeed, rearing up stiff as a ramrod while the Swedish girls alongside watched with appalled fascination. The Africans shed their uniforms, dark skins shining in the lamplight, breasts bobbing as they giggled and surrounded my prone form. The leader lowered herself over my erect dick, directing the crest to her parted thighs and thrust down. She crouched forward with tits swinging out as she impaled her cunt on me, immediately making rapid jogging movements and grunting out her pleasure.

There was no finesse about her actions, she rode my prick fast, bumping and grinding her fat mound against my pubic bone, breasts bouncing and her strong sweat running down in rivulets to my belly and thighs. With a loud cry of release she came and fell forward over me then was immediately dragged aside so my next molester could mount. It was the girl I'd heard called Moto, who thrust the more slightly built Yoti away as she straddled my thighs, eager to take my still erect stalk. It looked red raw and glistening with cunt juice in the lamp glow.

The girl who had just abused me reached out to hold my tool upright for her mate to squat over it and use her fingers to part the thick inrolling lips of her cunt to receive me. My aching balls nestled in the marble-hard cleave of her buttocks, as she grunted her approval of the stiff mass filling her and began a slow gyrating rhythm with her pelvis.

This one, I had to concede, was a connoisseur, a woman who appreciated a long unhurried screw. She ignored the impatient Yoti who complained about waiting her turn. The deliberate squirming of her arse, the grinding I was getting, set my own arousal soaring against my will. I groaned in response as the pace quickened, my fucker now moving agitatedly to match my involuntary twitches and thrusts. Then we were both lost in the throes, humping and heaving together as she screeched in violent climax and milked me with her cunt muscles and my come jetted in spurts to saturate her.

In the Groove

Already on my back, I cursed my lack of strength to resist, lying embarrassingly limp and sated with the two captive Swedish girls regarding me wide-eyed. Yoti, the guerrilla next in line, was not amused that she could not pleasure herself immediately on my now-drooping dick, berating us all furiously for being denied. While her companions laughed at her, she held my prick in disgust, no doubt hoping for a sign of life, giving it tentative strokes. The low moan I gave was of agony not pleasure, having been rough ridden and left sore. Yoti looked at the watching Swedish girls, grimly determined to get satisfaction.

'These white women,' she said to me in Swahili, 'I want one of them to suck you to hardness. Once in East Germany where I was trained an instructor showed me photographs of *mzungu* girls with a man's penis in their mouths. I was told that white women do not mind that, and their men like it too much. Tell them what I want them to do—'

Her look, directed at the Swedes, left them in no doubt that she'd been referring to their presence. There was added fear in their faces as they turned to me. The one I had learned was called Mai voiced her concern. 'What did she say?' she asked anxiously. 'It was about us, wasn't it? She is so angry we are afraid she wants to hurt us—'

'She wants one of you to suck me,' I said as Yoti looked on murderously. 'I'm sorry, but that's what she demands. She's heard white women do that. She believes it will get me erect again for her. The mood she's in, we'd better not disappoint her—'

Mai nodded, 'I think so too,' she smiled wanly. 'Do not blame yourself. We have both done it before many times. I hope it will work for you. We will try our best, won't we,

Carla?' Her companion nodded solemnly and Mai dipped her head over my middle.

Being sucked hard to order in a grotty hide tent that reeked of sweat, cunt and fear while three African girls sat up on their haunches watching with great interest, cradling automatic rifles, was a whole new ball game in my varied sexual experience. Mai took my flaccid member in her soft hand, dandling it a moment as if to get the feel of it, then gathered saliva in her mouth to lick me from the ball sac upwards along the shaft. She was giving her all, no doubt, and was obviously experienced in the art, dribbling spit to lave me sensuously as she lapped at my knob, wanking the floppy stalk gently with curled fingers, fearful of failure. For my part I decided to forget all else and enjoy such treatment, squirming my hips and reaching out to place a hand lightly on the back of her neck.

'Eat it, suck it,' I ordered in my effort to gain the stiff prick Yoti demanded for her use. Mai nodded her approval, poised to suck me, murmuring, 'Yes, yes, tell me to eat it, suck it for you. I love it. Go hard in my throat.' She lowered her face and took my slackness in a warm wet soft mouth, at first sucking gently with my prick imprisoned between her palate and tongue. For my poor abused dick this was like a soothing balm. To show its appreciation it gave the first responsive twitches, pulsed and throbbed, showed signs of thickening. Mai, scenting success, sucked harder, beginning to bob her head and drawing her lips back to my glans before going forward to deep throat me delightfully. I began to suspect that, despite the circumstances, she was getting turned on, enjoying what she was doing for its own sake. Her hair was falling over

In the Groove

her face as her bobbing increased.

I wondered if watching the African girls using me had had an effect on her. Certainly she sucked with a will and made the appropriate noises of pleasure in her task. Then another head was beside hers as her friend Carla joined in. Two pairs of lips, two mouths shared what seemed to be a delicious morsel. I heard them slurping over the growing shaft, taking turns to suck, as if reluctant to relinquish it to the other. My prick, as it was released momentarily to be transferred from one mouth to the next, reared up with its full girth and length restored. It did not go unnoticed by Yoti, who prodded the Swedish cocksuckers with her rifle to stop. Abashed for a moment, they retreated on hands and knees, leaving the field with a job well accomplished.

Yoti mounted me eagerly, spearing her tight, well-lubricated quim on my stander, jerking her arse in quickening motions. She settled on its probing length, bolt upright with tits flying as she brought herself to a first climax and continued thrusting for seconds. My own lech, thoroughly aroused by the expert dual sucking, makes me desirous of fucking Yoti with relish, loving the sensations surging in my loins as she lost control and bucked like a dervish on my prick. I reached up to grasp her tits, squeezing the firm globes tightly, gratified as she cried out and her spasms became wilder until she collapsed across me, spent with my jism deposited deep within her cunt. She made her companions squeal with mirth at her final flopping about, and I concluded that we would be allowed to settle down for the night at last.

Come the grey light heralding dawn, I saw our three guards fast asleep near us in the dimness of the tent. The

In the Groove

eyes of the Swedish girls were wide and white with alarm as I touched their arms and found them awake and alert. I noted the slumbering guerrillas had their rifle slings wrapped about their arms, which made a grab for a weapon out of the question. Bursting for a piss, I stole out of the tent, finding the once-bustling camp deserted. No doubt the various units had congregated to march south across the border into Uganda. My Cessna aircraft stood a tempting fifty yards away. Back inside the tent all was quiet but for the slight snores and deep breathing of the Africans. I motioned to the Swedish girls and they arose soundlessly to join me in the pre-dawn stillness.

'Walk,' was all I had to say furtively. I realised I was taking one hell of a chance, the hairs rising on the back of my neck as we proceeded towards the aircraft, our pace increasing almost to a run as we passed a few sleeping forms in blankets around the remains of fires. Then I was opening the aircraft's door, urging the Swedish girls in, climbing over them to get into the pilot's seat and praying the self-starter would function first time before a hail of bullets cut us down.

A twist of the ignition key and the single engine spluttered and thankfully roared into life. For take-off I taxied straight ahead on the flat baked earth, the wheels bumping over the ashes of previous cooking fires, narrowly missing our tent. I saw our guards rush out with mouths open in screams of fury as we flashed by. Then we were airborne and I banked steeply to dodge any fire coming in our direction, turned south as we gained altitude and breathed in relief at our easy escape.

I was congratulated excitedly by the two hostages I had

In the Groove

released, both girls hugging me and pressing kisses of relief and joy to my neck and cheeks as I flew to freedom. Their freedom at least, I gloomily reminded myself, wondering what awaited me on landing, having pinched two valuable hostages that Colonel Wasswa's chief wife intended to trade for monetary gain. I feared my good deed would probably cost me my life.

'Thank you, thank you,' the relieved girls kept repeating, but pleased as I was for them my future boded ill. 'You know why they slept so soundly for us to make our escape?' Mai said laughing in her elated mood. 'You fucked those girls so good that they were worn out! It is a fine prick you have, pilot. Now my friend Carla and I would like to finish off what we started last night.' Both girls giggled excitedly at the thought. 'We want to do it to thank you for saving us—'

'Christ, I've got to fly this thing,' I began, but both of them squirmed their bodies in the cramped space around my feet, unzipping me. As Carla brought out my prick, she kissed it and held it on offer to Mai, who sucked at the knob. No doubt they found it a great lark in their high-spirited euphoria at being safe. Each in turn took me in their mouths until at last I crunched up my body in my seat, trying to hold a steady course as Mai's expert deep-throating drained my balls into her gullet. Carla took over to get the last trickles and then lapped and licked my knob clean.

In time I saw the bush airstrip of Bombo below with its delapidated hut and windsock. I landed and taxied in to be received by the engineer, in the same filthy overalls and accompanied by the same two African girls, but with no sign of Wasswa or Amin. My time in Uganda was over, I decided. Either that or my life. Some choice!

Chapter Sixteen

I was no stranger to dire straits, and we're talking serious trouble here. In the past, the devil's own luck had always turned up to save my skin – luck aided and abetted by a strong survival instinct. While in the air I'd considered my options. Gallant it may have been to rescue the girls with me, but it was certainly foolhardy if ever I met up again with the vindictive Colonel Wasswa or his fearsome chief missis. On the other hand, I'd be a bit of a hero when delivering Mai and Carla safely to the Swedish Embassy in Kampala. Official gratitude might extend to giving me sanctuary there until it was safe to bolt from any retribution. That being so, I had flown directly to Entebbe, only to be refused permission to land and therefore had returned to use the Bombo airstrip.

'I didn't expect to see you in one piece again,' said the grimy engineer on my arrival. 'Back with passengers too. All hell has broke loose on the northern border, it's been on the local radio all morning. There's been heavy fighting, the Uganda Army is putting down rebels marching south to overthrow the government. It's a real attempt at a coup, it seems, led by your mate Colonel Wasswa.'

'He's no mate of mine,' I said, intrigued, hopes rising. 'This could mean that the bastard is *personna non grata* here any more—?'

Personna non fucking *alive*,' I was told. 'When they catch him they'll string him up by the balls. Of course the big hero of the day is Colonel Idi Amin, leading the loyal troops.'

'*Colonel* Amin?' I said. 'I thought he was in with Wasswa—'

'You know sod all about African intrigues and politics, chum,' he laughed. 'It was a set-up. All morning the radio's been bumping up Amin's military skills as he crushes the insurgents. The bastard wouldn't know a strategic concept if one fell on his thick bonce. Did you bring back the goodies with you?'

'Only these two Swedish girls,' I said, mystified. The engineer opened a small square flap near the tail of the Cessna and hauled out an ammunition box. As he pulled open the lid I saw it packed with banknotes. 'They must have put that there while I was in the tent—' I began.

'Payment for the weapons you took up,' said the engineer cheerfully. 'Loot stolen by the guerrillas holding up banks, post offices, Hindi shopkeepers, even Catholic missions. My pay is in there, even yours if you ever get any. The rest will no doubt be requisitioned by Idi. Do you and your two birds want a lift into Kampala? I'm going in to stock up on booze. That and my two young bedmates here makes this life tolerable.'

I got him to drop us at the Swedish Embassy. We were immediately escorted to the ambassador who was told of our escape by Mai and Carla. Glowing terms were used to describe my part in it all. I modestly waved aside the praise heaped on me, enjoying the attention. I was given a splendid room with a bath in which to rest and refresh myself. New clothes were laid out for me by a flunky, and I was invited to dine that evening with the ambassador and his wife. Beside me, Mai and Carla looked resplendent and gorgeous in chiffon and silk evening dresses. Once more, it seemed, my luck had held.

I finally got to bed in my luxurious air-conditioned room. I lay back and kicked my heels in the air like a colt. And no wonder. Beside the bed was a small fridge and on investigating I found it stocked with the finest liquor and wines. I was toasting my good fortune when a tentative knock came at the door and Mai and Carla looked in, their bright eyes glowing from celebrating their release. I waved them in, glad of the lovely company, noting that both were in dressing gowns as if prepared for bed.

'Our ambassador is going to recommend you for a medal,' Mai giggled, 'but Carla and I think you deserve a special Swedish reward tonight.' Both girls exchanged mischievous glances, slipping off their dressing gowns to stand before me gloriously naked. They could have been sisters – later I was to discover that they were – with the same smooth golden skin on curvaceous young figures, pert little rounded breasts with uptilted nipples, and last but definitely not least delicious cunt prominences with curled fair pubic growths nestling between their thighs. They crossed to me, taking the drink from my hand, lowering me across the bed. Mai's nimble fingers unbuttoning my pyjama jacket while Carla drew off the pants.

As naked as they were in no time, Mai held a taut nipple

to my lips while Carla licked my balls and rapidly erecting stem. 'We want to ravage you, rape you like those awful women did to you in that tent,' Carla informed me before taking my prick fully in her mouth and sucking avidly. I decided to let them have their wicked way with me.

One thing I hadn't told them about our escape was that, after my rape and while Mai and Carla had slept fitfully, the three guerrilla girls had drunk themselves to sleep on pombe, a strong native brew. Sneaking off in the dawn had not been so perilous as they imagined. However if it meant the grateful girls wanted to repay me with the bodies, so be it.

Carla's soft wet mouth worked its magic, making me groan my appreciation, grasp her head, move my hips in fucking motions at her face. With my prick bursting with tumescence, she withdrew her mouth to straddle my loins, directing the shaft to her cunt lips. At my other end, Mai was climbing aboard too, squatting over my upturned face so that the sight I got of her was the delightful parted cleave of her pert bottom, with its pouty wispy-haired cunt and tightly puckered-up anus. I was definitely about to be used.

The night was spent in fucking and sucking, and helping ourselves to the contents of the fridge to further refresh ourselves. A permutation the girls enjoyed, obviously from past experience, was for them to lie before me with legs widely parted and cunts on offer. I was ordered to fuck one for no more than a few vigorous thrusts, then to penetrate the other immediately while the disengaged sister waited her turn by fondling her breasts and fingering her cunt. I insisted we enact the same manoeuvre with their bottom holes and, to much mirth and giggling, the game sisters got in position side by side on their hands and knees, their rounded buttocks tilted and waggling at me in a cock-stiffening come-on.

Dawn saw me shagged useless and I slept until mid-morning. I bathed, dressed, was given a late breakfast and driven by an embassy limousine with a chauffeur to Entebbe and the Lake Vic hotel to report my continued existence to Sam Bishop at the driving school. If I expected to be welcomed with open arms, I was sadly mistaken. 'You can pack up your gear and go,' were Sam's opening words of greeting to me. 'I've employed another driving instructor, a local African lad, so I'm not forking out for your room and food at this hotel.'

'That's the second time you've dumped me, Sam,' I said, wondering if he'd discovered I'd been fucking his Marjory. 'So what is it this time—?'

'I can't afford to have someone working for me that's involved with the military here,' he grumbled. 'Nothing against you, Ty, it's just bloody dangerous. You'll have to pay for your bed and board if you're staying.' He held out a hand. 'No hard feelings—'

'Up yours too,' I said, refraining to add that I'd been up his wife, several times in fact. 'I'll survive.'

Despite my bravado it would be a struggle though, I knew, having little cash. Even the boxroom I occupied was beyond my means. As ever, it seemed I went from feast to famine, with little idea of my next move. Like Mr Micawber, however, I firmly believed something would turn up.

It did so shortly in the giant form of Colonel Amin, who entered the hotel foyer armed to the teeth and surrounded

In the Groove

by his bodyguards, all genial smiles as he accepted the applause of the people present. In the unlikely event that he had spotted me, I tried to hide myself behind a stand of postcard views of the beauty of Uganda. Too late, he waved in my direction and I had to approach the great man.

'Very good pilot,' he greeted me, crushing my hand in a warm handshake. 'You did very good. This morning I stopped at Bombo and heard you had returned. I was on my way back from the northern front, where I led brave Ugandan soldiers in putting down a very bad rebellion.'

'I'm delighted for you,' I said, disengaging my bruised hand. 'Also for your promotion to colonel—'

'Major-General now,' he corrected me, delighted with himself. The lad was getting on in his career, no doubt, in astonishing leaps and bounds. He was as crafty as hell too, using me to fly up arms and ammo for Wasswa and his rebels to attempt to overthrow Prime Minister Obote's government, then pocketing the payment. Obviously he was aware of every move. 'Join the Uganda Army,' he offered genially. 'You would be my official pilot with a captain's rank. Think about it, my friend, there could be high promotion and much money in serving me—'

'I haven't been paid for the last job,' I dared to say in my circumstances. This made him roar with laughter, slapping my back while his bodyguard and everyone in the foyer including Sam Bishop looked on in wonder.

'Come with me,' he said, an arm about my shoulder as he led me outside to a dust-streaked army lorry surrounded by armed troops. At his order they dropped the tailboard and he pushed me forward to see inside. I saw the floor awash with blood, and, in the dimness under the

In the Groove

canvas canopy, discerned strewn bodies. Wasswa was there with his chief wife Gulu Nkusi sprawled beside him. In shock I also made out the corpses of Yoti and her two mates who had ridden my dick.

'Wasswa told me he would be President of Uganda,' Amin said jovially. 'Look at him now.' I merely nodded, deciding the ambitious Amin had designs on that high office himself. He gave a pointed look at an aide and the officer handed me a briefcase. 'For service to Uganda,' Amin informed me, again with his broad grin. 'There will be more if you join my army – a Mercedes car, wives, a house with servants and a swimming pool—'

'Thanks but I'm strictly a civilian,' I said as his personal jeep mounted with a heavy machine-gun drew up for him to climb aboard. I felt I hadn't seen the last of him as he leaned out to shake my hand again.

'I need men I can trust, I like you,' he said. 'You knew me as a sergeant. Now I go to hold the airport in case of attack.' I was relieved to see him go, walking back into the hotel with the briefcase under my arm, wondering what it contained. In my boxroom I opened it to find it stuffed with currency, an untidy squash of Uganda banknotes ranging from the five shillings issue up as high as the one-thousand denomination. Suddenly I was rich, or at least very solvent. I saw a more conducive room in the hotel, a car, new clothes. In my elation I heard the muffled sound of small-arms fire coming from the direction of the airport. After the hectic past few days, I collapsed across my bed with the briefcase under my pillow.

In the evening I woke and showered before dining on the best the hotel could offer.

I found Sam Bishop in the bar, drinking heavily and

In the Groove

looking gloomy. The fact that he'd fired me so abruptly did not stop him joining me. 'Another bloody fine mess we're in,' he complained.

I'm not one to hold grudges, so I let him buy me a drink. I knew he wanted to moan on, so let him continue. 'Your pal Idi has been shooting up the airport, getting rid of soldiers there he don't want around. He's using the excuse of this so-called coup to tidy up the army with his own followers. There's a flaming curfew from dawn to dusk, did you know? I'm stuck here for the night if I don't go home before dark. After that, anybody outside will be shot—'

'I'm going nowhere,' I told him, but one should never speak too soon. I was approached by a waiter who announced I was wanted on the telephone. Not Amin again, I hoped. I picked up the receiver.

'Oh, Mr Wight,' came a tremulous female voice, 'This is Anne Gregory, your former driving school pupil. Do you remember me—'

Very much so, I could have said, recalling not only her aloof and superior attitude but her remarkable beauty – those breasts that thrust out rounded and prominent, not to mention her shapely arse and long limbs. 'I remember you,' I said. 'If it's about driving lessons I'm not employed at the school any more.'

'It's not about driving lessons,' her voice quavered. 'You're the only one I can call upon. I'm here in my cottage alone, terribly frightened. There's been shooting and there are soldiers around. Could you please, please, come and stay with me? I would be eternally grateful—'

How grateful, my salacious mind pondered? 'I'll leave

now, before the curfew,' I said. 'Sam Bishop can drop me off.'

Sam was not keen to leave the bar but, with the curfew hour upon us, he drove me to Anne Gregory's cottage, still moaning about his safari business while the country was in turmoil. 'You could come and stay at my place,' he said. 'There's all the drink we need there, and my missis welcomes company.' This made me wonder if Sam fancied a night of wife-watching if good-fellowship flowed and Marjory was flirtatious. I kept it in mind for the future as I knocked on Anne Gregory's door, calling out my name as she hesitated to unlock. She looked beautiful, if frightened, in a pretty print dress.

'Thank God you came,' she said in obvious relief, no longer the aloof United Nations official. I could smell drink on her breath, no doubt she'd been at the sauce to gain Dutch courage. 'I don't know what's going on but I feared for my life, or a fate worse than death.' She shuddered, as if finding the idea of being ravaged by black soldiery awful but exciting. 'Let me get you a drink, Mr Wight—'

'My friends call me Ty,' I told her, handing over a bottle of Bell's whisky I'd had the forethought to bring with me from the hotel. I added, 'I thought we could use this—'

'It's very welcome, although I don't usually drink,' she said, stifling a hiccup. I had a very vulnerable young lady here, I decided happily, watching her shaking hand as she poured two extravagant measures. 'I'm afraid I've drunk most of the little stock I had in. I've been terrified. Thank God you came,' she repeated. 'I'd have done anything to

In the Groove

have had company tonight.' Shots rang out from somewhere and she leapt in the air.

'Sit still,' I ordered her, playing the unflappable macho male while I pondered the best route to get into her knickers. More shots fired in the distance made her tremble, spilling her drink, which was all to the good to increase her dependency on me. 'Don't worry, they're only killing each other. This is Africa. You're an exceedingly lovely girl, you must know. Beautiful. I always thought so—'

'I must look a sight, I'm petrified out of my wits,' she simpered, liking the compliments. 'I took a chance in calling you; I remember seeing you with that drunken nude woman back in the hotel. What kind of man am I inviting here? That's what I thought. But I was desperate. I had visions of you raping me—'

And might you not enjoy that? I wondered, seeing her fluttering her eyelashes at me. There was more to the uppitty Anne than met the eye, obviously. The outwardly superior beauty probably fancied a bit of rough stuff. If she were forced, her conscience would be free of guilt.

She sank back in her armchair, relaxing now that my presence made her feel secure, legs out stretching as if in relief, parting and remaining parted as she drew up her knees to sit facing me. I could only do what is known as a double-take as I glanced at her. Beneath her skirt, I saw the white rounded flesh of her upper thighs and a plump hummock nestling at the fork, forested with downy hair through which peeped the pink crinkle of vaginal lips. The bitch wore no knickers! She was flashing her cunt at me! Deliberately!

She was flashing to the right guy. I enjoy viewing snatches, quims, cunts, love-nests, cockpits, hairy pockets, boxes or whatever that dear orifice so beloved of men has been called in its history.

In no hurry now, admiring the sight presented with her almost creaming herself under my direct gaze, I sat engrossed for long minutes. I considered my options: crawling over on my knees to tongue the offering; strolling over quite nonchalently to finger it, or sitting awhile to increase her lewdness and arousing her further with plain talk. I decided on the latter course.

'That's a splendid cunt, Anne,' I told her admiringly. 'I shall be forced to do something for it. While I'm enjoying you flaunting your snatch, why not give it a tickle. Play with yourself. I'm sure you'd like to—'

'How can you suggest such a thing?' she mumbled, lowering her eyes. 'I'm so embarrassed. What makes you think I'm like that—'

'Do you always sit with parted legs and no knickers?' I taunted her. 'Let's be honest with ourselves. You want it. Some rude and naughty sex. I won't let you down. So start with the fingers, love. Let's see you—'

'I will not,' she defied me, her face flushing. 'I think that is awful, and you are awful. You can't make me—'

'Don't be too sure,' I warned, pulling my belt from the loops of my trousers. 'Ever had your plump little bottom thrashed? I think you'd enjoy that—'

'You wouldn't dare,' she whined. I noted with satisfaction that her right hand had gone hesitantly to her crotch. 'I'm sorry now I invited such a horrible pervert here—'

'Come off it, you're loving every moment,' I said. 'You want me to come on strong so you won't feel so bad about

In the Groove

what's going to happen. I've met your sort before. Come on, work those fingers!'

'You beast, you filthy depraved creature,' she muttered as she fingered herself. 'I'll never live this down. Can I stop now, please? Please?' I noted her arse squirming as if unable to contain its motions. 'God, oh God, don't look at me like that, you swine. Oh, oh, I can't help myself—'

'Give yourself a good come,' I goaded her, settling back with my drink in my hand, my prick tenting my pants at the sight of the now helpless girl masturbating fiercely, in the grip of body-jerking spasms, buttocks rotating and pelvis thrusting to her fingering. She gave a long drawn-out *aaaagh* and flopped about in the chair, until finally she gasped and slumped back in extremis. Her legs stretched out straight, widely parted, and I saw her cunt actually palpitating and pouting, the inner flesh glistening wet and pink.

'You pig,' she berated me. 'I hope you are satisfied now.'

'The night is young, sugarpuss,' I told her cheerfully. 'And we ain't even started yet. That was just to get you in the groove and what a nice juicy groove you've got. Now I want to see that gorgeous body of yours. Everything – tits, cunt and arse. The lot.' I tapped my doubled-up belt lightly across the palm of my hand. 'Stand up and undress for me, Anne. Let me see you—'

'Do I have to?' she said meekly, but she was already on her feet.

'You do, whether you like it or not,' I said calmly, estimating that a cool approach, despite my own excitement, carried greater menace. 'Strip off. Men have seen you naked before. More than I've had hot dinners, I'll bet. So

In the Groove

hurry up. You've been fucked plenty too, so don't pretend that all this is against your will.' I gave what I imagined was a cruel laugh. 'You're the sort who needs an excuse – like getting your lovely arse spanked – so that you can kid yourself some nasty man forced you. I'll be happy to oblige,' I promised, swishing the belt against my leg.

'I've never been so insulted or humiliated,' she protested. 'I do this under duress, I'll have you know.' Bitter as she sounded, she drew her dress over her head, thrilling me with what she uncovered. The girl was *built*: big creamy mounds overflowing her lacy bra; a silky smooth belly with a deeply indented navel, shapely thighs and at their join the sweeping curve of her pubic delta. I forced myself not to exclaim in admiration, eyeing her lewdly as the bra was unclipped and her gorgeous tits swung free. 'Understand how much I hate this,' she said, nevertheless she was trembling with emotion. 'Can I dress now that you've ogled all there is to see of me? I've never been so degraded, you filthy beast—'

'Flattery will get you nowhere,' I laughed, unable to resist the well-worn cliché. 'Come closer.' To ensure she would, I reached out and clasped a wrist. She tugged her arm as if to wrench herself away. I drew her forward, stumbling. In one swift twist I had her face down across my knees and gazed upon the narrow curve of her back and the plump moons of a splendidly rounded backside. She screeched out and struggled, getting a taste of the belt for her pains. My arm worked, my aim true, the leather thwacking down and reddening both cheeks either side of their cleave.

'Oh! Ow! Don't, *please* don't!' she squealed. 'Please,

In the Groove

please—' Jogging about across my lap, squirming as if to avoid the blows, clenching her buttocks, I could see she was receiving what she craved. She did not attempt to scramble away and I did not hold her down – my free hand was under her body cupping a breast. The punishment meted out was not too severe either, the crack of my belt to cushiony flesh sounding worse than it was. I heard her begin to change her tune to a whining sob, as if the agony she felt was from other than the chastising. She shifted, jamming her cunt hard against one of my knees, pushing against it in time with the strap. *The bitch is bringing herself off*! I told myself with glee. Her tits swung like bells as she was lost to all but an urgent need to come. I thrashed the belt faster against the bouncing of her arse.

She climaxed with a loud series of grunts and only after her jerky undulations had subsided did she attempt to rise. 'I haven't finished with you yet,' I said, and she lay still but for the final tremors and twitches transmitted from her cunt. I dropped the belt, using both hands to part the well-reddened bum cheeks. I liked the view. Her rear-directed quim resembled a split peach festooned with wispy hair, the cleft slack and moist. An inserted finger slid into a juicy channel, finding a thickened clitty and bringing forth a low moan from her lips. 'You're drenched in there,' I taunted her. 'You came off a storm, didn't you? There's nothing like a good walloping to make a girl like you feel horny and depraved. You loved it all, I could tell—'

'You disgust me,' she replied, lolling across my knees with her head down and trying to sound dignified in that posture. 'Is it too much to hope you're satisfied with what you've made me do—?'

'It was interesting,' I admitted, the iron-hard erection in my trousers poking against her stomach and surely proof that I was not satisfied. 'By my count you've come twice to my nothing so far. Two nil for you. Is that fair? You should at least allow me the chance to even up the score—'

'Have I a choice?' she asked sullenly.

'Not a hope – you'll do whatever I want,' I said mercilessly, pushing her off my lap to the floor. I stood, legs straddling her as she sat up, at eye-level with the rampant prick I brought out. 'How are you at sucking cock? After that I'll take you to bed and fuck you rigid through the night. How does that sound?'

With apparent distaste she took my prick in her mouth. 'Protest all you want,' I told her, noting how delicately she sucked at first. 'To your heart's content if it turns you on. I like it.' I knew she wouldn't have wanted it any other way as she began to suck fiercely, bobbing her head as the lech rose in her. It made me determined to fulfil her every submissive desire, whatever it was. It would be fun finding out.

Chapter Seventeen

With the stage-managed rebellion quashed, and the suspected enemies of those in power all satisfactorily eliminated, the curfew ended and the situation returned to normal – or as normal as it would ever be in a turbulent Uganda. By mutual agreement I continued my role as protector and live-in lover with the gorgeous if grandiose Anne Gregory. I stayed on because, apart from her magnificent tits, I was turned on by the young lady's quirky nature. Such a psychological mass of complexes and strange desires had never before been my good fortune to find in one female alone. In many, yes, but not all in a single person. It made for an interesting relationship.

She was afraid of living alone and had already requested a transfer to a more conducive spot like Washington or Paris, but me sharing her cottage was an opportunity she could not pass up. Equipped with more degrees than a thermometer and on the outside a very self-sufficient and confident woman, inside her burned an unquenchable urge to be dominated and used against her will. I'm no psychiatrist but I do know shame and humiliation can be like a drug to certain women. They get high and wanton on the fix, drunk on the indignity, and are left feeling marvellously dirty and degraded by their submissiveness. I had sussed out the arrogant Anne's secret needs and intended to utilise the fact to the full.

On that first evening together, when I ordered her to strip, the softly murmured protest as she stood and undressed before me came out as if it had been rehearsed and spoken before. I wasn't fooled by the air of resignation and her suitably shamed downcast eyes. All the same, with her clothes discarded at her feet, despite the slumped shoulders and lowered head, I had rarely seen such beauty of the naked female form. I found myself giving a lewd whistle at the bountiful symmetry that was unveiled. Full and perfectly matched breasts hung out from her chest as she hunched in apparently abject shame. My eyes swept down over the flat white belly with its deep naval to the outswell of her hips and comfortably rounded thighs and the alluring elevation of her well-thatched quim.

Still seated and tapping my doubled belt idly against my leg, I ordered her sharply to straighten up. In obeying, she gave a little whine as if in utter misery while I rightly judged that her lower region churned with excitement. She could not disguise the noticeable thickening of her nipples as she drew her body to an upright posture, breasts thrusting out temptingly. Her cunt lips seemed to pout and throb in her evident excitement. 'Yes,' I informed her coolly. 'You were made to fuck. Don't move, I'm coming over to inspect you—'

I strolled around her in what I fondly considered a nonchalantly off-hand manner, lifting a firm tit as if to test its resilience and weight, idly stroking the fleece on her mound, cupping a splendidly curved buttock cheek. All the while, I said nothing. Her cheeks burned with genuine shame and her body twitched at my touch.

'You are as bad as my stepfather,' she suddenly announced. 'He is a beast too.'

'Tell me more,' I insisted, taking a taut nipple between finger and thumb as if threatening to tweak hard. Her admission of hanky-panky with her mother's present husband had immediately aroused my interest – as was no doubt intended. 'I should order you to stand facing the corner of the room, as naughty girls deserve,' I admonished her, enjoying every second of my dominance and her submission. 'I could make you stay there all night to consider your sins. On the other hand, I might be lenient if you come clean. Confession is good for the soul, you know.'

It is also compelling, I should add, to hear a woman reveal past sexual misdemeanours in the presence of a male as lewd as she. 'It was all his fault,' Anne began. 'Mother got friendly with this man after divorcing daddy. Even before they got engaged he came to live with us, supposedly sleeping in the spare room. I was sixteen and knew what was going on—'

'Which was?' I enquired, tweaking the nipple a little.

'He went to her room at night, I could hear them. I heard mother's moans and even her pleading him to – you know what—'

'Fuck her more,' I suggested. 'Lick her cunt.'

'That,' Anne agreed as if still ashamed of her mother's wanton nature, 'and worse. Some nights I could hear her cry out and I'm sure he was spanking her or using a belt or cane on her bottom. I actually found a cane hidden in her room. Then I'm certain that at other times he – he – abused her bottom in another fashion. Anal penetration, you know. I heard him calling out when he was in her—'

'Giving your mother a good corking, no doubt,' I said. 'How do you know all this? They must have thought you were asleep in your room. I bet you were in your nightie right outside their bedroom door—?'

'I had to know was was going on,' Anne pleaded. 'I thought it shameful and disgusting—'

'And highly arousing,' I taunted her, picturing the teenage girl standing wide-eyed and with her ear cocked outside the lovers' door. 'I bet you masturbated – played with your virgin cunt, didn't you—?'

She positively squirmed with embarrassment. 'Please don't use such crude language,' she begged. 'You're hurting my nipple, you sadist. It's so tender—'

'Then I'll pinch the other one,' I said malevolently, gripping it firmly. 'Big, aren't they? And you haven't told me whether you were fingering yourself off on those nights. I can make you talk, you know.'

'Yes, I did,' she admitted ruefully, her head lowering in mortification, only for me to use my free hand to raise it again. 'You are a beast, making me tell you that. I swear I didn't want to, it was just – just—'

'Too tempting not to,' I finished for her. 'So what about your new stepdaddy? How did he complete the double and have the mum and the daughter? You'll claim he seduced you, no doubt. Give me the gory details.' I watched her shudder as if to brace herself for the telling, revelling in the pleasurable affront to her dignity. I'd enjoyed Vera Steedman's confessions but she had wholeheartedly enjoyed her bouts with her doctor. Anne was the complete masochist, acting the reluctant party in our weird sequence of question and answer. Bone hard as I was and eager to fuck her, I was willing to continue the charade for the fun of it. There seemed no pretence about her humiliation, which no doubt added reality to the scenario. It was what she craved in her nature so I would give full measure before having her. 'Tell me how the beast seduced poor little Anne,' I insisted.

'I had showered after school one day,' she began falteringly. 'Thinking I was in the house myself I went back to my own bedroom nude to dress—'

'A likely story,' I said. 'Are you sure you didn't know he was in the house and you wanted him to see you? Sweet sixteen with swollen tits and hair on your cunt? I bet that thrilled you—'

'I wasn't sure that he was at home,' Anne admitted. 'I mean, Ronnie was in and out at all times. He was a television producer and went up to London most days.'

'Ronnie, is it?' I taunted her. 'Sounds like a set-up to me, with mum safely out of the way somewhere, and you and he alone. So he caught you in the buff – accidentally on purpose—'

'It wasn't like that,' Anne whispered reproachfully. 'It *was* accidental. He came out of his room naked too on his way to the shower, thinking he was alone. So we were standing like that, without our clothes, Ronnie and I—'

'I'd say the bastard was lying in wait for you and horny little Anne played along,' I charged. 'What did you do then?'

'I did nothing,' Anne wailed. 'He did it all, taking my

arm and leading me to my bedroom, sitting me on the bed and standing before me—'

'He'd be standing, I'm sure,' I reckoned. 'So let's just enact what happened.'

I led her to the bedroom and made her sit on the bed while I stripped before her, then stood with my rearing iron-hard prick inches in front of her face. 'So this is how it was. Was he very hard and big?'

'I'd never seen the like,' Anne said, actually wringing her hands. 'It looked so huge and mean, frightening me. He took my hand to it, made me grasp it and rub it for him. I didn't want to—'

I clasped her hand to my stander, working her wrist so that she masturbated me gently. She continued to do so when I let go of her hand. 'What did it feel like for you?' I asked.

'It felt hot and throbbing, yet so stiff, like yours. You are both the same kind of filthy beast. He made me say I liked it, rubbing it and holding it—'

'And did you?' I demanded, enjoying her cool fingers stroking my engorged stalk quite expertly.

'I went all weak and trembly inside. I didn't know what I felt. I suppose I liked it, even though I hated it—' She paused, looking at me with appealing eyes. 'He made me say awful things like, would I like it between my breasts, in my cunt, even in my mouth? Then, while I was holding it, he drew my face down and told me to suck it. I felt so dirty doing that, but he made me, moving his hips against me. He told me my mother loved doing that to him too.'

My own prick was poised at her lips by then, and with a low moan of resignation she gave it several delightful sucks. 'Like mother, like daughter,' I could only mutter, holding her head. 'I'd have loved to have known her. Time for this later, now I need to fuck you.'

'No, no!' she managed to protest with her mouth full of dick and she increased her suction, gobbling away like a kid with a lollipop. Ronnie had taught her to perform expertly and she swallowed my spunk like it was nectar as I came helplessly down her throat.

'I didn't think I could ever swallow the beastly stuff,' she said almost apologetically as I collapsed on the bed beside her. 'What girls have to do to please you awful men.'

'You horny cocksucker,' I accused her, 'I wanted to screw you, but you love it in your mouth more. Don't think you've got away with it, just give me a rest and I'll have you all ways, front and back. That should give you more to feel humiliated about, and won't you enjoy that?'

'You can do nothing to me that Ronnie hasn't already done,' Anne said, and I took that as boding well for my future stay with her.

The days passed and I was made to realise just how little I knew of her salacious mind, as she came up with tricks that both amazed and amused me. She was a lovely fuck, protesting loudly while being used each time as if rape were taking place, then losing control as the thrill overwhelmed her, urging me on, ordering me to fuck her, using the coarsest language as her spasms increased. I made use of her tits, mouth and cunt at will, at all times of day, simply by taking her elbow and leading her off to bed. She would grumble and resist before complying and enjoying a strong orgasm or several. Often I would put her across my knee for a lesson in obedience that we both enjoyed. If she was especially defiant at times, the spanking was followed by a good fucking in her warmed-up arse just to humiliate her further.

There seemed no end to her foibles. She had an African housegirl who came in every morning to make our breakfast and tidy up before Anne left for work at her office. We would be awake, hearing the rattle of cups and saucers from the kitchen while the girl made tea to serve us in bed. Almost without exception, knowing her servant would be coming through with the tray, Anne would cuddle up to me provocatively, the only instance when she made advances to me. It was not hard to get hard, with both of us sleeping naked and her marble-smooth tits pressed to me, her hand groping for my prick. Hence it was Anne's lewd pleasure that, when the girl came through, the sheet would be thrown back and she'd be sucking me off or getting fucked. Fucked front, back or sideways according to her choice.

I didn't mind and the housegirl didn't seem to either, merely placing the tray on Anne's bedside table and wishing us good morning before padding off. It was a time when I was living high again, in a comfortable rent-free billet with all the fucking I could manage – and that included the housegirl as I was often alone in the house while Anne was at work. I screwed the girl on Anne's bed before she made it, the black girl tickled pink that her mistress's bloke was having her.

I had money too, enough to buy myself a reliable Peugeot estate and there was enough left over to keep me solvent. I knew, however, that the good times would end. Soon, Anne got her posting to Paris and I had to vacate her bungalow, moving back to the Lake Vic hotel. I knew I'd have to find work as my bankroll was decreasing, but then work found me.

Chapter Eighteen

During the next few weeks I found myself flying for Amin again, piloting the Cessna from Bombo airstrip on deliveries to the former Belgian Congo – now renamed Zaire. Its independence was marred, however, by a bloody struggle for power by a dozen factions. Tales that emerged into neighbouring Uganda were of horrific massacres – of doctors, nuns, priests, intellectuals, both whites and blacks – of anyone unlucky enough to be in the wrong place at the wrong time. Several provinces, including the rich Katanga area, had become battlefields, with Zairan troops, Simba rebels and companies of white mercenaries shooting it out. I didn't want to know what cargo I carried but guessed it was Ugandan Army weapons flogged for bars of gold and silver 'liberated' from ex-Belgian mines.

The aircraft was always fuelled and loaded when I was driven to the airstrip by an army driver, where the grimy engineer Len Parker greeted me as if for the last time. It could well have been, for my destination was Stanleyville airport, where the whole city was in the hands of a so-called Popular Government and the garrison was a thousand-strong mix of witch-doctors in full regalia and a ragtag army of Simba rebels dressed in monkey-skin headgear. It was always a relief to return from this nightmare of a place. I would steady my nerves with a good slug of Len Parker's Scotch before returning to Entebbe and fucking Vera, Marje or Beverley to set me up before the next trip. The pay was good but I wondered how long I'd survive, sometimes weaving and ducking over jungle as Sam ground-to-air missiles soared up.

To make the most of an unavoidably hazardous existence – for there was no denying Amin my services – I spent my loot like a drunken sailor, staying in the best appointed room in the hotel and partying there every night in orgiastic pleasures as if my time would run out. Following one session that had lasted until dawn, the afternoon saw me recuperating on a sun-lounger beside the swimming pool, iced drink in hand, shaded by a huge umbrella, a waiter hovering nearby in case my glass needed a refill. The pool was invitingly blue with bright sunlight dappling the surface. At such times I dismissed the thought of escaping Uganda in a midnight car dash south into Tanzania, considering occasional danger perhaps worth the price of living so regally. And then I was regaled with the cock-stiffening sight of Beverley Marchbanks in a bikini top that overflowed with luscious tit and a triangular scrap of material around her sumptuous loins moulding her prominent mound.

'You had a wild party in your room last night and you didn't invite me,' she complained. 'Shame on you, Tyler.' She held her arms open, her breasts threatening to burst free of the constraining bra. 'Wouldn't I have been welcome? I could have come like this.'

In the Groove

'I got drinking with a PanAm aircrew at the bar,' I explained. 'Then I invited them to my room. We just took it from there, nothing was arranged—'

'Were the air hostesses willing?' she asked.

'Drunk and randy. I note none of 'em have surfaced yet.'

'You could have phoned me. Will the party continue tonight?'

'They'll be flying out tomorrow, so drinking is out for them,' I said. 'You look extremely seductive in that bikini, Bev. It looks two sizes too small and all the better for it. What are you doing tonight?'

'I thought you'd never ask,' she chuckled wickedly. 'It so happens I'm at a loose end. We're leaving here. Jumbo has got the ambassadorship of some ghastly South American banana republic. He's in London now being briefed. Jovial has gone back to her village and I fly to England tomorrow?'

'The end of an era,' I said. 'We must do something to mark the occasion. Dine with me tonight, then we'll take it from there.'

'Yes, I want my stay here to end with a bang,' she laughed. 'Could you lay on something special? Out of the ordinary—'

'A bit of black to stop you wondering?' I suggested. 'I've made friends with an American negro chap staying in the hotel. Calvin something, I don't know his last name. He's a US Airforce air-traffic controller on loan to train the locals. A nice guy. What's more, I saw him operate at my party last night and he's all they say about black studs. You want to try him?'

'By all means,' Beverley agreed, 'but I don't have to

wonder about black men. A few of our more presentable Ugandan friends have had me, including one handsome houseboy I couldn't resist. That was before my dear husband caught us together and learned to appreciate me, of course. You corrupt everyone. To think I once thought I was madly in love with you—'

'That was just my dick you fell for,' I laughed with her. 'So we invite Calvin. Anyone else you fancy as a farewell gift?'

'Vera,' she said surprisingly. 'Vera Steedman, that simple little piece I've seen you with here at the pool. I presume she fucks or you'd have nothing to do with her. Invite her. I'd like to see your American negro friend roger her. She shouldn't die wondering, should she—?'

'You horny bitch, Beverley,' I said. 'I'd like to see that myself, but don't let Vera's respectable façade fool you. She's as keen to take the dick as you are. I've actually heard her say in her fantasies she's fancied a big black dong up her. She's adventurous. She told me that the lesbian scene intrigued her too and that she'd like to try it with a woman—'

I saw Beverley's eyes light up. 'Make sure she comes tonight,' she urged me eagerly, with mischief in mind no doubt.

Eight o'clock saw all four of us seated at a lavish dinner accompanied by champagne with liqueurs to follow. In the carefree mood I led my party towards the stairway that led to my room, where I'd ordered more champagne to await our arrival. Vera fell behind as if to adjust the back strap of a shoe, signalling me with her eyes to wait with her as Beverley and Calvin walked on ahead, chatting most animatedly.

In the Groove

'Your friends,' Vera hissed at me so that only I could hear her. 'I sat between them and at times both of them were feeling my thighs. One on each side, the black chap *and* the woman too. Her!'

'They must like you,' I grinned. 'Did you mind—?'

'Well, no, I suppose not,' she giggled. 'I've had too much to drink. It excited me. A black man and a woman—'

'Could be your lucky night,' I suggested, taking her arm and following the other two. 'It shows how attractive you are to both men and women.'

When we entered my room, Beverley chose some smoochy music to get the party going while I poured champagne. Not bad going, I considered, looking about with some satisfaction at my expensive room and my attractive guests in evening dress, recalling how I'd arrived in town broke and homeless. As Sinatra began to sing *Embraceable You*, Beverley took a startled Vera in her arms and began to dance her around the room, pressing her ample breasts to Vera's firm and pointy ones, their cunt mounds grinding together.

'Never mind these men, my dear,' Beverley insisted sweetly as her partner, unsure how to react, tried to disengage from such blatantly sexually contact – only to be hugged closer by the determined woman. I saw Bev's lustrous eyes gleam with lewd intent as she gazed at the girl in her arms as avidly as any man set upon seduction. 'You are a poppet,' she exclaimed. 'You must know I want you terribly. A kiss, my darling, I demand a kiss—' She ceased the erotic motions of their dance to clamp her full open wet lips hard to Vera's.

Throughout the duration of a long, passionate kiss, I stood with Calvin, drinks in our hand, enjoying the view.

In the Groove

'She sure has a lech for that girl,' my companion decided. 'Randy as hell, isn't she? I'm hard as blue steel watching them. I presume we'll get the chance to fuck both later, or is this strictly their scene? Not that I mind an entertaining show—'

'They both screw like rabbits,' I assured him, 'so take a seat and enjoy what will count as a warm-up for things to come, if you'll excuse the pun. It should be interesting. It's Vera's first time with another woman. I think she'd not too sure about it, but Bev will get her going, I hope—'

Vera still looked apprehensive as Beverley's mouth drew away after the wanton kiss. She held up trembling hands as if to ward off a further assault, but Bev was set to have her way with the girl, slapping her smartly but lightly across the face with her fingertips as if an uncooperative attitude would not be tolerated. 'Don't be a silly little bitch, Vera,' she ordered sharply. 'You know you really want this as much as I. Let's have no fuss. I don't want to get angry with you—'

It was getting better and better for us men, privileged to watch the seduction proceed. Vera stood stock still, mesmerised, as Bev undressed her completely, cuttingly told at times to help by lifting her arms as her dress was drawn off or to lift her feet for her briefs to be removed. All this Vera complied with as if she was unaware of what she was doing. At last she stood naked with her face and pert uptilted breasts the same blushing shade of pink, either through mortification or arousal. It was a helpless mix of both, I considered, for she remained transfixed while Bev hastily shed her own clothes.

Calvin nudged me, appreciating the sight, the neat slim

In the Groove

Vera and Beverley's strong back tapering to the waist and flaring out to fine buttock mounds. Her flesh had that dimpled softness of womanly maturity, jiggling alluringly as she advanced on Vera.

Her hands went to Vera's shoulders, urging her gently but firmly to stand upright against the wall. Little mewing cries and whimpers sounded from the tormented girl, which no doubt added as much to Bev's salacious pleasure as it did to ours. I had no doubt that, among other treats, Vera was to be put to Bev's tongue, and I eagerly awaited her reaction, having never had her cunt tongued by a woman before. But first, prolonging her victim's delicious agony, Bev merely stroked the uneasy Vera's face quite tenderly, smiling fondly on her, gentle fingers sliding down over chin and neck to pause at her breasts, cupping each in turn, palms rotating over each pear-shaped projection in a circular motion.

'My dear, your nipples feel so *erect* and quite beautifully *stiff*,' Bev said soothingly. 'Have I made them so? How nice and slim your body is, and *so* delightfully smooth to touch. Such dear breasts, I'm quite infatuated with them. I'm sure you like them kissed and sucked. I want to so very much—'

'You shouldn't say such things, really—' Vera croaked, lifting high the pointy tits that Bev was praising as if to offer them. The girl breathed in short gasps in her agitation. As Bev's lips flitted from nipple to nipple in swift little pecks, kisses and sucks, Vera sighed as if faint with reluctant desire, no longer able to resist. 'Please, please—' her strained voice pleaded, but to no avail. Bev's left hand sidled behind, now lightly caressing Vera's trim bottom cheeks, the right hand engaged in stroking her cunt lips and beyond. Such expert and unhurried titillation had poor Vera arching her back, sobbing in a delirium of ecstatic pleasure.

'Don't you just love it,' Bev taunted her victim as her fingers continued to titillate, making Vera cry out a groan of anguish, unable to contain her true feeling, tilting her quim and wriggling her hips and arse to the other's expert fingering. 'Such a divine cunt you have, so drenched with your juice, girl. That tells me everything. Clench my fingers, grip them and work against even harder, give yourself the come I know you damned well want—'

'Yes, yes,' Vera admitted, 'but I didn't mean this to happen, not with you—' as she allowed herself to be led to the bed. By now resigned to the fact that a woman was about to make free with her, Vera shot me a look of uneasy reproach. 'You set me up, Tyler you beast, inviting me to dine with these people. There was nothing said about there being others—'

'Shut up and stop pretending to be the little innocent, Vera,' Bev snapped, playing the dominant role perfectly. 'Do you want to be put across my knee? You've got a pert little bottom, just ripe for a spanking—'

Even as Vera mournfully denied that she deserved such treatment, I spoke up, with Calvin nodding agreement, that a warming of her bum by another woman was entirely necessary to stop her childish fuss. We wanted to see it and, from the look Bev flashed us, it was evident she was dying to do it. Vera was pulled unceremoniously across Bev's lap as the older woman sat on the edge of the bed. We two men arose from our seats to look closer as Vera squealed in protest, her tight little arse pointing upwards and tits hanging. Bev's first strike sounded like a thunderclap and Vera howled, more with humiliation than pain, I supposed. Smack followed smack.

'Bitch, swine,' the punished girl sobbed. 'That hurts and stings, let me up – I want to go home!' Certainly her bottom cheeks had turned from pink to red, creating a heat that no doubt penetrated to her whole lower region, permeating her already titillated cunt. Think of the galvanising indignity, the delicious humiliation, for a modest girl to be naked across another female's lap and her bare bottom smacked in front of two avidly spectating males! Vera's tortured groans came as if the humbling was more of a pleasurable affront. She squirmed and ground her arse and pelvis as if unable to contain a climax. It did not go unnoticed by any of us.

'See the little bitch wriggle, she's rubbing her cunt on my thigh,' Bev announced wickedly. She parted Vera's cheeks, inviting us to inspect the darker flesh of the cleave, the cunt lips on the rear-viewed split bulge pouting and salivating with arousal, the tight serrated arsehole puckering up and closing as it pulsed. 'Don't fret, my love,' she promised the girl, 'I don't intent to leave you in such an unfinished state. You'll get to love what another woman can do for you—'

'I want Tyler now,' Vera protested meekly, but Bev lolled back on the bed, legs overhanging the edge, turning her partner over and drawing her over her body until the startled Vera's face was poised over Bev's parted thighs. At the other end of the bed Vera's cunt hovered momentarily over Bev's mouth before it was clamped and sucked, tongued with eager relish, making the recipient gurgle as if in blessed relief as she worked her bottom wildly.

'Oooh, God, yes, yes,' mumbled Vera and, unable to resist the succulent tit-bit Bev's quim presented under her very nose, she crushed her mouth to it and began sucking, lapping and licking as if greedy for its taste.

'Christ,' Calvin said to me as we enjoyed the erotic perspective. He drew out a monstrously engorged prick and held it as if ready to join in the fray. 'Do you think there'll be any left for us? You know what they say – once a girl has tried another female's tongue, who needs a prick? They look like fully paid-up lesbians to me. Now that Vera's had a woman, she won't want a man.'

'Don't you believe it,' I promised. 'We have before us two of the horniest switch-hitters I've ever seen. Get out of your clothes, Cal, stand by and we'll apply the dick at either end of 'em. I'm getting up behind Vera for starters, I fancy her arse. You give one to Beverley, then we'll change places.'

The die cast, we stripped and, as surreptitiously as I could without disturbing the engaged women, I crawled to the head of the bed. Vera's tight little bottom bobbed and pirouetted to Bev's tongue-fucking. The 'sixty-nine' position suited their present lech admirably, I saw, Vera's face being buried deep between Bev's thighs as she gorged on cunt. Vera's gyrating hindquarters showed she was receiving as good as she gave, with Bev noisily eating her out in a gobbling frenzy of lips and tongue.

I laid hands on Vera's bottom to still it somewhat for my poker to have a steadier target. This made her raise her head and turn to see what permutation was being added to the act in progress. Before she could speak, Calvin had drawn her face back to him as he stood at the end of the bed, feeding his huge black weapon to her lips, insistent that she take it in her mouth.

'You must!' I heard Bev call out, seeing what was intended. 'Suck him and wet his prick for him to fuck me with, Vera.' Her hands reached around and parted Vera's cheeks for my access. 'You fuck her cunt and arse, Tyler – oh, aren't we beasts, dirty beasts – but we all love it so—'

I heard muffled sucking noises as Vera obediently lubricated Calvin's monster in her mouth, the black American grinning across at me as he enjoyed the treatment. My own dick was drawn down and given several strenuous sucks by Bev, laving it with her saliva before releasing it to bob up level with Vera's cunt. It was puffy with her excitement, the outer lips thick with tumescence and open as nature decreed to accept a cock. I went into her at first thrust nestling comfortably between her nether cheeks, holding her fast with an arm ringed about her waist. Thus was Vera taking a big dick at either end and obviously loving it, hollowing her back and bouncing her arse to my lunges while her head bobbed over Calvin's crotch.

But Bev was not to be denied her pleasure. 'Fuck me, Calvin, fuck me now!' she cried out urgently. 'Vera is getting enough at this end, pull it out of her bloody mouth and put it up my cunt, damn you! Oh, shove it in—' The way I felt her body stiffen as if getting a shock, and the whimper of disappointment from Vera, told me that Calvin had done the deed and shafted her to the hilt. As Bev thrashed, accepting the bar of taut flesh in her, I felt the heat in my balls generating an oncoming surge and I decided to loose my load up Vera's rear. I withdrew and the vexed protest she began to voice changed to a muffled squeal as I let my stalk glide the inch or so up between cunt and arse, pressing my crest home on meeting her back orifice.

'Oh, no, oh y-e-e-s,' Vera grunted as I embedded sufficient of my prick up her tight passage to give her the feel of it, hot, hard and filling. She positively quivered in ecstasy, her bottom lifting to my belly, desiring the full penetration. As if to show to Bev that she was every bit a wanton creature, she crowed out that I was up her bottom hole. 'He's fucking my bum, the brute, right up my arsehole! Did you ever—? Oh, God, it's splitting me, burning me – ride me there, shove it up, shove it up, Ty—'

I did, aroused beyond sanity by the voluptuousness of Vera working her bottom so deliciously, the girl encouraging me loudly in her own delirium. Bev was crying out too, that it was heaven, heaven, being fucked by such a huge black prick, while Calvin was grunting and thrusting in his tremors. As I came, Vera bucked her arse in violent undulations and screamed that she was THERE! and sobbed out that it was killing her! I pulled back to my knob so that she could better feel the strong spurts I was jetting into her back passage.

I sat on my knees, chest heaving as Vera rolled aside from Bev, Calvin slumping forward on the bed so that we formed a breathless sprawl of naked perspiring bodies. Beverley was the first to rise, crossing, with her magnificent buttocks waggling at us, to pour refills of champagne.

'There's no stopping now,' she warned us. 'Don't forget that tomorrow I have to fly off and leave you all. Goodness knows when I'll enjoy such a lovely orgy again.'

'Goodness has nothing to do with it, Bev,' Vera chuckled slyly. 'If we exhausted the boys, we've got each other, haven't we?' Never was a truer word spoken!

Next morning we all saw Beverley off at the airport, satisfied that she had left Entebbe with a real bang – a night-long sequence of explosive fucking and sucking to mark her farewell.

Chapter Nineteen

Over a week passed after Bev's departure with no further call on me to fly arms into the Congo. I began to hope that Amin's cache had dried up. The time passed pleasantly as I caught up on sleep, relaxing by the hotel pool, calling on Vera and not forgetting to visit Mrs Dulip Singh for mutual sexual relief. I also got a surprise invitation from Sam Bishop to dine at his house one evening. 'I'm having a few friends in,' he said. 'Come along, it should be a good night.' Having nothing else on, I agreed to attend. His wife was always worth admiring and I also hoped to arrange another romp with her when Sam had left on his next photo safari.

Going into the hotel bar for a quick one before leaving, I found Len Parker, the Bombo aircraft engineer, surprisingly clean shaven and smart in a lightweight suit and tie. 'Don't tell me,' I said. 'You got all dressed up to spoil my evening. Are you here to say I'm flying tomorrow?'

'You won't be flying for a while,' he grinned to my relief. 'The old Cessna is in bits. It needs an engine rebore and a new prop for starters. You can relax. I'm here because I've been invited to a dinner party.'

In the Groove

'Me too,' I told him, delighted to hear his good news. 'Let me buy you a drink for a change, Len. You've always been generous with your whisky. Who's managed to get you out of your filthy overalls? It must be a woman. I thought you were strictly faithful to your two little African wives—'

'They do me,' he stated, accepting the drink I ordered, 'but that doesn't mean I wouldn't throw a fuck in any other woman's direction if she was worth it. Like the wife of the bloke who's throwing this dinner tonight, for instance. Marje Bishop, now there's one I'd like to screw anytime—'

'I've been invited to eat there, too,' I said, 'and Marje is a lady built for fucking. I wouldn't mind giving her one myself,' adding that to disguise the fact I already had. We drove off in our separate vehicles, arriving at Sam's bungalow to be met at the door by Marje looking splendidly curvaceous in an amply filled evening gown with such a low neck that her large bosom and tight cleavage excited the imagination. She had already been drinking, I noted, getting a long kiss of welcome from her and tasting the alcohol on her breath.

'Tyler's an old friend,' she informed Len, seeing him noting the kiss with a shrewd look. 'He once worked for us. Drinkies first and then dinner. Sam's in there with our other guest – a Captain Spilsby. Let's join them.'

Bad pennies frequently turn up and I knew Ed Spilsby of old, a cashiered army officer and later an ivory poacher in Kenya. As ever when I saw him, he had a drink in his hand and the wild-eyed look of a dangerous nutter. Although I had worked with him, flying out his tusks and skins from bush airstrips, he merely nodded in my direction, paying more attention to Marje's lush wobbly bits, her big breasts and cushiony arse. As we gathered around the array of booze set out on a sideboard, Spilsby manoeuvred himself next to our hostess, his free hand gliding over the plump moons of her bottom and giving both a suggestive squeeze.

Marje giggled and I saw Sam frown though he said nothing of Spilsby being so familiar with his wife. It was going to be one of those nights, I considered, degenerating into a wild free-for-all once enough alcohol had been consumed and hair and everything else including knickers and trousers had been let down. As the sole female present among a group of lechers waiting their chance, Marje was all tipsy smiles and smirks, anticipating her fate. Her husband, meanwhile, acted as if nothing was amiss or expected to happen. I sensed damned well it would, with the opportunist Marje not likely to miss out on being the centre of attraction, and Sam knew his extrovert missis better than anyone.

I watched with interest as the evening proceeded, Marje flirting with each of us, standing so that her ample tits brushed our arms, sitting on our laps as she grew more outrageous, while Sam resigned himself gradually to accepting her behaviour with his guests. That was his defence, I knew – it was out of his control and therefore he was no longer responsible for his wife's actions. Thus he could enjoy seeing her fucked by all and sundry without apparently making it so obvious. It was an unspoken agreement between them.

Our appetites were satisfied by an excellent curry meal

served buffet-fashion, and then Sam and Marje removed the used plates to their kitchen in the absence of their servant – another clue to me that they expected sexy fun to ensue now that other appetites had been well aroused. 'I'm going to fuck that woman before the night is out,' Ed Spilsby declared, nursing his umpteenth neat Scotch. 'Whether her old man is here or not to see it. I get the idea he wouldn't mind either. Suits me, I'd screw her in front of anybody the way she's been asking for it. What say we all have her—?'

'Business before pleasure, though I don't mind admitting I fancy a shag at her myself,' Len Parker spoke up. 'What about this foray into the Congo you've arranged, Spilsby? That's the purpose of this get-together, not to screw a horny woman. You say there's gold there for the taking—'

'Loads of it knocking about,' Spilsby enthused, 'waiting to be picked up for trade.' He looked up as Sam Bishop came back into the lounge alone. 'Where's your good lady, Sam? We were enjoying her company—'

'Gone to do up her face,' Sam replied, 'so let's make the most of it.' He turned to speak to me. 'Are you with us, Ty? We're making an expedition into the Congo to sell goods for gold. It could make us all rich men—'

'Dead men,' I said, horrified, as the others fixed their eyes on my reaction. 'Christ, I've been down there. What I've seen are bloody wild men from way back murdering and raping. You asked me here for dinner, Sam, not to commit suicide—'

'Show him some gold, Spilsby,' Len Parker said, and Spilsby handed me a small ingot about the size of a bar of chocolate which felt weighty in my grasp. It was stamped with the impression *Republique du Congo*. 'Worth about five thousand quid,' I was told.

'I don't give a shit if it's worth a million,' I said. 'My skin's worth more than that. Count me out—'

'Fuck your skin, think of the loot,' Spilsby argued. 'You were flying to rebel territory. We'd be travelling through parts held by loyal troops. Piece of cake. I've been there this past six months leading a mercenary company of infantry. I got paid with that gold.'

'It gave the captain an idea to get more of it,' Sam chipped in. 'He says at the military base at Maganga there's a total shortage of everything except weapons: whisky, cigarettes, coffee, sugar, you name it. So we go there with several vehicles loaded to the roof and barter for gold. A quick dash in and out and we're wealthy.' He looked at me defiantly. 'Spilsby knows the route like the back of his hand. You've got money to chip in for the supplies and a good Peugeot estate car to make the trip—'

'And I took your aircraft to pieces to make sure Amin couldn't use you for the next few weeks,' Len Parker said. 'I was getting to admire you, thinking you were a real daredevil—'

'The best of British to the lot of you,' I laughed. 'You see before you the original scared-shitless coward.'

I was glad at that moment to have their attention diverted by Marje's grand entrance, swaying tipsily around our seated group in the manner of a seductive slow dance. She was absolutely bare bollock naked except for two silk scarves that she drew across her body seductively, big tits bouncing and wobbling with each flounce, giggling at her display of wantonness. She finally plonked herself down on an elated Spilsby's lap, facing forward and squirming her bottom into his lap as his hands came around to cup each breast.

'Don't let me stop what you gentlemen were discussing,' she insisted wickedly. 'Or have you other things in mind? Sam won't mind if you all want to fuck me, will you, my love? Should we draw lots? Who will be first—?'

'My wife is drunk,' Sam excused them both in a quavering voice. 'In the morning she'll hate herself for – for—'

'For being exactly what you men want me to be,' the gregarious lady said, parting her thighs wide to display her muff, a thick crisp growth on a thrust-out mound. Spilsby was kissing her neck, flicking her nipples, moving his hips in grinding motions at the plump backside ensconced in his lap. 'Eat me, somebody!' Marje ordered urgently, sliding forward with her toes digging into the carpet. 'For God's sake use my cunt – tongue it or fuck it—'

Len Parker slid forward on his knees, widening her thighs to the limit and diving in with his face, slurping away at the offered orifice like a starved man. Marje groaned and whimpered as Spilsby played with her tits and Len pleasured her below. 'This has gone too bloody far,' her husband croaked to me, his voice thick. 'I suppose you'll want to fuck her too before the bitch comes to her senses. Go on, you might as well.' He stamped agitatedly around, his eyes never leaving the action.

Marje was muttering 'Yes, oh yes!' and working her groin into Len's nose and mouth ever faster, head twisted so that she was sharing the lewdest deep kissing with Spilsby, who in his ardour was crushing her tits in his

In the Groove

hands. Finally her spasms stilled and she looked around for approval.

'Cow, bitch, whore, slut,' her husband spat at her, pulling his belt from the loops of his pants. She was all those things but I admired her all the more, seeing Sam throw the belt aside as if giving up on her, too hopeless a case to punish for her waywardness.

Marje was not to be denied, getting to her feet with a bounce of her superb breasts, smiling contritely at her husband and picking up the discarded belt to hand to him. 'I agree I've been a very naughty wife tonight, Sam dearest. Oughtn't I to be punished for disgracing you—?'

The game woman turned, bent over, and waggled her wide bottom at him in taunting invitation. She presented a magnificent target, waiting until she was certain no blow was to fall and then turning to press her naked form to his body, moving her tits hard to his shirt, her cunt mound rotating against his crotch.

'Fuck me then, Sam,' she urged, while the rest of us stood around them with straining erections tenting our trousers. 'I know you want to, I can feel you're iron hard. Fuck me and show them how it should be done. Right here, we'll throw cushions on the floor.' She began to peel off Sam's shirt, glancing about at us, smiling as if she was now in complete command of the situation. 'Gentlemen, cushions on the floor for my husband to fuck me, please. And do you think that I should be the only one here naked? Undress, all of you—'

To hear was to obey, of course, our clothes being shed to reveal three horny men with upright erections that made Marje nod and grin approvingly. 'I'll attend to you lot

In the Groove

after my husband,' she promised. She seemed now to be intoxicated by completely uninhibited sensuality rather than by drink. During her absence she'd no doubt showered, made up her face afresh and, while changing her dress, had decided to start the ball rolling by appearing nude. It was a master stroke that had my full approval and, from the elated look on her face, she was delighted by its reception. This was many a woman's secret fantasy, I imagined as I watched her flaunt her beautifully mature charms; full tits, buttocks and inviting hairy snatch. She got down on the scattered cushions, pulling them below the curve of her back and buttocks to tilt her proffered cunt, parting her legs and drawing up her knees, arms out spread.

'For God's sake screw her or let me at it,' Spilsby shouted, cock in hand as Sam Bishop hesitated to mount his wife, standing with a short stubby erection poking out of a mass of gingery hair. I suspected his reluctance was to do with his fear of an instant ejaculation on penetration, and from the wicked smile on his spouse's face she knew it. Sam was no doubt more than ready to go off at half-cock, aroused as he was by other men ogling his Marje's body, and she intended to give him the ultimate humiliation, that of not being able to satisfy her in the presence of other men. She began to finger her cunt lewdly, raising her arse and parting the outer lips as if daring him to accept the challenge, pursing her lips in his direction and taunting him.

Sam bowed to the inevitable as Len Parker placed a guiding hand on his back and pushed him down between Marje's legs. 'Get on the nest, man,' Len urged. 'Don't

In the Groove

keep her waiting, we all want at it. Fuck the horny cow—'

'Yes, fuck the horny cow,' Marje cried jubilantly. 'They all want at it. Show them how it's done, Sam darling!' She curled strong legs about his back, cradling him in her parted thighs and directing his prick to her cunt. You bitch, I thought. Sam would have done better belting her plump arse as she effected penetration by hoisting her crotch in one savage jerk, producing a groan and long shudder from her husband as his immediate climax drained his balls.

'That's no use to me!' the devious Marje howled to further embarrass Sam, who sat up on his knees between her thighs in a picture of dejection. 'If you can't fuck me properly, others will—'

'Too bloody true,' Len Parker rejoined, pushing Sam aside to take his place between the spread thighs before Spilsby could make his move. His first thrust went up Marje fiercely, making her moan her appreciation and arch her back. 'That's a well juiced-up gap,' he announced as he began shafting. 'I'm going in on a wet deck as we used to say in the Fleet Air Arm. Oh what a lovely woman you are to ride, what a great fuck—'

'Don't be all bloody night at it,' Spilsby complained. 'Leave some for others—'

As for me, I was content to wait, bull-at-a-gate tactics not being my forte, standing with what seemed a permanent hard-on as Marje and Len humped away strenuously. I went to the sideboard where Sam was morosely pouring himself a drink. I put a hand on his shoulder solicitously.

'This has really got out of hand,' he grumbled, jerking his head in the direction of his wife being screwed. She was loving every inch of it, judging by her cries and undulations. 'This was supposed to be a business meeting about the Congo venture—'

'Don't come it, Sam,' I said. 'You know the score with a wife like Marje; you wouldn't have her any other way—'

'Takes some satisfying, don't she?' he agreed trying not to sound proud of his promiscuous woman. 'I'm just ashamed I didn't manage to last out longer—'

'You were set up, mate,' I assured him. 'The bitch had you going and she knew it. Whoever fucked her first would have come off like that. Relax and give her a good going over later, show her who's boss. Use that belt on her arse if it helps get you up again. She said herself that she deserved a walloping.'

We both glanced across the room to see Marje being rogered by Spilsby, her legs over his shoulders and matching him thrust for thrust until he slumped forward spent with is face between her breasts. 'You next, Ty,' the randy creature called out to me, pushing Spilsby off her. 'I haven't really had a good come yet. Let me try that big cock of yours—'

'She does deserve a good arse-warming for her behaviour tonight,' Sam decided, exactly what I hoped he'd say. A disciplining of the buxom Marje would be worth witnessing. 'She's gone over the bloody top this time. Four men and wanting to have us all. Where's that belt—?'

I retrieved it from the floor, handing it to him as he advanced on his wife splayed out on the cushions. 'I want Tyler,' she pouted. 'You had your turn, Sam, and made a fool of yourself.' She sat up as if to reach for my dong but I

In the Groove

drew back. 'You're not using that belt on me,' she argued. 'Not after refusing when I offered nicely—'

'I've changed my mind,' Sam declared. 'If ever a woman needed a belting, it's you, Marjory. Turn over and tilt up your big arse, woman. You've got it coming for being such a slut—'

'Make me!' she defied him. 'Just you try and use that belt. You're not man enough to do it—' As if to taunt him further, or because she enjoyed the thought of being punished before an audience, she did roll over and waggle her behind in the air. Sam dropped to his knees, the belt doubled, and whacked at the offered target, the leather cracking across both ample cheeks like a pistol shot. 'Bastard!' she screamed, 'that stung—'

Sam eased off, strapping her more lightly than the first crack but still effecting a bright pink striping of the rounded flesh. Marje moaned, cursed him, flinched the muscles of her moons and twisted about as if in agony. 'Bloody good show,' Spilsby congratulated the belt-wielder. 'Not before time with a wife like that, Sam, though I must say she's a marvellous hostess. Promiscuous, lewd, wanton and uninhibited, everything a woman should be. You're a lucky chap—'

'I know that,' Sam said, turning his wife over on her back. She noted that he'd regained a sizable erection and in his kneeling position it was level with her mouth as she sat up on an elbow. Like a dutiful wife she clasped it and pressed it between her tits, kissed the tip and gave it a gentle suck.

'Why, Sam, beating me has given you a lovely hard-on,' she said sweetly. 'Don't waste it, dear, I want *you* to fuck me. Lie back so that we do it the way you like best, with me on top.' No doubt she was eager to perform again before her captive audience. Sam lay back obediently with his cock upright while Marje straddled his waist, directing the stalk to her cleft and grinding down to squat over it. She gave low moans, glancing about to make sure we were appreciating the sight before rotating her arse. This set her big tits jiggling as she savoured the prick impaled up her.

This time Sam stayed the course, allowing her to arouse herself to a frenzy on his shaft, twisting her pelvis to swallow his intruder deep within her capacious cunt. She soon became vocal, crying out her pleasure in the crudest terms, now sitting bolt upright, now falling forward to press her great tits to his chest. It was in one of these forward shifts of position that I decided my turn was overdue, admiring her big firm buttocks as they tilted up on her up-stroke. I stood directly behind her, seeing Sam's swollen stem being shunted in and out of a down-hanging, peach-like bulge, an inch or so above it the winking anal circlet begging for attention. I wet my finger thoroughly with saliva and curled it into the tightly serrated orifice, going up to the second knuckle.

Marje groaned, a different type of groan from that produced by riding Sam's stalk. She stiffened her back, stilled her bottom for a long moment and recommenced her up-and-down movement more cannily, as if savouring the feeling of something up her arse as well as her cunt. She gave out low moans and sighs, dipped her back to raise her bottom to me, and then plunged down on Sam's prick, delirious with lewdness. 'What's happening?' he wanted to know. 'What's going on back there—?'

'Tyler's got his finger up my bottom,' she whined. 'Oooh, God, more than his finger. He's fucking my bum, the bugger! His big prick's up there now – it's splitting me – oh, aaagh, it's so tight, filling me up. I'm fucked in both holes—'

She was indeed, my lech getting the better of me, unable to resist so fine a posterior waving under my nose. I had withdrawn the finger and replaced it with my knob, pressing home until the tight portal gave, admitting the first inch or so. I clasped the firm rounds of her cheeks, easing up inch after inch, aided by her own back-and-forth jerkings until I was fully engulfed up a warm and tight back passage. Marje went berserk, craning her neck and whinnying, braying and bucking away completely out of control, squirming her arse to my lap one moment and then thrusting down on her husband the next. I felt Sam's prick nudging mine through the thin membrane separating arse from cunt and then, in the madness of our dual coupling, we began to come off all together. I squirted jet after jet deep into Marje's back recess as Sam writhed below us, giving her his donation and grunting throatily as she screamed out her climax. The three of us still shook in violent spasms for long moments after we had disengaged.

'You took unfair advantage of me,' I was chided by Marje when she'd recovered sufficiently, but it was said with a wry smile. I could not but admire the spirit of such a willing woman as she rose to her feet. Her splendid build mesmerised us all; the beautiful white belly and thighs, the soft curly-haired cunt with its parted pink slit, the massive tits with red engorged nipples. 'Come along then,' she urged us men. 'Let's go through and be more comfortable doing it on the bed. Who's going to fuck me next? You all won't be in such a big hurry now—'

Next morning Marje slept late, deservedly so after keeping a quartet of randy men supplying her wants. I managed an hour or two sleep on Sam's couch, to be awakened in bright sunlight by his smiling housegirl bearing a cup of strong coffee. I used the shower, going out onto the verandah to join the others who were devouring ham and eggs. 'Thought about our offer to join us on our Congo trip?' Sam enquired, bringing up a subject I'd hoped had been forgotten. 'We're talking serious money. We need another warm body, one with a big car to help cart down all the supplies we'll be taking—'

'That's what I intend to stay, a warm body,' I said. 'You guys will be lucky to get out with your lives, let alone any gold. That's serious trouble, not serious money. I already said count me out—'

'For an arse-shagger like you the Congo is just the place,' Spilsby put in. 'There's more women, black and white, flogging it in the present circumstances than you can shake a stick at. We need another driver with a good car who can handle a gun. So join the club, Ty, you're it. Listen to Len's proposition—'

'Just a suggestion,' Len began, looking pleased with himself. 'This is for your own good. You want to lay your hands on some real moolah, don't you? Well, I might just let slip, if you ain't with us, that the reason Amin's aircraft is grounded could be because someone's fucked about with it. Sabotage, you know? If he somehow got the idea it was his pilot, you'd really be in deep shit. So I guess you're with us—'

'You wouldn't—' I began, ham and egg sticking in my throat. I saw from the evil grins all around that they would. 'You're devious bastards, all of you,' I cursed. 'So when do we set off, if you insist on this madness?'

'You can relax for a week or so,' Sam said. 'I've a photo safari booked to start today, and while I'm away Nanji Singh is going to buy all the supplies we'll need from her uncle's grocery store. I've given her a list: booze, ciggies, coffee, tea and sugar, tinned meat. You'll be getting a bill for your share. Then when I'm back from safari, it's shit or bust to lay our hands on big money. You'll be told when to be ready.'

'I can hardly wait,' I said unhappily. As ever it seemed, fate had decided I'd had my share of the good life for the present and now I must pay. And this time I had a presentiment of disaster.

Chapter Twenty

'Tyler,' said Marje Bishop as I answered the phone in my hotel room, 'I want you to fuck the little bitch. Fuck her thoroughly, mind. Fuck the tight little arse off her too.' She had been drinking and on saying her piece couldn't suppress a loud hiccup.

'Hang about, Marjory,' I replied, amused by such an outrageous request. 'Glad to help out, I'm sure. Always happy to bonk for a good cause, but who is the chosen one? No one you like from the sound of it—'

'Damn right,' Marje slurred venomously, 'not exactly my favourite person. Remember I told you about Sam's kid, my hateful stepdaughter?' I made an appropriate noise, recalling being told how she'd caught the girl having it off with big Callum, whom Marje had ran off to England to be with. 'Well, Christine is here, the little cow. Out from her bloody expensive boarding school. I want her fucked and buggered all ways—'

'Intriguing,' I admitted, 'but if you detest her so, and she's the horny little piece you claim, wouldn't that be doing her the kind of favour she'd like—?'

'No doubt,' Marje agreed maliciously, 'but wouldn't I

just have something to hold over the slut if she plays me against her father while she's here. He thinks the sun shines out of her virginal little cunt, that she only uses it to pee. When she gets on his knee and bad-mouths me, one look from me to remind her that you've had her back and front will shut her up—'

'You already have the fact that Callum screwed her,' I said.

'Then Sam would blame me for her meeting Callum,' Marje pointed out, devious even when tipsy. 'No, she'd probably claim it was rape, and say I arranged it. It's got to be you, and with me around, and photos of the fucking to prove it all happened—'

I didn't owe Sam a damned thing, I felt, after he and his two mates as good as blackmailed me into joining their lunatic foray into the exceedingly dangerous territory of the Congo. When trouble found me, I reflected, I sure got into it for real and with the biggest bunch of losers too in this particular case. Apart from risk to life and limb, I had already had to shell out all of my cash for the supplies we were taking. My newly acquired car and its contents, including me, would be a prize for any trigger-happy rebel or bandit encountered on the road, which would be jungle tracks mostly. As for Spilsby knowing the land like the back of his hand, I was only too aware how much it trembled when lifting a drink to his mouth.

'Fuck Sam,' I said wholeheartedly, ruminating on a bleak future, 'why shouldn't I make the most of my time?'

'It's his daughter I want you to fuck,' Marje said. 'You'll do it?'

'Gladly. Are you sure she'll let me?'

'Who cares about sure,' Marje giggled. 'I'd tie her up and hold her down for you if necessary, but it won't be. The little cow would probably enjoy that. She'll oblige, and you owe me one for having my bottom when Sam was up me the other night.' I heard her giggle down the phone as if savouring the memory. 'Christine will want you if she thinks she's taking you away from me—'

'Why should she think you and I are an item?' I asked. 'How could she know that—?'

'Because while Sam's off on safari this afternoon, you'll be dropping in for drinks,' Marje insisted. 'A big handsome hunk like you will soon get her cunt drooling. Think what she'll be able to boast about to the girls at her boarding school when she gets back. If I make a big fuss of you, she'll bite. Then you invite us both to dinner at the hotel, with drinks to follow in your room. Get the picture?'

I did, arriving at the Bishop's bungalow later in a crisp drill safari suit, looking the picture of a bronzed white hunter. Reclining on the verandah on a sunbed was a very pretty girl of seventeen or eighteen, flame-haired like her father, in a bikini bra that showed a nice swell of prime young tit. Below a flat white belly of the kind of skin only maidens can boast, there nestled a triangular patch of nylon that barely covered the sweet prominence at the vee of her rounded thighs. I saw a few wispy reddish hairs curling beyond the bikini line. All this I took in, well noted by the attractive girl as she shaded her eyes and gave me a long appreciative scan.

'My father is away,' she said sweetly, sitting up and allowing me a good look down between her breast cleavage. 'Can I be of help?'

She sure could, but I asked to see Marje and got a good reaction, a sulky frown and a pout. When her stepmother appeared, also in a brief bikini, I was hugged, kissed and invited in, which prompted the girl to rise and come through with us in case she missed anything. I flirted with them both, flattered them outrageously, and made sure she knew Marje and I were apparently more than just good friends. Then I made a further impression on the girl by including her in my invitation to dine at the hotel that evening. From her quick look of triumph at her stepmother it was obvious she concluded that I was already preferring her as my company.

We wined and dined, and I danced with both females in turn. I was aware that, with Christine in my arms, she nestled close, her pliant young boobs pressed to me and her cunt mound deliberately rubbing my crotch to induce a hard reaction.

'What is my stepmother to you, Ty?' she asked innocently. 'She is too old for you to find – find – *attractive*, surely?' She reached up to press her cheek to mine, my ear close as she whispered, 'Look at her, drinking herself stupid. Can't we dump her somewhere and spend some time alone?'

Marje, I knew, though appearing to get sozzled, was keeping an eye on proceedings which, particularly now the girl had virtually offered herself to me, was going to plan. At my suggestion we went to my room, plonking Marje into a deep armchair and standing back as her head lolled and she pretended to fall into a deep drunken sleep. 'You can't take her anywhere,' Christine said spitefully. 'Now we could do almost anything and she wouldn't be the wiser.' She clasped her arms around me and moulded her delicious breasts and pussy to my body, my prick responding at once to the warm pressure. 'I do *like* you, you know,' she cooed naughtily. 'I'm sure you much prefer me to that drunken old bag—'

I kissed her long and hard, my lips rolling on her sweet fresh mouth, tongue probing, working my erection against the fork of her thighs. The arrogant little bitch needed a good spanking for her jealous and unkind behaviour, I decided, and I'd have much pleasure in paddling her cheeky little bum among other things before I was through with her. Right now she was returning my kissing with expert tonguing and a loose wet mouth. She was already highly aroused, and probably all the more so with her father's wife evidently out to the wide before us. 'Strip off,' I said urgently. 'I want to see you, all of you, your pretty young tits and cunt. Then get on the bed, I'm going to fuck you—'

'Oooh, what naughty talk,' the young vixen said, eagerly pulling off her clothes as I did the same. 'I like that. Will you talk dirty to me when we do it? She won't know. Tell me all that you want to do to me. Use words like prick, fuck and cunt—'.

'Tits too,' I mumbled, unable to resist the bouncing pair with uptilted nipples that she'd uncovered. I grasped them and felt their firmness, kissing each in turn, sucking hard on the teats as she moaned her pleasure. She fell back on the bed, regarding me with a greedy light in her eyes as my prick reared up before her. 'That's for you,' I told her. 'All of it. Between your tits, in your mouth, up your cunt and even up your bottom. Get up and leave now if you think that's too much for you—'

She shook her head and held out her arms, widening her

In the Groove

knees so that I was presented with the neatest, sweetest fig-like young twat I could recall. She impelled me to worship it with my mouth and tongue. As I licked and lapped she placed her hands on her knees, drawing them up and thrusting them apart for my full access. Each probe of my tongue brought a strangled moan of delight, a thrust of her raised cunt, cries for more, and subtle shifts of her pelvis to bring her taut little clitty forward to be pleasured. I soon felt her stiffen, going into spasms that told me she was spending, and to prolong her pleasure I moved over her, guiding my prick to her pulsating quim.

The rude intruder was welcomed by her loud gasping sigh of utter satisfaction, legs clamping my back to the rocking cradle of her thighs, cupped hands reaching down and pulling my thrusting arse harder to her. If ever a girl gurgled taking the cock, she did, squealing out her delight, urging me on. 'Oh, aaah,' she groaned between her third or fourth come, as I ploughed her velvety folds, containing myself to bring her to added heights. 'What a lovely big prick you have. Did my stepmother ever take it? I don't care, I love it, love it—'

'The little bitch certainly does,' said an unexpected voice and suddenly Marje was beside the bed, making Christine shout in anger as she saw her stepmother. 'She adores it, every inch of your prick, Tyler. Don't stop for me, let her have it!'

I had no intention of stopping. My flanks heaved as I pistoned stiff flesh into the girl, noting that after the momentary surprise she resumed fucking, wantonly meeting my thrusts. 'Fuck you, Marjory, you fat whore,' she screamed. 'I don't care what you think! Fuck me harder,

Tyler, never mind her—' She bucked against me, increasing her wild pace. 'God, I'm coming again, coming again! You can shoot up me, I'm on the pill – fill my cunt, flood me—' Such was her urgent writhings that I let go, firing a series of spurts into her adorable honeypot as I surrendered to the wilful girl's entreaties.

She lay back as weak as a kitten as I rolled aside. Marje sat beside her on the bed and smiled. 'Don't look at me like that,' Christine said moodily. 'And don't you dare tell my father about this either. You'd better not, or I'll swear you brought me here and got me drunk so he could seduce me—'

'This is our own private little party, Christine,' Marje insisted, speaking kindly as if to mollify the girl. 'We should be friends, a family. Of course no one will ever know of this. You did enjoy Tyler fucking you, didn't you? And he would enjoy you, such a sweet and pretty thing you are. I find you quite irresistible myself.' Her hand idly flitted across Christine's breasts and the girl looked alarmed. Watching from the bed beside them I decided, from the flushed look on Marje's face and the soft glow in her eyes, that she meant what she said. She fancied her stepdaughter. She laughed at Christine's look of shock, bending to kiss her forehead, fingers lightly brushing the girl's raised nipples. 'I think you like that,' she whispered.

'Leave me alone,' Christine said weakly, all the while with her stepmother fondling her breasts, making the girl shiver as if the pleasure was nice but not welcomed. 'What makes you think I would let you do things to me? With him here,' she added, 'with what he's got? I would rather have that—'

'But he'll have to revive first,' Marje said wickedly. 'Of course we females could do that with our hands or mouths, but let's let him watch us for a while. That will give him another erection for you, as I'm sure you want him again. He'll certainly want you again, you sweet young thing. You like me feeling your titties, don't you? I can tell.' She bent to kiss each one lingeringly, then put her mouth to each nipple to give little sucks. 'No secrets here, my girl. I'm sure at your boarding school you girls pleasure and play with each other as a matter of course, and quite naturally too when young women have no recourse to boys. I did as a young girl—'

'No, not with you,' Christine sighed weakly. 'It's not right.'

'Nonsense,' the older woman insisted, her voice lulling her victim, all the time pecking little kisses at Christine's mouth, neck and tits. 'You like to come, I know, I saw how how excited you got. I can make you too. Let me, I know you'd like that.' Christine gave a little moan that I took to be the start of a protest, but Marje had slipped back and was directly facing the girl's cunt. 'Such a sweet one,' she murmured, her nose brushing the bushy mound. 'It will taste of pure nectar, I'm sure.' I saw a warm wet tongue-tip part the rolled lips of Christine's fig and enter the pink channel. The girl stiffening her body for a moment then relaxed with a compliant sigh before uttering *no, no*, almost too feebly to be heard. Marje glanced at me as if to say, how am I doing? Then she ignored the softly whispered protests and proceeded to suck hard on the tit-bit presented.

Christine began to surrender, tilting her cunt and sob-

In the Groove

bing, finally she grasped Marje's head and began to buck uncontrollably. Her face became deeply flushed, and her sweet titties rolled and wobbled as her chest rose and fell, faster and faster. The spectacle had its effect on me as predicted – watching Marje sucking and tonguing cunt while her pretty stepdaughter writhed in a haze of high arousal made my dong lift and stiffen to await its call. Then the loudest groan of all told that Christine had climaxed, shaking from the power of her orgasm as Marje kissed her and soothed her. The girl was putty in her hands, trembling, allowing herself to be rolled over and positioned on elbows and knees, the pert globes of her smooth apple-rounded girlish buttocks raised.

I could not help becoming lecherous at the sight of the twin columns of her upper thighs, the dipped back leading to the swell of ivory-white moons, the tight cleft dividing the full buttock cheeks. 'Remember, front *and* back,' I was reminded.

'What was that, what did you say to him?' Christine blurted out, still on heat but not too sure about being manipulated by her stepmother. The conniving little seductress was now being forced to submit to the older woman's salacious caprices. 'I won't, I shan't, not that way, it's too big!' she howled. 'You beasts, you animals, it would split me. Fuck my cunt if you must—'

She struggled to turn around but Marje held her neck, forcing her head down and her buttocks to rise higher. 'Still, girl!' she was ordered sharply, at the same time Marje's right hand delivered several good smacks to Christine's pretty posterior. 'Less fuss, for goodness sake, you know you're really enjoying this.' The girl's arse stopped its gyrations and lifted obediently, as if admitting surrender. I watched with growing interest, my cock swollen and ready. Marje's hand went between Christine's rear cleave, gently trailing loose fingers over the pouted quim lips and arsehole, making Christine jerk and expel breath in a sigh of restrained pleasure. Never, I decided, was a girl needing to be put to the cock more.

'On the bed behind her,' I was ordered by Marje. 'I want to see you both naked together. Don't fret, dear,' she promised Christine, 'your cunt will receive full measure first. Hasn't he got a lovely big one?' Then both hands were smoothing the tilted pert moons sensuously. 'And you have a divine bottom. Has it never been corked? I've always found with your father it's naughty but nice. Properly introduced to it a young girl can get a great fondness for bum-tailing. Fuck her, Ty, and I leave the rest to you at the appropriate moment. You'll know when—'

'Stop it,' Christine moaned weakly. 'I know I won't like it.' All the same her arse remained in position for me.

The enticing sight made me impatient to be at it and I closed in behind the girl and parted her twin cheeks to look down upon the split hang of her cunt. Stiff as a ramrod, my knob slipped between the outer lips easily and entered a cranny slippery with juices, such was her arousal. 'Yes, do, do,' I heard whimpered and her bottom balled back to my belly as the eager recipient took my full length. I let it soak, unmoving for long moments, feeling her grind back her gorgeous plump backside urging me to shunt my prick inside her. In return I began my first easy thrusts, altering the angle of my cock, making her squirm and gurgle with ecstasy at such poking. 'Feel my tits,' she said throatily. 'Squeeze them tight. Fuck me faster. Oh, God, it's up to my throat, heaven, heaven—'

From her ever wilder undulations, it was evident she was building up to a body-shaking climax, the first surges of the sensation bringing forth loud demands that I fuck her, fuck her, fill her, fill her! 'You two have made me so lewd, you—' she screamed.

Glancing aside I saw Marje nodding, pocket-sized camera in hand, indicating that now was the time. I withdrew my stiff rammer glistening with her sticky lubrication and getting a loud protest for depriving her cunt of its presence. As it rose the inch necessary to place bulbous knob to puckered ring she trembled, bracing herself. A gentle push forward and my crest was inside, gripping tightly.

Christine gasped, hollowed her back, and further inches of thick tool worked into her rear entrance. 'Hold it, please,' she begged, but not in any outraged tone. 'Let me get used to it there. It feels so hot and huge – oh, it's filling me up – can you get it all in there?'

Content to let her savour the new experience and encouraged by her evidently finding it pleasurable, I remained still with four or five inches held captive by the tightness of her hole. Marje was impressed too, enquiring if it was her first time that way, since she was taking it bravely. 'Careful now, Ty,' she urged me, 'you have a virgin bottom, I believe. Did Callum not have you that way, Christine, or some other—?'

'No, truthfully,' Christine grunted, getting the feel of it and moving her bottom against me gingerly to get more cock up her. 'Only at school, you know, we sometimes fingered each other there to see what it was like. One girl tried her vibrator on me—' She wriggled back to me and I met the movement by insinuating a couple more inches. 'I quite liked it,' she admitted, groaning. 'Yes, it's delicious. Tyler, feel my body, my tits and cunt – shove, shove it up me. Oh, you're really up my behind, fucking my bum, and it's fantastic.'

It was fantastic for me too as I increased the power of my strokes. The pair of us were now given over to the lustfulness of the act, crying out our delight together. Then I could hold back no longer, my cock jetting off globs of jism deep into her receptive arse as it worked back furiously to slap against my belly. As I rolled off, Christine fell forward, backside pulsating and leaking from the glorious bout.

But what should have been a moment of relaxation was rudely disturbed by a persistent banging at my door. Both Marje and Christine looked at me in some alarm. I wondered if our noisy rutting had brought the management to complain and I cursed the interruption.

'Ignore it,' I advised. 'Whoever it is can go away.' But the knocking continued more urgently. Marje was by then gathering up Christine's clothes, indicating that she and the naked girl go to my bathroom. Once there and safely out of sight, I pulled on my robe and sullenly opened the door. Sam Bishop stood there, the husband of Marje and the father of Christine, the last person I wished to see. 'I thought you were on safari,' I complained. 'What the hell are you doing back already?'

'I cut it short,' he announced, looking in on my room with its rumpled bed but all sign of my female guests' visit

In the Groove

had been removed. 'Spilsby phoned me to say all's ready to move out. Things are quiet there in the Congo right now. You car's loaded, so it's the gravy train for us first thing tomorrow—' He sniffed the air. 'Christ, this room stinks of cunt—'

'It usually does when I've entertained a woman here,' I said. 'As a matter of fact you've just missed her. Thanks for giving me such long notice of this blasted trip. Now if you'll piss off I'll get some sleep.'

'Sharp at seven in the morning then,' Sam warned. 'We'll be outside the safari office loaded up for gold. I tell you we'll be rich—'

'Dead more likely,' I replied gloomily, shutting the door on him.

'I'll be in the bar drinking our success with Spilsby and Len Parker if you care to join us,' he said as it closed. Marje and Christine emerged from the bathroom looking relieved at their escape. While in there Sam's wife had tidied up, combed her hair and made up her face. Christine remained naked and made no move to dress.

'That was a close shave,' Marje declared giggling. 'At least we've had our fun and can get home while he's in the bar. Dress, Christine, and we'll leave by the back stairs. My car's parked out there anyway.'

'I think I'll stay,' Christine decided saucily, ignoring her stepmother's annoyed frown. 'I want to sleep with Tyler the whole night too. You can tell daddy I went to a tennis party in Kampala and am staying the night with friends.' She got into my bed and pulled the single sheet up to her middle, showing off her pretty tits, as if waiting for me to take off my robe and join her. 'You don't mind, do you,

In the Groove

mummy dear?' she smiled mischievously. 'I'm sure Ty fucks you all the time, but I've got to go back to boarding school soon. Fair's fair, isn't it?'

'Bitch,' Marje said good-humouredly, going to the door to leave. 'We evidently understand each other. Enjoy his big dick all night then, for I take it every chance I get while your father's out of the way. Goodnight, you horny little tart.'

'I think we're going to be good friends from now on,' her stepdaughter declared. 'What a shame Tyler is having to leave tomorrow—'

You can say that again, I thought gloomily, remembering what was facing me as I shed my robe and made to climb in beside the waiting girl. At the door Marje paused, eyeing my nakedness, walking back into the room and starting to undress.

'We *both* went to that tennis party in Kampala and stayed the night,' she declared. 'You can be piggy in the middle, Tyler. Christine, let's give him a send-off he'll never forget!'

Chapter Twenty-one

With jungle, dirt tracks, steeply forested hills and a maze of tumbling streams to ford, our little convoy of four vehicles made painfully slow progress once we had crossed the Congolese border. Leaving the flat Rift Valley plain with its stunted umbrella trees and abundant herds of game, I wished a reluctant farewell to Uganda and drove a dark forbidding route where sunlight barely filtered down to the forest floor. At the rear of the others as the Tail-end Charlie, I'd been given the short straw. I was the one who was more likely to be picked off and therefore I was apprehensive in the extreme as my overladen car bumped and bounced in the wake of Sam Bishop and his cronies.

Overladen was an understatement, for even the seat beside me was piled high with cartons of canned beer and the rear was stocked to the roof with other supplies. I feared the Peugeot would collapse on its wheels and I'd be left to my own devices while the others bowled on ahead. Already we had met armed men in ragged uniforms who claimed to be manning a customs post, and we'd handed over whisky and a carton of cigarettes so that we could proceed. The expedition would have ended there, no

In the Groove

doubt, but Captain Spilsby had rehearsed us to show a display of our weaponry at such times. With shotguns and automatic rifles poked out of our vehicle windows during the interview, we were waved on as being too formidable to rob and kill. 'Fuck this for a game of soldiers,' I thought, envisaging a shoot-out somewhere along the way when encountering more determined armed bands. And all the time the forest grew denser. It was perfect ambush country.

The heat was oppressive and I was not feeling too alert, as I negotiated deep holes in the winding tracks, having spent the previous night trying to satisfy the demands of Marje and her stepdaughter. 'Wight, you'll never learn,' I told myself grimly, but it had been a romp to remember, especially as it could well be my last. Both females had been in that wantonly wicked mood inspired in women sharing one male between them, something I had always found to be the case. They can fuck all night, while a mere male can just rise to the occasion so many times. They were insistent, sucking my dong in turn and together to resurrect it, putting stiff nipples in my mouth, demanding more fucking long after I was ready to sleep. They had taunted me, tickled me and smothered me in tit and cunt. It was hardly preparation for the trip I was now undertaking, but truly a dream come true for any man.

We bivouacked that night in a clearing by a stream populated by hippo and crocodile, but I feared more what might come charging out of the surrounding forest with blazing guns. Much as I desired sleep, it was only fitful and, instead of Marje and Christine to cuddle, I hugged the pump-action shotgun. Thankful to see daylight, I joined

In the Groove

Sam, Len and Spilsby for an al fresco meal around the fire, certain that the rising smoke would give us away. The others, happy to think they were on the make, dug into beans and bacon. I felt starved too, scraping my tin plate and drinking mugs of strong coffee. It was remarked that our fly-boy, the daring pilot, was beginning to enjoy the adventure. Think of the lolly we'll bring back, I was reminded.

'We'd better,' I said. 'Every bean I had in the world is gone.'

'Piece of cake,' Spilsby assured me. 'We're all ex-servicemen, used to action. We can handle anything they throw at us—'

'Sure,' I said cynically. 'I flew Lancaster bombers over Nazi Germany; Len Parker here served on light fleet aircraft-carriers on the Russian run, up among the ice-cap; and Sam, he's told me he sat out the whole war in Gibraltar on an anti-aircraft gun. That makes us skilled jungle fighters, I don't think.'

'You'll fight if it's your skin they're after,' said Spilsby, and he was right. That morning we drew into a village of mud huts with a ramshackle shop with a Coca-Cola sign hanging outside. I pulled up as the vehicles ahead halted. The next moment shots were coming at us from the huts. One at least entered my off-side door and struck the piled cartons beside me. I banged off several volleys with my pump-action shotgun and saw running men throw themselves to the ground. Then I realised that my companions were driving off at speed. I put my foot down, racing past startled black faces daubed with war-paint, monkey-skin caps on their heads with dangling tails. These were the

In the Groove

rebel Simba soldiers that Spilsby had claimed were not in the area. Beyond the village I found myself alone on a track that forked in two directions. It was no time to stop and think. I drove on, pushing the car to the limit.

By mid-afternoon it was certain that I was completely lost. I was surprised, therefore, to see a white woman emerge from the bush and wave me down. She was blonde, in her thirties, wearing a white dress that was dirt-smeared and ragged from her wanderings. I drew up, glad to see another human face, deciding that it would have been an attractive one, round and fair, in other circumstances. Her body too was ripely rounded, the torn dress showing a large expanse of one thigh.

She introduced herself as Maria Poincet, the Belgian wife of a mining engineer; she'd become separated from her husband in fleeing from the Simba advance. Surprisingly calm, obviously an educated woman, she spoke in fluent English on learning my nationality. Almost her first words were, did I have a cigarette? Thousands, I was able to tell her, seeing her light up and sit at the side of the track, not caring that her dress, torn at the neck, showed an expanse of her full left breast. I gave her a can of lager and opened a tin of ham loaf which she wolfed down, wiping her fingers on her dress and raising the hem to dab the juice from her wide mouth. I found she was as lost as to her whereabouts as I was. Only then did we hear the engine of a vehicle approaching. We looked at each other in alarm.

I got her to crouch down with me behind the Peugeot, facing the arrival, making sure my pump-action was fully cartridged and determined to shoot it out if an enemy hove in sight. Asking if she'd prefer we hide in the dense bush, a shake of her head told me she was resigned to her fate. 'Shoot me,' she said coolly, 'if you can't hold them off. They'll kill you slowly and do what they want with me. Get as many as you can before that.'

I found myself giving a grim laugh, admiring the lady, yet still hopeful that it would be Sam or one of the others come to find me. But the vehicle that came into sight was a former US Army jeep mounted with a machine-gun, driven by a swarthy type, definitely not African. As he drew up alongside the Peugeot and got out to inspect it, the pistol he carried still holstered at his belt, I walked around from the other side and levelled my shotgun at his face. Maria came with me and, on seeing her, the soldier raised his cap and gave a low bow, putting me off shooting the bastard.

'Captain Emilio Alvarez,' he introduced himself, speaking in accented English. I told him to forget the niceties and raise his hands while Maria took the pistol from his belt. Suave sod, I thought, noting his broad grin and the white teeth, the hairline moustache on his upper lip. 'At your service, of course. Do not attempt to shoot me, I beg you. It would bring my men here at the double and I would not be alive to stop their excesses—'

'He's right,' Maria said. 'Cuban, no doubt. I'd heard Castro had sent officers here to train and lead the Simba rebel army.'

'Then we understand each other,' Alvarez smiled, taking back his pistol and holstering it. 'As a good Catholic I am on my way to the Mission of Saint Angelo, where there are priests and even nuns, I believe, held hostage. I hope I do not arrive too late.' He made to climb back into his jeep. 'For a consideration, I should be glad to lead you there. I would like your woman. I have not had a white one for too long.'

'An officer and a gentleman, obviously,' I said. 'Go fuck yourself. If the mission is held by your bloody Simba troops, we'd be worse off than we are here. We'll take our chance on the road—'

'Then you are dead for certain,' Alvarez said with his constant smile. 'I can control the Simbas, even if I have to shoot some of them. I have also radioed for some of my Cubans to go there. As Catholics they would wish no harm to come to ones of our faith. Do you agree now to my proposal, that I enjoy your wife—?'

'Let the pig have me,' Maria spoke up matter-of-factly. 'A worse fate awaits me if you don't. I'll bet he comes off at once, anyway—'

'That is not my style,' Alvarez assured her, bringing forth a blanket from the rear of the jeep, pulling it from a sleeping African girl who sat up, dazed, as her drugged slumber was interrupted. If he had been hastening to the mission to rescue endangered members of his own faith, I concluded, a fuck at Maria was top priority. He laid the blanket on springy grass at the verge of the track, unbuckling his belt and preparing to strip off. Seeing him, Maria gave me a shrug, then drew off her dress, shaking out her blonde hair, discarding her bra and briefs as if committed to the task. Despite our situation I could admire her not only for her courage but for the ripe firmness of her body; she was well-built and curvaceous at breast and buttocks. She held her clothes out for me to hold and took up position on the blanket.

In the Groove

She sat up, naked to our eyes, large breasts tilted. Alvarez knelt before her, the broad masculine shoulders obscuring her parted thighs as he moved them apart. Noisily, his mouth went in to her cunt, hands upstretched to paw and pull roughly at her sumptuous big tits. For a moment she seemed to resist, mouth set against uttering either distaste or reluctant arousal. She glanced at me, eyes appealing, as if to beg that I not judge her, while the Cuban lapped and tongued fiercely, groping at her tits, inducing a low whine from Maria that told she was responding against her will. Many women, I know, like to be taken, to have things go beyond their control.

She deliberately stretched out her lovely long white legs, lolling back with her arse twisting, lifting up from the blanket. Even engaged fully with pleasuring her cunt with mouth and tongue, Alvarez gave out a hoarse cry of triumph, a *haaargh* that indicated the woman was his.

'Now, now,' Maria gasped urgently, no longer able to deny her mounting lust. 'Take me now, fuck me!' I had watched with mixed feelings, sorry for her and despising Alvarez for abusing his position of power. Now she was pulling at his shoulders to drag him over her, legs splayed wide to receive him. I was jealous of him, my prick tautly erect at the exhibition provided by her wantonness. He went into her with a lunge, the impact of his body knocking the breath out of her, yet immediately she began to return his thrust for thrust, panting and straining to get more of him up her cunt. Alvarez began fucking her hard, but he was obviously making her come time after time, increasing her ecstasy. I had to admire his staying power, he was poking a woman to distraction as I loved to do myself.

In the Groove

Maria humped back to him, all trace of restraint, pride or wifely dignity gone, lost in a state of abject submission, getting a surfeit of what she craved, climaxing continuously until at long last I saw the Cuban's flanks shudder, his thrusting arse go wild, then slow as he emptied his load within her.

'Mercy, mercy, you're killing me!' Maria screamed, but clung on to him until he disengaged, sitting up on his knees while she slumped back limp and dishevelled. He stood to dress, grinning at me as if to say *There, now your wife knows what real fucking is like.*

His African girl sat up, picking her teeth unconcernedly as he got back in the jeep. I helped Maria to her feet, handed her her clothes as she dressed unsteadily, then drove off, following Alvarez as he proceeded on his way with a wave of his hand, disappearing in a cloud of dust.

Maria sat beside me, smoking reflectively between sips of lager from a can I'd given her. I concentrated on following the cloud of dust ahead, as ever dodging the deep potholes that made up as much track as the level parts. I left her to her thoughts, realising she was still somewhat dazed, her cunt no doubt still pulsing from the spasms brought on so repeatedly by his incredible staying power. Like it or not, she had proved a magnificent fuck, one I'd very much like to match. She saw me glance at her and blushed, smiling wryly back at my look.

'I'm sorry,' she said shyly, 'if I disgusted you. I couldn't help it. God knows I only agreed to it to help our situation. But once he started, I don't know what came over me. I wanted it—'

'Why not?' I said kindly. 'You probably saved our necks.

In the Groove

The bastard was no novice, he set out to get you going. There is no shame in that. I envied him—'

'Did you?' she laughed softly. 'He thought you were my husband. My husband never fucked me like he did – I got so excited—'

'How many times?' I asked cheerily. 'It seemed endless.'

'A dozen at least, but I lost count, I'm sure. I just came and came,' she admitted. 'He was good at it, wasn't he?'

'Bastard,' I cursed him lightly. Then in front of us, on a winding road leading up to a hill top, stood a brick building of church-like proportions. I drew up beside the jeep, disturbed at the number of wild-looking Simba troops gathering around us. Alvarez stood up, firing his pistol into the air and making them fall back a few yards. To my relief a good dozen or so Latino-looking soldiers in jungle green and armed to the teeth with modern automatic weapons joined us.

Right away, with at least several rifles poked into my back, I was ushered into the mission house, the stout wooden door slammed behind me and I found myself amidst a group of anxious white-clad nuns and one old priest. Several of the women were kneeling in prayer and fingering rosaries, as well they might. Beyond the door came wild tribal chants and stamping of feet as if the Simba troops were working themselves up for a spot of rape and slaughter. Maria had been separated from me but I was not surprised as Captain Alvarez undoubtedly wanted to further demonstrate his sexual prowess on her. At such times I felt compelled to admit I should never have strayed from the family home near Brighton, but then I'd have missed out on a whale of a life. The wizened old priest put a consoling arm around my shoulder, a carved wooden crucifix around his neck and wearing a dirt-stained white robe unchanged for weeks.

'We are in God's hands, my son,' he said solemnly. 'I am Father Ignatius and my companions are of the order of Sisters of Mercy. Are you Catholic, young man?'

'No,' I admitted, 'but I'm liable to become one right now. At least some of your lot are here now. I hope those Cubans were taught right from wrong back in some Havana convent. Whether they can control the wild mob with them is another question. It doesn't look good—'

'Pray,' the old man suggested, 'at least we still survive while others of our order have been mutilated and suffered worse indignities.'

No doubt they had prayed too, I thought grimly, as I was shown to a small cell in a corridor. It still had a mattress, but elsewhere the furniture and fittings of the whole mission, including religious statues, had been smashed and thrown about obviously in some wild frenzy.

'Rest, my son,' I was told kindly. 'Later you will be brought food and water. It's maize meal porridge, all we have, but you are welcome to share with us.' My mattress was about an inch thick and as hard as iron, no doubt the ideal for a dedicated nun. The one who came to me later with a tin bowl of the thick glut and a mug of water was fair of face, serene in her composure. Outside the chants and stamping had increased in fervour, while the glow of fires showed through the bars of a tiny window high up in my cell. Any moment now, the captives would be dragged out and made sport with, I had every reason to believe. With a steady hand, the nun placed the food and water beside me, hesitating before she turned away. I could imagine what they would do to her and gave her slim hand a squeeze, for once quite genuinely concerned for the fate of others.

'Do you not recognise me?' the woman said in a strong Irish accent. 'It is indeed a small world, Tyler Wight, isn't it? Do you remember Soho and the photographic studio, and what you and I did to earn money—?'

'Moira,' I gasped, 'Moira Lafferty?' Of course I remembered her, a beautiful red-haired nurse helping to maintain a brood of younger brothers and sisters back in Galway by posing and fucking with me for porno studies. 'Moira,' I repeated. 'Good God!'

'Sister Luke now,' she said proudly. I knew she had always been staunchly true to her faith as we had lived together for some months before I'd deserted her. I still held her hand, drawing her close, her breasts to my chest and one thigh pressed to my upper leg. 'No,' she said, her voice trembling. 'You can't, you mustn't. Those feelings are not longer part of me. Please, please, let me go—'

'Oh, but you were such a lovely fuck, Moira,' I said, my own voice thick with emotion. 'You and I, we had such good times—' My mouth found hers and I felt her relent, opening her mouth to allow passage for my tongue while my hand went up under the long coarse cloth of her habit, feeling the delightful smoothness of the skin of rounded thighs, meeting no undergarment and reaching the mass of curled hair at the plumpness between. 'Let me,' I urged. 'One more time – let's die happy for Christ's sake—'

'It would be for our own carnal sake,' she protested, but I sensed in her struggle that a long period of celibacy had made her in conflict with her vows. 'No, no,' she repeated time and again between the deep kisses pressed to her lips, giving a low moan as my finger curled into the recess of her cunt, shivering as I found her clitty, even moving her thighs to the titilation. My prick surged and I rolled her below me, hoisting her garb, meaning to have her, but like a slippery eel she squirmed out from under me, getting to her feet and breathing heavily as she adjusted her habit.

'God forgive us both,' she said, crossing herself. 'You have not changed one whit, Tyler Wight. Shame on you. I'm a nun—'

'And you're a woman with the feelings of a woman,' I said, frustrated in my desire but willing to concede to her. 'Don't tell me there aren't times when you need sex, or think about it?'

'I try to put such thoughts out of my head,' she said, standing back as Father Ignatius came into the cell with Alvarez. The Cuban indicated that we be left alone, saying he had business with me. 'Goodbye, Tyler,' Sister Luke smiled bravely. 'I shall pray for you.'

'I have inspected your car,' Alvarez said, oily as ever. 'It contains much of what comforts are in short supply here. I could, of course, confiscate it anyway, but I am a gentleman. Therefore I will trade. Your goods for your freedom and that of the priest and his nuns. There is one of my company's trucks and a Cuban driver waiting at the rear of this mission to take you all to the Ugandan border. File out of the rear door now and take this chance while I'm able to offer it—'

'You're taking my car too?' I said.

'Go,' he ordered, 'for we Cubans are leaving ourselves,

not trusting what these savages with us will do as they get more out of control. Maria will stay with me,' he smirked. 'I know now you are not her husband and I have promised to help find him—' He held out his hand. '*Asta la vista*, Englishman, you are one lucky *hombre*.'

Dead lucky, I thought later as I bumped along in an army truck's canopied rear with the nuns packed in beside me. At the fork of the track Alvarez led his men off in a little convoy that contained my wheels and my fortune. At least my skin was whole after the fiasco I'd been conned into.

The next night, safe in lodgings at the mission at Fort Portal, showered, shaved and settling down in another tomb-like cell on an iron-hard bed, once more I was visited by Sister Luke. She bore a candle and placed her fingers to her lips as she closed the door.

'I have come to say goodbye again,' she said, sitting on my bed. 'Tomorrow some of my sisters and I cross back into the Congo, for there is work to do for trained nurses.' She made no attempt to stop me as I reached out for her, placing the candle on the floor.

'Is that what you've come to tell me?' I said, drawing her down beside me. 'Or have you been thinking about us and what nearly happened? Would that have been such a sin?' I held her close, kissing her forehead, smelling the clean aura of her, one hand cupping a shapely breast that I'd known so intimately of old. 'Don't stay if you're going to fight me off,' I warned, 'come to bed with me. You're as lovely, as beautiful as ever, Moira. Say all the Hail Mary's and do all the penance you like after, this once give in to temptation—'

I drew off her habit, aware of her reluctance in allowing me the liberty. Naked beside me, my mouth went to hers, then to her breasts and nipples. I felt her hand reach out to grasp my huge erection and her body move to cover mine. 'God help me, for I can't,' she said in a low whisper, impaling herself on my shaft as if now desperate for the coupling to proceed. I grasped two firm tits as she began to writhe and thrust down against my pubic bone, remaining still so that she could savour the feel of a prick deeply embedded in her cunt once more. 'Now push it up me,' she ordered in a strangulated voice. 'Like you always did. Oh, help me, help me, it is too good. Fuck, fuck me, I will pray for forgiveness tomorrow—'

Tomorrow came with the sudden East African dawn and I awoke to find her gone, only the burned-out stub of the candle beside my bed. We had kissed, fondled, sucked and fucked until I slept and she had slipped away in the night. Calling for breakfast, I found the party of nuns had already left to return to the Congo and God knows what fate. The money for my fare to get me back to Entebbe was given to me by a priest from a fund to help the poor and needy. Once more I sat in a bus packed with humanity and livestock in the exact same parlous state in which I'd arrived in Entebbe all those months before.

Chapter Twenty-two

Bleak indeed was my outlook once more. I was penniless and homeless, fast running out of options, unsure even where I would lay my head that night. As a last resort, hoping for a lucky break, I got off the bus as it arrived at Entebbe Airport. There I offered my services again to Lake Airways as spare pilot, booking clerk or anything. I offered to sweep out the office and hangar or wash down the fleet of three Cessna aircraft. Whatever you've got, I told the ex-RAF Wing Commander, Bill Dove, who ran the small private flying outfit.

'I've been meaning to get in touch,' I heard to my great relief. 'We've been busy with safari flights, flying lessons, business trips, and one of my employees is going on UK leave soon. There'll be six months flying for you at least. Look me up next month, Wight, and I'll take you on the payroll as a temporarily employed pilot.'

A mix of gratitude and pride forbade me from saying what was I to do in the intervening weeks or even asking for an advance in pay. 'Can you handle a chopper?' Dove asked. I told him that was my speciality before realising he meant a helicopter.

In the Groove

'There may be a permanent job for you then,' he added. 'We're considering buying a Bell Jet Ranger for our business, it's the latest thing. Part of the package in purchasing it would mean a trip to their factory in Houston, Texas, where the pilot would receive training. Would you be willing to spend some time in the States? My married pilots aren't too keen. They're not chopper men, preferring fixed-wing.' I said I was free to go anywhere and would jump at the chance to visit America.

We shook hands on a future deal and then, having no other means of transport I hoofed it in the mid-day sun to Sam Bishop's bungalow, wondering if he had survived the trip to the Congo. My reason for going there was twofold. If Marje was alone I hoped to share her bed that night. If Sam had made it back, I intended to throw myself on his mercy and borrow some money to tide me over.

On arrival I saw Sam, Len and Spilsby celebrating around a table on the cool verandah, a table ladened with bottles and glasses and, much to my envy and chagrin, a pile of gold ingots the size of bath-sized bars of soap. The sight of me coming through the garden, perspiring and dishevelled, brought forth a roar of ribald laughter and raised glasses from the gleeful trio.

'Where the hell did you get to?' Sam bawled out, flushed with success, raising high a gold ingot in each hand. 'You dipped out, Tyler, we're rich men. We thought you'd be hanging out to dry, skinned alive in some Simba encampment—'

'I might well have been,' I said drily, gratefully accepting a glass of wine from Marje, who at least did not join in the general crowing at my predicament, shaking her head in annoyance at the display of hilarity. 'I'm so broke now I couldn't get back without robbing a poor box. My car's gone and everything else. You bastards ran out on me—'

'No, you didn't keep us with us, Wight,' charged Spilsby. 'We pushed on to Maganga that day and traded like I said we would. Gold,' he said holding up an ingot. 'Stamped with the official mark of the Katanga mine. There's well over sixty grand on this table. Tough luck you didn't get any of it.'

'I need a loan to tide me over,' I said, the words choking me. 'I'll pay you back with interest once I'm on my feet—'

'And when will that be?' Sam laughed. 'You're a loser, Ty. No dough, no place to stay; you're a bad risk.'

'Sam,' his wife put in. 'Give him a break.' This made him laugh louder in his triumph. I was about to tell him that I'd fucked both his wife and daughter but refrained. It was hard to put up with his shit.

'Your old job is available,' he said. 'I mean as instructor at my L Passo Driving Academy. The African I employed sold the bloody car, but Marje got it back while we were away. It's in the hotel car park as usual and there's a waiting list of eager pupils. The job's yours at the old terms, bed and board in the hotel annexe where you lived before.'

I nodded acceptance, deciding for the time being at least I'd have a place to live, free food and a small salary until the job at Lake Airways was available. Nanji Singh would have the keys to the car, Sam told me, and I could tell the hotel receptionist I was to have my old room. No one offered to drive me there so I began the long walk leaving Sam and his friends to continue celebrating. Some ten

In the Groove

minutes down the road I saw Christine Bishop draw up in her father's Oldsmobile. Someone was happy to see me at least, her pretty young face was wreathed in smiles.

'You're supposed to be dead,' she laughed. 'What a waste of prime cock that would have been. Why are you walking in this heat? I can think of a better way to use your energy—' She simpered at me. 'I fly back to school tonight. Fancy a quickie?'

'You have a way with words,' I said, getting in the car beside her. 'Tell me, would your old man really go berserk if he knew I was screwing his precious daughter?'

'And his beloved wife,' the wanton creature giggled. 'He would do his nut, go completely bonkers. I've discovered a quiet spot by the lake. Shall we have a back-seater? The car's roomy enough.'

We drove off the road to a track narrow with encroaching bush, emerging beside the wide expanse of Lake Victoria. Without hesitation, Christine hopped out and stripped off in broad daylight, throwing her clothes across the driving seat. For a moment she stood and impudently shook her shoulders, wobbling her pretty tits at me, before diving head first into the back seat. Pausing with her knees on the seat, a delightfully pert apple-smooth bottom was tilted up for my approval.

'Stay like that, you horny little baggage,' I ordered, charmed by the sight, dropping my pants and kicking them aside. Already my dong reared stiff as a hammer's handle and almost as long. She glanced over her shoulder, giggling wickedly and bracing herself on elbows and knees for what she was about to receive. I stood feet apart on the baked earth beside the open car door, my hands cupping both cheeky moons, drawing them apart to reveal the split

In the Groove

fig of her young cunt. It looked sweet enough to eat so I drew my tongue along the ridges of her nether lips, felt them part for me as if expelling breath and delved in to taste the flowing juice.

'Oh, yes, tongue me, tongue-fuck me,' the excited girl moaned. 'You do it so much deeper and harder than the girls at school—'

'They haven't got one of these, either,' I boasted, straightening up to direct the plum-crest of my engorged knob to her cunt, teasing the outer lips. 'Put it in,' she urged me in a breathless voice, 'shove it all up!' Her arse lunged back but I withdrew, giving her a playful smack to further increase her impatience. 'Beg for it,' I said meanly, thinking of her old man having me at his mercy. 'Say please and I might just give you a good fucking. Say "Fuck me, I want to be fucked—"'

'You bastard,' the spirited girl howled. 'Of course I want to be fucked. Get that thing in, you sod. Fuck me all you want!' Her lunge back caught me off guard, my shaft penetrating her full length with her smooth arse hard to my belly. 'Squeeze my tits,' she screamed, almost out of control. 'Go on, give it to me, fuck me harder.' With her girlish bum thrashing back onto my spike and her spine dipped to tilt up her cunt and me on tip-toe to give her the last centimetre of my greedy rammer, it was indeed a memorable coupling. One I was sure that would be recounted sparing no lurid details in the dorm of her school for young ladies. Her quickening gasps and helpless undulations told me she had come off at least twice, but she gamely continued to ball her bottom back to receive my poking.

I wished that Sam could have witnessed the scene, but

In the Groove

now I was as engaged as she in the animal lust of our bout. When my spunk boiled up from my balls, such was the immense delight I found in fucking this young and wanton bitch on heat that I yelled a hoarse cry, swamping her innards, I'm sure, with a gallon of spunk. 'What a fuck, what a magnificent fuck,' I praised her, drawing back a pace and noting she remained with arse cocked, frowning back at me.

'You've come!' she exclaimed, sounding greatly disappointed. 'I was wanting more. How long before that thing gets hard again?'

'That depends on what you can do to revive it.' I said, laughing at her enthusiasm. I shucked off the rest of my clothes and got in the rear of the car beside her, noting her smooth young flesh and the erect raspberry nipples on tits yet to reach full maturity. We lay along the seat, mouths fused, my hands squeezing and fondling her breasts, her fingers hopefully stroking life back into the object of her desire. Of her own volition she bent her head to suck it, head bobbing as she felt the stiffening process taking place, clamping it between tongue and palate to increase suction, until at last she withdrew her mouth with a look of triumph at the stander she'd procured.

'Both ways, this time, like before,' she hissed wickedly. 'Up my bottom too—' Eager to fuck the lithe vixen, I was between her thighs and up her cunt again in a flash, beginning with a slow shunting that had her lifting to me and sighing. She came even with such easy fucking, writhing around to get my probing knob against the parts she found particularly arousing.

'The other way now,' she commanded. 'Shall I turn

over?' No need, I told her, withdrawing a steaming cock saturated with her lubrication and nudging open her bottom hole. Her knees rose, she clutched my shoulders, gamely pulling me forward. 'I didn't know, didn't know, it was possible that way—' she moaned. 'It feels lovely up there, put it all up!'

Later, when I was alone again in my box-like room with its single bed and coffin-like wardrobe, the tiredness brought on by the past few hectic days made me glad to lie down even though it was still afternoon. I awoke to find sunlight streaming in from outside. My watch told me it was after eleven the following morning. I felt wonderfully refreshed and had a tremendous hunger, realising I'd missed the previous evening's dinner and that morning's breakfast. I showered and shaved, looking forward to lunch on Sam Bishop, ruminating that I'd given his hot little daughter a good sending off. I was wrapped in just my bath towel and horny at the thought of her smooth young body when a tentative knock sounded at my door. Was this my employer coming to see if I was ready to start work? I wondered as I opened the door. But there stood Nanji Singh looking very appetising with dark mascaraed eyes, rings and bangles, filling out a light blue sari most seductively.

'Welcome back,' the Asian girl greeted me, entering and trying to avoid looking at my half-naked body. I noted a ghost of a smile on her wide lips. We stood mere inches apart, admiring each other I like to think. 'I came to tell you that a pupil of the driving school has a lesson booked for two this afternoon,' she said, handing me the car keys. 'A very very pretty white girl. I suppose you will flirt with her and chase her like my mother says—'

'It was you, Nanji, she said I wasn't to chase,' I teased, the nearness of her and the cloying perfume she wore causing my dick to tent out the towel about my waist like a sarong. 'You asked what was stopping me once, I remember. Now you are at my mercy in this room. Should anything stop me?' I saw her eyes flick nervously at the door so I closed it and turned the key, the towel around me falling to the stone floor and revealing the upright erection thrusting out from my groin. I had not contrived it but it seemed appropriate.

'Ayee, it is too big!' Nanji squealed, covering her mouth to stop a flood of giggles. She hesitated, then cautiously stretched out her right hand, clasping it gingerly as if it would bite. 'Put it away. I don't want to see it—'

Oh yes, you do I thought, seeing the look of awe she gave my uncovered stalk. I had always flirted with her and had a lech to fuck her, but thought that as a dutiful Asian wife it was not on. But here she was in my room, not trying to leave, with me bollock naked before her and what looked like a huge and permanent cockstand in her brown hand. As if suddenly aware of that, she let go as if my prick was red hot. I immediately replaced the hand on my cock, curling her fingers about its girth, moving her wrist up-and-down surreptitiously to let her feel its warm throb and the sliding of the outer skin.

'My husband,' she began in a voice so low it was a mere whisper, 'my husband does not compare with this – this – but his penis is the only one I have known. Also he is too quick, I mean that he finds his satisfaction so soon when he takes me—'

In the Groove

'Have you never had a proper orgasm, Nanji?' I asked, playing the sympathetic friend while itching to fuck her. 'I'm sure it can be very frustrating—'

'I've never had any kind of climax at all with my husband,' Nanji admitted. 'I have read of such pleasures and thought about it, of course. But only by myself have I felt—'

She left the rest unsaid, her light dusky face darkening in what I took for a deep blush. The girl was mine, my instinct told me. She was not flaunting herself and was unsure, but she was intrigued enough to remain when all she had to do was turn and leave. The ball was in my court, as they say. Her interest was purely sexual, a fact-finding mission so to speak. Insincere sweet talk was not the way to proceed with her tuition, I decided.

'This must not be rushed, Nanji,' I said masterfully. 'You must do whatever I tell you, then you'll know how good it can be for a woman as well as a man. If you find out what you've been missing then you can get on to your husband and tell him what you want.'

'I do want to know what I am missing,' she agreed shyly. 'Shall I lie on the bed for you—?'

'Take off your sari first,' I said. 'And everything else. I want to look at you, and you'll feel the pleasure of standing naked while I admire you.' Her hands dropped to her waist as if to unwrap, but hesitated and she remained dressed. 'I like your sari, it's very becoming on a beautiful young Asian woman such as yourself, but I'm sure you're more beautiful with it off.' I went to her, standing chin to chin, firm breasts to my chest and my erection nestled in the fork of strong thighs. Hands on her shoulders, I kissed her full upon the lips and heard a submissive moan as my tongue went into her mouth. I fondled her back through the folds of cloth, running my hands from her small waist, over her swollen buttock cheeks, then I clutched the succulent globes, pulling her closer to me. 'Undress, Nanji,' I repeated.

She did as I asked, fingers working as she unwound the sari and let it slip to the floor. It was joined by her bra and brief panties until she stood gloriously naked.

'Superb,' I cried. 'Full-fleshed, magnificently curved, you really are a beauty, Nanji. Did you come here wanting this to happen? Knowing me well enough to think that it would—?'

She lowered her eyes as I approached again, taking hold of her breasts, flicking my thumbs over taut and elongated nipples, admiring the fine smooth texture of light-brown skin and her profusely forested cunt, the thick black hair growing in a triangular bush on a plump forward-thrusting pussy mound. I made her turn around so I could enjoy the rear view and trailed my fingers down her spine to the supple flesh of her brown buttock cheeks, parting the cleave. I stood against her, prick upright and pressed to the cheeky divide, my hands around her body, each palm overflowing with the heavily rounded orbs of magnificently high-set tits. Her body trembled, bottom pressing back against my erection. 'Yes, you hoped this would happen,' I told her.

'I wanted to come before,' Nanji groaned throatily, as of now so committed and worked up she could not deny the fact. 'I was afraid, afraid that it would be like this – that I would lose control, maybe get pregnant – that I would not

In the Groove

want you to cease.' Her arms had gone behind her, hands drawing apart her arse cheeks, making deliberate squirming movements of her bottom to get the knob to penetrate her. 'Put it in, Tyler,' she begged. 'You are being unkind—'

'You don't mind getting pregnant now?' I teased her. 'Not at this precise moment?' That precise moment coincided with my shaft sliding up a warm slippery cunt to give her a taste of it. 'I wouldn't do that,' I promised. 'Nice as that would be—'

'It doesn't matter now,' Nanji gasped, working her bottom back to me in urgent flurries. 'Joginder has me pregnant already, that is why I wanted you. Oh, what is happening inside me? Push, push it all the way! It is killing me – my stomach is leaping – oh, aaargh, oh, I come, I come! I cannot stop it—'

'Let yourself go, Nanji,' I encouraged her, mightily pleased with myself for bringing her off in such record time. All the frustrating fucks with her husband, all the climaxes she'd been denied, combined to have her juddering and jerking in my arms, backside thrumming to my belly as the sensations surged through her cunt. At last she fell forward on my bed, sprawled ignominiously with legs trembling to her toes, quim still palpitating and breasts heaving with each breath. I sat beside her and took her hand. When at last she raised herself, sweeping long dark shoulder hair from a flushed face, she looked at my still mightily erect cock with disbelief.

'It is ready again so soon?' she said. 'After it made me come to strongly I thought I would faint. Were you not satisfied?'

'I like to save the best until last,' I grinned at her. 'One fuck doesn't make a session and I trust you're in no hurry. You have a lot of catching up to do. Sit closer.' She moved so that our outer thighs met and bare flesh mingled. I drew her hand to my lap, placing it around the unstanding shaft, so vibrant in her clasp. 'Do you like the feel of it, Nanji?' I asked.

'I like to feel it so stiff,' she agreed shyly. 'But I like it inside me better.' She stroked it gently, my flesh throbbing beneath her fingers, stiff and thick to her touch, exciting her. 'Will you do it to me again?' Nanji enquired. 'I want to—'

'All in good time,' I promised, relishing such an eager pupil for my own pleasurable brand of tuition. 'First you must have it in your mouth.' I saw her hesitate. 'You must,' I insisted. 'Have you never done that? Try it, get to like it; your husband would love you doing it to him. Think of him,' I urged her selflessly. 'How pleased he'd be.'

Not to mention how pleased I'd be, of course, seeing Nanji bend her head and pause momentarily before covering my knob with her lips. 'Joginder has asked me to do this, but I've always refused,' she admitted. 'Tell me if I'm not doing it right—' The hot flesh of my prick was then on her tongue, lips circled to its girth, the stiff length smooth to her sucking. For a beginner she showed great promise, increasing her suction and making gulping sounds of mounting pleasure in the act, drawing me back to her throat, bobbing her head as if to fuck her own mouth with my hardness. I murmured and groaned, grasping her head and thrusting into her. Nanji gamefully sucked on, taking my gushing, the thick glut spurting upon her tongue until I was limp and slipping from her lips.

In the Groove

Such was the lech on me for the girl that I lowered her onto her back and pressed my face between her thighs, licking at her source, tonguing the pungent furrow, going deep into the cunt. Nanji's groan, the tilting of her mound, the jerks of her pelvis matched my thrusting in her crevice. She draped her legs over my shoulders, clutched my hair, crying out her pleasure. I felt the flow of sensations in the cunt I tongued. It pulsed like a beating heart. She urged me on brazenly, igniting me with her wild lust, working the miracle of returning tumescence – the iron-hard stiffness required to give her the ultimate. Still with her legs bent at the knees over my raised shoulders, I went forward with her cunt exposed, piercing it to the cervix with my first thrust. Welcoming its thickness, she gripped my stem with her pussy mouth as if to milk me, making me fight to halt an immediate ejaculation.

Before I'd allow that, I intended to give the gorgeous Asian girl a fucking that would have her returning to my humble room for seconds on future occasions. I cupped her firm bum cheeks as I went in determinedly, pulling her to me as I thrust, then I used an old trick I'd always found highly arousing to women I was in the process of cunt-fucking. My right hand slid into the cleavage of her arse, middle finger insinuating, breaching the tight anal ring, pushing in to the knuckle and beyond. At the same instant I thrust forward full-cock, giving her every inch. Nanji gasped, arched up against me, squirming her bottom on my finger, hoisting her cunt to my poking, ooohing and aaahing at the double sensations created.

'You love it, don't you?' I said lewdly into her face, making a mental note that in time I'd put something much more substantial in her tight bum-hole. 'Tell me when you're coming, shout it out, so that I'll come too. That's the way to finish a good fuck, together.'

'I'm coming, I'm coming!' Nanji howled. 'Fuck, fuck, fuck me more, don't stop—' Such was her excitement she nearly threw me off her and I rode her hard as she peaked and shot my volley deep into her writhing body. 'It's a good job I'm already pregnant by my husband,' she said as we slowly recovered. 'Otherwise I bet I would be now. Now I really must go, the time has flown so fast—'

'It always does when enjoying yourself,' I said as I watched her dress, enjoying the expert way she wrapped her sari about her figure. 'Who's been minding the shop while you were here? Don't tell me our boss is standing in for you while we fuck? I'd like that—'

'Oh – I meant to tell you before but I got carried away,' Nanji said, pinning back up her long tresses, her lovely face flushed with the afterglow of fucking. 'There's no hurry for me to return to the office. Mr Bishop was rushed to Mulago Hospital during the night. He collapsed—'

'Something serious, I hope?' I suggested. 'When I last saw him the drunken bum was celebrating his good fortune rather liberally—'

'No,' Nanji said. 'It was his bad fortune that made him drink so much. Last evening he sent for my uncle Amrit Singh to come from Kampala to value the gold from the Congo trip. Uncle is a jeweller, a goldsmith.' She rattled the bracelets on her arms at me. 'He made these, all twenty-four carat. He knows about gold—'

'Don't tell me Sam's ingots didn't make the sixty-odd grand he figured they were worth?' I asked cheerfully.

In the Groove

'They didn't make anything,' Nanji replied, unable to resist a grin. 'All the ingots are worthless. My uncle was suspicious when he weighed them on his scales. He drilled holes in them, sawed some in half, used his acid to test them for purity. Base metal every one, he said—'

'Old iron tarted up as gold,' I rejoiced, seeing the funny side of it. 'Sam and his cronies have been taken by smarter cookies than they imagined.' I fell back across the bed laughing until my sides ached and I had to wipe away tears. 'You've really made my day, Nanji. A lovely fuck and then hitting me with that interesting bit of news. Whatever can I ever do to thank you?'

'Let me come to your room again soon,' she suggested, sounding quite mischievous. 'You have made me like it too much—'

With that retort she slipped from my room, leaving me to ponder how often, in my seemingly darkest hour, either somebody up there liked me or the devil's own luck had come to my aid. In a few weeks I'd be back flying again and possibly training as a helicopter pilot in the United States. My future in Uganda seemed at last set to take off. Little did I know just what hazards that future would bring in the continuing saga of my rude lewd life. But that is another story.

A selection of Erotica from Headline

SCANDAL IN PARADISE	Anonymous	£4.99 ☐
UNDER ORDERS	Nick Aymes	£4.99 ☐
RECKLESS LIAISONS	Anonymous	£4.99 ☐
GROUPIES II	Johnny Angelo	£4.99 ☐
TOTAL ABANDON	Anonymous	£4.99 ☐
AMOUR ENCORE	Marie-Claire Villefranche	£4.99 ☐
COMPULSION	Maria Caprio	£4.99 ☐
INDECENT	Felice Ash	£4.99 ☐
AMATEUR DAYS	Becky Bell	£4.99 ☐
EROS IN SPRINGTIME	Anonymous	£4.99 ☐
GOOD VIBRATIONS	Jeff Charles	£4.99 ☐
CITIZEN JULIETTE	Louise Aragon	£4.99 ☐

All Headline books are available at your local bookshop or newsagent, or can be ordered direct from the publisher. Just tick the titles you want and fill in the form below. Prices and availability subject to change without notice.

Headline Book Publishing, Cash Sales Department, Bookpoint, 39 Milton Park, Abingdon, OXON, OX14 4TD, UK. If you have a credit card you may order by telephone – 0235 400400.

Please enclose a cheque or postal order made payable to Bookpoint Ltd to the value of the cover price and allow the following for postage and packing:
UK & BFPO: £1.00 for the first book, 50p for the second book and 30p for each additional book ordered up to a maximum charge of £3.00.
OVERSEAS & EIRE: £2.00 for the first book, £1.00 for the second book and 50p for each additional book.

Name ....

Address ....

....

....

If you would prefer to pay by credit card, please complete:
Please debit my Visa/Access/Diner's Card/American Express (delete as applicable) card no:

Signature .... Expiry Date ....